# Praise for Jessica L. Webb

"Intense, realistic stoi⋯⋯⋯d each other during a fight for justic⋯⋯ ⋯⋯p, Bookseller

This is an excellent tension filled suspense novel with a strong romantic thread that adds to the overall sense of anticipation. The combination of the kids unease, the emotional withdrawal of one of Jordan's key team and the building expectation of some violent act, mixed in with a classic "will they/won't they rekindle their old love" romance gives this a wonderful atmosphere and is excellently written and paced."—*Lesbian Reading Room*

"As heavy as the subject is about kids that are in desperate need of better representation and social services this book gives you lightness and hope as well. At times this book is heavy but the counterbalances are done well. The secondary characters add so much to the book but never out shadow the mains. That is hard to pull off and Webb did it flawlessly. More than anything this one keeps you hooked."—*Romantic Reader Blog*

## Lambda Literary Award Winner *Pathogen*

"Where did Jessica Webb come from? This is the second Dr. Kate Morrison book, the first is *Trigger*, and it was amazing. A reader should really read them in order, because they are both fantastic. I would sign up today to read the next ten books Webb writes."
—*Amanda's Reviews*

## *Troop 18*

"*Troop 18* is the third in the Dr. Kate Morrison series and is another winner…The story is a fascinating mystery that had me stumped and I loved how it was told in a very understated way with so much going on under the surface."—*Kitty Kat's Book Review Blog*

"Jessica Webb, you are so good! I love a book that makes you feel, even if it hurts."—*The Romantic Reader*

## Trigger

"The book reads very well and is full of heart pounding, adrenaline racing moments. I have zero clue if human bombs can be actually made, but Webb 100% sold me on the possibility through her story. I was held captive throughout the book, desperately needing to know how this was all resolved…This book has action out the wazoo, but it doesn't stop there. Mystery, intrigue, and a fantastic couple are in full force as well."—*The Romantic Reader*

"[A] really clever, intricate, and extremely well developed story line that has conspiracies, betrayals, and enough excitement to whet any reader's appetite. I cannot commend this book highly enough."
—*Inked Rainbow Reads*

## Lambda Literary Award Finalist *Repercussions*

"[A]lthough this is such an action-packed book, Webb still balanced it with some romance in such a way that the chemistry leaps off the pages in this intense, steamy kind of way. Webb is someone you can count on for accuracy and realism in her books, which I love because it makes it so much easier to fall into the story and forget the world around you. Her dialogue is well written and sounds conversationalist. She has a fast pace, good writing style, developed characters, plenty of action, and an exciting plot."—*Artistic Bent*

"I loved this book! The author has balanced suspense and romance perfectly. The plot is edge-of-your-seat exciting. The writing immerses the reader. The action is plentiful with lots of twists and turns and there are some very interesting, creative ideas within the book."—*Melina Bickard, Librarian (Waterloo Library, London)*

# By the Author

## *Dr. Kate Morrison Thriller Series*

Trigger

Pathogen

Troop 18


Repercussions

Shadowboxer

Storm Lines


Visit us at www.boldstrokesbooks.com

# STORM LINES

*by*

Jessica L. Webb

2020

This Trade Paperback Original Is Published By
Bold Strokes Books, Inc.
P.O. Box 249
Valley Falls, NY 12185

First Edition: July 2020

**Credits**
Editors: Jerry L. Wheeler and Stacia Seaman
Production Design: Stacia Seaman
Cover Design by Tammy Seidick

# Acknowledgments

Thank you to Bold Strokes Books for everything you do to create community and a space for queer books. Huge thank you to Jerry L. Wheeler, not only for being an incredible editor, but for providing all the words I needed to hear when things got hard. Thanks to Katie, beta reader and bestie. And thanks to readers for sharing in the joy of my stories.

For my wife, Jen. You make me happy every single day.

# PROLOGUE

Water streamed and gushed, the sound swirling and eddying in rhythm with the pain in Marley's side. It was too fast, too constant, too loud. Marley couldn't think. Every thought was a thickness, sluggish like her heartbeat. The rain was warm, too warm. Mixed with the blood pooling on her lap. Rain filled her eyes, dripped down her face. The rain had soaked through her clothes long ago. Maybe she'd been sitting here for hours, dirty concrete beneath her wet jeans. The pipe above her spewed dirty rainwater from the roof. Marley thought about moving but she couldn't. Her body refused the message from her brain, and she didn't want to break the cocoon of warmth. Summer rain and her own blood. Ugly and peaceful.

She shouldn't be here, though. Something important was in that thought. More important than the knife wound in her side, the bruises on her neck, or the pain in her hands. Fault and blame formed a sharp line, dividing her world into then and now, into consciousness and sleep. Marley shuddered, the first movement she'd made in a long time. She shouldn't be here in this alley in the rain. The knife should never have come between them. It was the last in a long line of mistakes.

Marley moaned, and the sound dislodged some of the heaviness. The effort to open her eyes felt huge and impossible. Her body felt numb, the hurt replaced by nothingness. *Move. Move.* But nothing happened, and Marley could only be grateful her tears didn't mix with the warmth of the rain and blood before she slipped down into sleepiness. Summer rain pattered against her neck, the sound of the water out of the drainpipe receded, and Constable Bridget Marlowe lost her fight with consciousness.

## CHAPTER ONE

E verything was fine until it wasn't.

Devon Wolfe dodged the hypocrisy of the thought even as she dodged puddles on the nearly empty streets. She was thankful the rain had driven most people indoors or into cafés or cabs. She and her somber black umbrella had the sidewalk to themselves. The rain meant she had a reason to keep her head down and avoid looking at anything other than the square of sidewalk in front of her.

Agoraphobia was tough.

*An aversion, not a phobia.*

She'd patiently explained that to her therapist last week. Devon had developed an aversion to being out in public. She had no real sense of dread or panic. She was just strongly disinclined to be out of her house and around other people. Temporarily. Everything was fine.

Except it wasn't. Hence the therapist.

Devon skirted the edge of another brackish puddle on the sidewalk. She pictured her therapist, Ash. She was young, not even thirty, and her streaked brown hair, heavy tattoos, and infectious grin made her look even younger. Ash did not care about Devon's distinction between aversion and phobia. She didn't care Devon was a psychologist who had spent her last five years focused on the mental wellness of the entire health care team at Hamilton's busiest trauma centre. No, Ash only cared about digging down into why everything had started crumbling in Devon's world and how she was going to rebuild. Devon cared about getting back to work.

That's where she was heading now, a meeting with Human Resources to discuss her return. She hoped for another month of leave, and then a gradual reentry. Allow some time to build up her stamina again, to carry the weight of others' pain. To run the programs meant to keep front line health workers at work and feeling okay without running herself into the ground again.

Another gust of rain tugged at Devon's umbrella. She wiped her hand on her pants, a useless gesture since she was soaked. Maybe walking today had been a bad idea, but she hadn't wanted to be trapped in her car then trapped in an office. Just then a delivery truck sprayed water as it sped down King Street, and Devon edged closer to the buildings, eventually stepping into a small alley. The world greyed as the truck roared past in a fascinating, disgusting spray of dirty water. An odd vacuum of sensation followed the truck's passing, and then she heard a whimper of breath.

Devon peered down the alley toward the bare, hurt sound. She could see a pair of legs, boots and jeans, sticking out from behind one of the bins. The legs moved in a convulsive twitch and then went still. Devon entered the alley, the sound of the street swallowed by the brick and stone and concrete. She heard whimpering again, a moan. Devon's breath felt trapped in her chest.

It was a woman, maybe thirty. She was bleeding, her white button-up shirt soaked with rain and blood. Dark blond hair was plastered against her face, her skin pale except for the dark patches of trapped blood. The bruises made Devon angry, the blood made her scared. The woman's eyes were half closed, her eyelids flicking rapidly. Was this a good sign or bad? Devon knelt in the puddle made by the gushing downspout.

"Hey, I'm going to get you some help."

She raised her voice to be heard above the storm and the interminable gushing of the downspout. The woman didn't respond. Devon dialed 9-1-1, hunching her shoulder, trying to keep her phone dry in the downpour. She answered eleven questions about the time and place and the patient's condition. The woman was still now. Even her eyelids barely flickered, and Devon's chest went tight with an odd, disassociated panic. Devon reached for the woman, pressing her fingers gently against her neck, feeling the warmth and strength of the artery. The woman groaned, and her arms collapsed to the ground, moving restlessly, shakily. Devon realized the woman was trying to sit up.

"Hold still," Devon said, the gentlest of commands. "I've called an ambulance. They won't be long."

The woman didn't seem to hear as she lurched forward and gasped, her eyes flying open as if suddenly aware of every pain and assault to her body. Devon leaned in when self-preservation told her to move away. She put a hand on the woman's shoulder, crouching lower to get into her line of sight.

"Easy. You're hurt. The ambulance isn't far. Sit back. Easy."

The woman leaned back, and she seemed even paler than when Devon had arrived. Devon felt the sickness of worry, the heaviness of responsibility.

The woman closed her eyes and groaned, the attempt at sitting up causing her blood to seep again. The sight of fresh blood had stopped affecting Devon long ago. The smell of it, though, earthy and primal and wrong, still made her pause.

Devon considered what she had that could possibly stop this flow of bleeding. Nothing—everything was soaked. She picked up the woman's hand and placed it over her abdomen. Then she placed her own hands on top and pressed, slowly and with a mimicked sureness.

"My name is Devon," she said, hoping to distract the woman from the pain. "I work at Centennial Hospital, and I know someone is going to be here any minute."

"Doctor?" The woman's voice was low and scratchy.

Devon smiled. "Not the kind that will help all that much currently."

She applied a little more pressure, and the woman's eyes dimmed with pain as her body slumped. Devon wondered if she'd passed out. She didn't think she'd lost enough blood to be dangerous, but what did she know? A psychologist who worked in an ER didn't know much about emergency medicine. *A broken psychologist. Who* used *to work in the ER.*

The faint stirring of sirens sounded above the din of receding rain. Hope bubbled in Devon's chest, but she kept even pressure on the woman's wound. She prepared herself for the lecture she was going to get on universal precautions. She scanned the woman's face—her lips were moving, but she seemed to have no energy for sound.

"What's that?" Devon said. "I didn't quite catch it."

The woman moved her free hand to her pocket and pawed weakly.

Devon reached past the woman's hand into her pocket, aware of the unasked-for intimacy of every shared movement. She pulled out a wallet and flicked it open. A thin black wallet was tucked inside. A badge, Hamilton Police.

"This makes things interesting, doesn't it?" Devon said. The woman gave the hint of a smile. Her eyes were a greyish blue, and Devon could see a world of hurt there.

Devon looked back at the wallet.

"Constable Bridget Marlowe," she read.

The woman closed her eyes. "Marley," she said, the name quiet but distinct.

"Marley," Devon said. She placed the wallet on Marley's lap and put her hand back to apply pressure. Marley flinched but made no sound.

The sirens were loud and constant, and Devon knew this odd, dark isolation of theirs would soon be broken. Sound filled the alley first, then people and equipment and the hustle of competence. The first paramedic crouched shoulder to shoulder with Devon and listened to everything she'd seen and done in the last ten minutes. Then he took over, Devon thanked him, and she stepped back, allowing the scene to unfold as it was meant to. As it always did, with Devon offering silent support in the background.

Marley's pain pulled her into consciousness, but she refused to open her eyes. She could use a few more minutes before she needed to evaluate the damage—the double layers of stitches to close the knife wound in her side, the bruises on her neck and the soreness of her throat, the ache at the base of her skull. And now the IV jabbed into her left hand. Marley sighed. There was more than just the damage to her body to evaluate.

"Faker."

Marley opened her eyes. She was in a semiprivate room, the curtains drawn around the hospital beds in a sad attempt at privacy. Marley's sister, Audrey, was sitting in the plastic visitor chair drawn close to the bed. She had her phone in her hand, and she tapped away while looking at Marley. Audrey looked worried. And mad.

"Shut up," Marley croaked through her dry, sore throat. Not a great comeback, but it's what she could manage.

Audrey grinned and stood, pouring Marley some water. She waited for Marley to take a sip before she spoke. "I've told Mom you're awake. So, prepare yourself for the onslaught."

Marley groaned and closed her eyes. She wasn't sure which she was dreading more—answering to her mother or her sergeant. At least she'd seen Sergeant Crawford already. He'd come into the ER as they'd decided to admit her for a day or two to watch for infection. He'd listened gravely to the doctor's assessment of her injuries, asked a few questions in his deep voice, then stated he could get a full report later and that he would phone her emergency contact himself. That's when Marley had closed her eyes. Looked like her reprieve was over.

"Mom sent you?" Marley said.

"I was closer," Audrey said with a shrug. She worked downtown at a swanky investment firm. Audrey's eyes crinkled at the corners as she grinned. "And she was mad, so she sent me."

"Scared mad?"

Audrey nodded. "Oh, yeah. With a little Mama Bear mad thrown in."

She and Audrey and their two younger brothers, Caleb and Jamie, had categorized their mother's versions of mad over the years. There was disappointed mad, I-raised-you-better mad, scared mad, protective mad. Grace Marlowe was a strict, loving matriarch. And she was a force to be reckoned with.

"How long?" Marley said.

"Ten minutes. She was already on her way down when I texted. I couldn't hold her off any longer."

Marley said nothing and closed her eyes. *Shit. Fucking shit god damn.* The enormity of her last two days felt like a weight sitting on her chest. She pushed against it, trying to breathe, but her thoughts pushed her back to the alley, humid and hazy at six in the morning.

Rain had been in the air, and Marley was hoping to be back at her apartment by the time it hit. It had been her day off but she'd promised to deliver a few days of groceries and was winding her way back to her car, parked this time behind the twenty-four-hour grocery store a few blocks away. She thought she was being careful. Not careful enough. They blocked her at the mouth of the alley, two figures dressed in jeans and beer logo T-shirts. They were silent, which unnerved Marley more than anything. She took two steps back as they advanced, and she caught their pale, light grey eyes. Warren brothers. Marley had helped put away their older brother two years ago for gang-related activity. The Warren brothers were exactly why she shouldn't be in this part of town when she wasn't on duty.

Marley had run. She was fit and fast and unarmed. Marley never saw who had tripped her, then hauled her up by her throat and held her as the Warren brothers had punched and kicked her. Marley had fought, taking some of the sting out of their blows. But she started to weaken. That's when she felt the knife in her side, a piercing, ripping pain.

"Bridget? You okay?"

Audrey's voice startled Marley, and she opened her eyes. The hospital. Late afternoon. Stitches. Sergeant Crawford's questions. Her mother. Her responsibility.

"Yeah," Marley whispered.

Audrey stood and put herself in Marley's line of vision.

"You're such a bullshitter. What happened?"

Marley indicated she wanted more water. She took a sip, and even the room-temperature tap water felt glorious on her throat.

"I was thinking about getting stabbed."

Audrey winced but held eye contact. "I don't even know what to say to that." Audrey's voice sounded shaky, and Marley immediately felt bad for speaking the truth.

"It's just pain. I'm okay." Marley tried to reassure her big sister. "You know I hate hospitals." She smiled a little, the action easing a little of the memory of the morning.

Audrey looked like she was going to take the bait. But she didn't. Of course she didn't.

"They'll make you see someone, right? A counselor or something."

Marley sighed again. She wanted to close her eyes, but that hadn't ended well a few minutes ago.

"Yes, probably."

They sat in silence, the noise and smell of the hospital seeming to press in on them and fill the space with a mixture of relief and worry that made Marley itch.

Then her mother was in the room, grey hair swept back off her face and behind her ears. She managed to look serious and summery and fierce and sweet, a combination Marley knew she would never master in her lifetime.

"Hi, Mama," Marley said, pretending tears weren't trying to surface. "I'm okay."

"Of course you are," Grace Marlowe said. Her eyes snapped to the monitors and IV poles, the former nurse taking in the readouts with practiced precision. Her expression softened as she leaned in to kiss Marley's forehead. "Stubborn child."

Marley was glad no one else was around to witness this moment. It was private, nothing to do with her job, her badge. Or her mistakes.

"Your nurse has been in since you woke up?"

Grace would care more about a nurse's evaluation of Marley's status than a doctor's.

"Not since I've been here, Mama," Audrey answered.

"Hmm. I know Sgt. Crawford has been in, though he was a little hazy on the details of why you were in an area of town you've been told to stay out of at six in the morning on your day off."

Only three decades of practice allowed Marley to maintain eye contact with her mother. "We'll have a full debrief when I'm released," she said.

"Of course you will." Grace closed her eyes and pinched her nose. Marley glanced at Audrey, who widened her eyes comically. Marley tried not to laugh. This was not-in-my-control mad.

"I should be released tomorrow," Marley said, trying to steer her mother clear of the stabbing and back to the safer subject of her recovery. "I wouldn't mind some of your lasagna in my freezer when I get back."

Her mother opened her eyes and glared at Marley.

"Bridget Vivian Doris Marlowe, don't you push it," Grace snapped. But her eyes were bright with humour. "You girls have been ten times the trouble of your brothers."

"That's what you get for raising strong women," Audrey said as she stood. "Here, you sit. I'm going to go grab some tea for us."

Once Audrey had left, Marley scratched at the bandage on her side, some of the tape pulling uncomfortably at her skin.

"How many stitches?" Grace indicated Marley's injury with a nod of her head.

"Eleven," Marley said. Grace raised her eyebrows, and Marley sighed. "Eleven epidermal and ten deep dermal." Her mother winced and Marley's stomach dropped. She hated doing this. But her mom would not relent until she had all the information. "It was a mess, but nothing got past the muscle layer. They're watching me for signs of infection."

"And for those contusions on your neck, I imagine."

"Yes, Mama."

The shared discomfort of each other's pain filled the silence until Grace cleared her throat. "I imagine you can't give me the details of what got you into that alley, but maybe you can share how you got out."

Marley wished she could. She had only been in the alley about twenty minutes, leaning against the brick wall, trying to stem the flow of blood and searching for the energy to find her phone, when the woman had showed up. Devon. Marley remembered her eyes, warm and brown. She had been so calm amidst the rain and blood and grit. Marley remembered feeling embarrassed, wanting to apologize to this professional and put together woman. *I'm sorry you're kneeling in a dirty puddle, I'm sorry my blood is on your hands. I'm sorry I can't help myself. I'm sorry I got this wrong, again.* All she'd managed to give was her name.

"A woman walking by found me," Marley said. "She said she worked here at the hospital, I think. Devon. She called EMS and stayed with me until the paramedics arrived." Marley started to shrug but the tight, aching muscles in her neck stopped her. "I didn't see her again after that."

"We'll have to find her and thank her," Grace said.

Marley was conflicted. She very much wanted to say thank you to the woman who had helped her this morning. But the embarrassment surfaced as well, the awkward and vulnerable need to apologize. Marley closed her eyes.

"I'm going to rest for a bit, I think," she said to her mother. "Don't stay here all night, okay?"

"Sleep, love," Grace said.

Marley slept.

## CHAPTER TWO

Devon was shaking by the time her meeting at the hospital was done. She couldn't expect much else given how this day had unfolded. She walked to the Tim Hortons kiosk outside the entry to the hospital. It was mostly frequented by patients and family, rarely by staff. Devon wasn't hungry, but she needed something to occupy her hands while she sorted through the chaos.

After the cop, Marley, had been taken away by ambulance, Devon had stayed to answer the questions of two Hamilton Police officers. They had been on edge, demanding accuracy and honesty with an underlying vague threat if she didn't comply. This was hardly surprising, given one of their own had just been rushed off to hospital. Once she'd been released from the street-side interrogation, Devon felt a sense of loss or disconnect. As she walked home to change, she evaluated this sense of loss. Perhaps she had felt so disconnected for so long, this brief and somewhat traumatic connection to Marley in the alley had made Devon feel centred and grounded—two aspects missing from her life of late.

Devon crumbled the too dry cheese biscuit she was holding, annoyance surfacing in the flick of her fingers. *Perfect. More evidence that the only time I'm centred is when I'm reaching out, when I'm taking my energy and supporting others.* Devon took a sip of her green tea and cursed. Too hot. She put her tea down with a little too much force and some splashed over her hand. *Enough. Pull yourself together.*

Leaving her tea until her hands had stopped shaking, Devon pulled out her phone, opened a news app at random, and started scrolling. She breathed, pulling air deeply into her lungs, expanding her diaphragm with slow, measured breaths. It was a technique she often taught to others to manage anxiety or stress when out in public. Controlling Your Nervous System 101, Devon thought. She felt a little calmer in a few moments, and her hands didn't seem to be shaking quite so much.

Devon glanced outside as an ambulance, silent but with its lights flashing, pulled into the lane and disappeared from view. It was raining lightly now, and the afternoon sun pushed its way in filmy swaths through the clouds. It would be nice to get a little sun on the walk home. More than anything, Devon wanted to be home and out of these clothes and away from people, comments, and questions. She had one more month of leave to learn how to stop hating being out of her house.

"Devon? Hey, Tiger! Haven't seen you in ages."

Devon flinched at the sound of her nickname, her muscles tensing so much her stomach hurt. She looked up to see Leo, a nurse from the trauma unit.

"Hey, Leo." Devon thought she sounded calm, even managing a smile. "It's good to see you."

Devon could feel herself gathering the energy to build a wall of wellness around her, an illusion of calm and competence, ready to absorb whatever she needed to help others feel more comfortable.

Leo tugged at the bike helmet swinging from the strap on his backpack and ran a hand through his hair. Devon had been off work for five weeks now and hadn't been in once to see her colleagues. This first, accidental meeting was awkward. Devon breathed through the impulse to allay his discomfort. *Sweet Jesus, this is hard.*

"You're good?" Leo said. "I mean, even the Zen Tiger needs some time, I guess."

Integrating a workplace wellness plan into a busy city ER had not been easy. After the staff had begun to accept her, though, they'd nicknamed her Zen Tiger. Chill but with a hint of no bullshit, as one of the nurses had described her.

Devon smiled at Leo, a real smile this time. She appreciated his bringing up her absence instead of dancing around it.

"I'm working on being good. I'm getting there." Devon chose to believe this was an expression of hope rather than a lie about how well she was coping.

Leo's smart watch beeped and he checked it. "I gotta go. Stop by and see the gang when you're up to it. We miss having you around."

Devon waved as he walked away, the metal of his cycling shoes clinking down the hallway. Ash would be happy with this day, Devon thought. Successfully leaving the house, coming to the hospital, navigating an interaction with a colleague.

There was something left, though. She hadn't gone directly home after meeting with HR about her leave of absence because Marley was somewhere in the hospital. And Devon wanted to see her.

Devon grabbed her still hot tea and began walking. The reddish brown takeout cup with the familiar Tim Hortons logo was camouflage more than anything. Devon needed a concrete reminder of who she was in this space. A visitor at the hospital. She had a purpose and a goal, and she looked just like everyone else. Even if she didn't feel it.

One of the officers had left a voice mail with Devon while she'd been in the meeting with HR. He said he'd need her to sign some paperwork in the next few days and had mentioned Constable Marlowe was doing well and was being admitted overnight. He also mentioned the constable would like to thank her in person. Devon thought now seemed like the right time. Put all the hard stuff in one day, then she could go home. Devon had a dark suspicion she wouldn't be leaving home for a few days after this. She shook her head, wiping sudden sweat from her forehead. Maybe a call to Ash wouldn't be the worst idea.

General Admitting was a maze, but Marley had come to know almost every corner of this hospital in the last five years. She was attached to the trauma unit but also consulted and connected to other teams, especially those who worked closely with the ER. It was a part of the mandate she'd pushed for, to move beyond the silos of health care specialties and try to make the units more cohesive and functional. This not only eased the burden on individual units but also added to the sense of hospital unity Devon was working so hard to achieve.

The third floor was quieter than Devon had expected. Nurses pushed med carts with practiced efficiency and singular focus. Devon waited for a nurse behind the desk to look up from her computer, a process that required patience and remembering her needs were not more important than the nurse's current focus.

"I'm looking for Bridget Marlowe?"

"Room 208, love," the nurse said, then went back to typing.

"Thank you."

Devon's stomach churned with anxiety as she checked the room numbers down the hallway. She stopped and took a sip of her tea, working on a mantra in her head. *Five minutes, check in, say you're welcome, act okay, act okay, act okay.* Maybe not the best mantra, but she needed something.

Devon stepped cautiously into room 208. An officer stood beside the bed of a pale but alert Marley. Devon prepared herself to take a step back, not wanting to interrupt.

"Hey," Marley said, her eyes brightening as she saw Devon. "My rescuer."

Devon smiled. "I wanted to check in on you. But I don't want to interrupt."

"No, no," Marley said, motioning for Devon to come in. She winced and leaned back into the pillows at her back. "Oof. Okay, so add waving to the list of things I can't do right now."

The officer laughed. He was a young guy, generically handsome in a way that often made Devon suspicious. "That list is getting long."

Marley lifted one hand off her side and gave him the finger. "Oh good," she said. "That still works." Marley looked back to Devon. "Come in. It's Devon, right? My memory is a little hazy from this morning."

Devon walked to the other side of the bed, feeling awkward, like she was taking up too much space. "Yes, it's Devon. Devon Wolfe."

Marley looked up at Devon, her grey eyes direct. "Thank you, Devon. You really saved my butt this morning."

"You're welcome, Marley," Devon said quietly. The moment felt intimate again, like this morning. They were total strangers with too many intimate moments between them already. Devon needed distance. "You look like you're on the mend."

"Stitched and pumped full of antibiotics and pain meds. And ready to get out of here."

The officer snorted. "Rushing home for bed rest. Sounds thrilling."

"Ugh," Marley groaned. "Bed rest." She motioned at the officer. "Devon, this is Constable Stills. We mostly call him Superman."

Devon and Constable Stills exchanged polite nods and hellos. Stills turned back to Marley, who was trying unsuccessfully to adjust her sitting position.

"Oh yeah, you're off duty for a good few weeks," he said.

Marley seemed to stiffen. "Fuck, that's a long time," Marley said, staring down at her bandages.

"What, you've got something to do in the next few weeks?"

"No, I just…I hate being forced out of commission."

Devon knew what that felt like, but she held her silence. She was also intrigued by her suspicion that Marley was hiding something. But it didn't matter. This wasn't her job.

"I don't want to interrupt your visit," Devon said, stepping away from the bed. "I just wanted to see you were okay."

"Wait," Marley said, with a hint of panic in her voice. Devon held still and waited. "If you could stay for a few minutes? I know I've already pretty much messed up your day." She looked down at Devon's clothes. Devon had showered and changed after Marley had been taken away in the ambulance. "And your pants. I must have ruined those. I can pay for those."

Devon held up a hand. "Hey, no. You're fine, really. And yes, I can stay for a bit longer if you like." The words were out of her mouth before she'd completely thought them through. She waited for the spear of panic, but all she felt was a waver in her belly, nothing more.

"Yeah, yeah, that's my cue," Stills said, pulling on his Hamilton PD ball cap. "I'll check in with you tomorrow." He tipped his head toward Devon. "Thanks for saving her bacon today. She's a pain in the ass but she's one of us."

Marley tried to swat the officer but seemed to think better of it. He laughed and walked to the door. "Wait, one more thing," he said, before leaving the room. "What the hell were you doing out in the east end? Crawford never said."

Marley blinked twice. "I was dropping off food to the Mission."

The officer cocked his head. "At six in the morning?"

Marley shrugged. "I was awake. And their breakfast program starts at seven."

The officer nodded like he understood. He gave a lazy salute. "Marley Saves the World, my favourite show. Catch you later."

They were alone again. Devon studied the perfectly made up, empty bed in the next cubicle. She wondered how long until Marley had a roommate. She wondered what she was still doing here. She wondered why Marley had just lied to her fellow officer.

"You can sit down," Marley said. Her voice sounded raw, scratchy. Devon walked to the other side of the bed and held up Marley's water cup and straw.

"Thanks," Marley said as Devon brought the cup closer. She took a sip and cleared her throat. "You're saving my life all over the place. Caller of paramedics, stancher of bleeding wounds, bearer of water, and getting ridder of well-meaning colleagues."

Devon laughed. She liked Marley's humour, a little self-deprecating, a little sarcastic.

"I'm happy to help."

Marley lowered the cup to her lap. "You are, aren't you? A helper."

Devon felt a moment of embarrassment. Marley didn't know how true it was.

"I was in the right place at the right time," Devon said, aiming for friendly but neutral.

"You said you worked here at the hospital. I remember that."

"I'm a psychologist. I work with the trauma team." Present tense felt acceptable in this moment. No matter HR had just signed off on one more month of her leave.

"The integrated staff health team, yes?"

Devon was surprised. Few outside of the hospital had heard of it. "That's right. That's my baby."

"I read about it in the paper, maybe last year? I was curious about how it might apply to other front line professions."

"Like police work?" Devon said, smiling.

"Yes," Marley said, smiling also but looking earnest. "We keep compiling stats about PTSD and stress leave and depression for first responders, but nothing seems to get done. Your integrated team finally looked like some action."

"I actually did ride-outs with the Toronto Police Department as a pilot a number of years ago. It's where this idea germinated, really."

"Tell me more," Marley said, her eyes bright.

Devon smiled at her eagerness. She didn't often get this kind of audience to talk about her work. "The pilot paired up mental health workers with street cops, since so many of the calls involved citizens struggling with mental health and addictions issues."

"Sixty-three percent in Hamilton last year," Marley said.

"Really?" Devon said as Marley nodded. "That's high."

Marley tried to shrug, and her hands fluttered for a moment then were still. "So you liked doing the ride-alongs?"

"I did, though they were hard. It made me think about front-line workers and the stressors these kinds of experiences put on them. And I wanted to design a system where someone on the front line had their own ride-along, someone who is there solely for them, making sure they're okay."

"Amazing," Marley said softly. "It's so good to hear about something that actually works from a ground roots level."

Devon felt her chest fill with pride even as her heart sank with knowledge of her own failure.

"Sorry, I'm babbling," Marley said. "It must be the pain meds."

"Are you in pain now?" Devon said, thankful for the turn in conversation.

"No, as long as I sit still." Marley sighed. "Very still. God, this is going to suck."

She closed her eyes for a moment, and Devon studied her. She was very pale, her dirty blond hair hanging in twists around her face and jaw. Like most people, Marley seemed to shrink in a hospital bed, dwarfed by pillows and IV stands and monitors.

Marley opened her eyes and looked right at Devon. Devon's heart stuttered a little in a way she recognized. In a way she did not want. Not now.

"I should go."

"Okay," Marley said quietly.

Devon didn't move. She wanted to say she would come back, that she would check in with Marley and follow her progress. But this wasn't work, and Marley was not a job. The impulse must be personal, then. Would it be an okay thing to say on a purely personal level?

"You're worrying," Marley said, watching Devon. "You don't need to. Nurses and doctors are taking care of me. I've got a good support network, and I'll...I'll figure out bed rest." She smiled a tired strained smile. "I'm okay."

Devon nodded and stood. "It was nice to meet you, Constable Marlowe."

"Just Marley. And it was nice to meet you, too. Thank you again."

"You're welcome."

Devon tried to let that closure be enough, let those words of assurance and thanks be exactly what she came here for. But she looked back before she left, saw the forlorn and hurt and anxious expression on Marley's face before she sighed and closed her eyes.

"Would you mind if I visited again?" Devon said, her throat tight.

Marley opened her eyes, and Devon read some kind of relief. "God. Yes, please. You can save me from my mother next."

Devon laughed and the tightness eased. "I'll come by tomorrow?"

Marley's eyes, still tired, looked happy. "Tomorrow."

Devon eased her way out of the room, a little bit of her own happiness in her chest.

## CHAPTER THREE

Devon's visit and her brother Jamie sneaking her French fries later that night were the last moments Marley felt any semblance of happy. Infection stole into her body in the middle of the night, an invasion that made her vomit and sweat. Each retching movement sent a streak of hot pain through her wound. By three in the morning, she was dehydrated and crying and exhausted from the pain. Her wound was now hot and swollen, and the nurses checked her constantly. The vomiting had stopped by the time her mother arrived at eight, but uncontrollable chills racked Marley's body. Marley could only feel relief, distant and nearly primal, as Grace Marlowe took charge.

They changed Marley's sheets and gown, and propped her body up to untangle her monitor leads and IV lines. Marley's whole body felt weak, and the room spun alarmingly. She was soon tucked back in under fresh sheets with another dose of pain meds and antinauseants and her mother's hand on her forehead. Thoughts of Sergeant Crawford coming by surfaced and disappeared. Devon was a sweet slip of a dream. There was something else, though. A worry that made her stomach lurch and plummet. Something she needed to do. But the world spun in a sea of worry and sick, and Marley let the meds pull her down into unconsciousness.

It took three days for Marley's body, along with a sledgehammer swing of antibiotics, to fight the infection. On the second day, they talked about taking her into surgery to clear out the infection. But her body finally started responding to the antibiotics, the redness around her wound slowly starting to recede. Marley still couldn't put her arm anywhere near her abdomen. She couldn't do much of anything.

"You're going for a walk today," Grace said, as Marley surfaced from another drug-induced sleep. She was filling up Marley's jug with fresh water.

"Oh, joyous day," Marley mumbled. She evaluated her body and her sluggish thoughts. Her body was a trembling, sweaty mess of pain. She was so weak. But her head felt a little clearer. The nurses had said she'd feel more like herself once the infection started to clear.

"Do you know what day it is?"

"Thursday?"

"Friday."

"Shit," Marley mumbled.

Grace lifted her eyebrows but said nothing. "Monday morning was your...accident. The infection started Tuesday, they wanted to take you into surgery on Wednesday, but by Thursday afternoon, the infection began to abate."

"Friday I go for a walk and Saturday they send me home," Marley said, then coughed. The bruises on her throat were starting to fade, but the soreness was still there.

Grace handed her some water. "We'll see," was all she said to Marley's prediction.

Marley sipped, the tang of the city's tap water settling on her tongue. She'd lived her whole life in Hamilton, a city built on the steel industry. Gritty and tough streets, gorgeous nature trails, the expanse of Lake Ontario, smog in the summer and blasts of snow in the winter, blue-collar workers and university students—Marley loved it all. And she loved the taste of the tap water. It meant she was home.

"Earth to Bridget," Grace said, dumping a cloth bag on Marley's hospital bed.

Marley rubbed her eyes. "My head is stuffed with cotton."

Grace rubbed her back, at once gentle and prodding. "You've taken quite a beating, daughter. Let's start getting you back on track."

They'd had a few days of practice sitting Marley up without tangling her IV lines. Grace produced a pair of Marley's track pants and a maroon McMaster Marauders T-shirt.

"Real clothes," Marley groaned happily.

It took longer than Marley thought possible to get her into pants and a shirt and she was sweating by the end of it. She had to push her pants low to avoid the bandage around her abdomen, but the worn cotton of her shirt felt heavenly against her skin.

"Ready?" Grace said, keeping her arm around her daughter's shoulders.

"Ready."

Marley shuffled more than she walked, but she made it to the nurses' station in the centre of the ward. Sure, it was only three doors down from her room, but it felt like an accomplishment. The nurses smiled and waved, and an older man in a wheelchair with a plaid housecoat wrapped around his shoulders cheered her on.

Exhausted and happy, Marley was concentrating on turning around when she saw Devon approach.

"You've got a lot of fans," Devon said, smiling sweet and shy, her hands shoved into her dark jeans.

"Devon, hey." Marley's tongue felt twisted all of a sudden, as if words were as impossible as sprinting down this hallway. "Thanks for coming."

"Devon's been by every day, dear," Grace said, tugging on Marley's arm to get her moving again.

Marley made the mistake of trying to walk and look over her shoulder at Devon. "You have?" she said to Devon, then gripped the IV pole hard as the hallway started to spin a few degrees off course. "Oh. Shit."

Grace took one arm firmly in her grip, and Marley felt Devon's steadying presence on her other side. This was embarrassing.

"Open your eyes, Bridget," Grace was saying in that calm, demanding way Marley had been listening to her whole life. "Find your balance, then we'll get you back to your room."

"Yeah, I'm okay," Marley said. They began a slow and awkward three-person shuffle back to Marley's room, Devon steadying Marley and pushing the IV pole. Marley wanted to make a joke to cover the humiliation of this moment but her legs felt weak, her side hurt, and her stomach was starting to roll. All she cared about was getting back to her bed.

Finally she was there, sweaty and exhausted and embarrassed, but safely back to bed. Grace said she was going to find a nurse and left the room. Marley took a moment to breathe before she looked up.

"Sorry, that was a bit of a show," Marley said to Devon, who stood by the foot of Marley's bed, looking concerned and a little bit guarded. Marley's stomach plummeted. Maybe Devon was tired of coming to her rescue.

"It's okay," Devon said, running a hand through her short curls. "It's good to see you awake and moving around."

"I've been pretty out of it," Marley said, fighting back the urge to cry. Devon sounded distant, detached. Marley let the disappointment swallow her up. "I didn't know you'd been in every day. Thanks for visiting, it's really good of you." She adjusted herself on the bed, the movement sending a fresh wave of pain through her wound. "You don't have to keep coming, though. I'm good."

Devon didn't say anything for a moment, and Marley's polite release of Devon's responsibility hung in the air between them.

Before Marley could try and work through what this helpful, distant woman was thinking, her mom returned with Sergeant Crawford in tow.

"Looks like it's a day of visitors," Grace said.

Devon took a step back from the bed and, to Marley's surprise, held out her hand to Crawford. "Good to see you again, Sergeant."

"Same to you, Dr. Wolfe."

*They know each other?*

"Why don't I head down and pick up some coffee and tea," Grace said.

"I'll join you, Mrs. Marlowe," Devon said. "If you don't mind."

"Not at all, Devon."

Everyone knew each other. This was a bizarre fever dream. How out of it had she been? What else had she missed?

Marley knew what she'd missed. The vague worry and responsibility that had been tugging at her turned into outright worry. She knew who she should be taking care of. She had to believe they were okay. They would be okay for a few more days. Maybe.

Sergeant Crawford cleared his throat, and Marley looked up. He stood somewhat stiffly at the foot of her bed. Marley respected her commanding officer of the last three years, but they had never been close.

"How is the recovery, Marlowe?"

"Slower than I'd like, sir."

Crawford nodded, like her answer was just the right combination of detailed and impersonal.

"I wanted to give you an update, and I have some questions about a case." He paused, clearly assessing the sweating, pale mess Marley currently presented. "Are you up for that?"

"Yes," Marley said, lying. "Go ahead."

Crawford pulled out his phone and read something then looked back up. "The Warren brothers were picked up two days ago, both arrested on battery of an officer."

"I was off duty, sir. Doesn't that make a difference?"

"No," he said evenly. It was hard to rile up Crawford. "You were targeted because of your role as a police officer. So they'll be prosecuted on those charges."

"Which brothers were they?" There were only four actual Warren brothers, but the Hamilton police included all the cousins, which brought the number closer to twenty.

Crawford checked his notes. "Cody and Stacy."

Marley forced herself to think. "The bowling brother and the one who's always eating protein bars?"

Crawford cracked a smile. "I believe you are right, yes."

Making this connection felt like a big accomplishment. It was a morning for accomplishments.

"Next up is the Fleming Street drug bust."

Marley's body went cold, and her muscles tensed. She did not think she had the energy to field these questions. And keep her secret.

"I thought we got all the major players last month, sir," Marley said, hoping the slightest shake in her voice could be chalked up to her current state.

"Distribution, yes," Crawford said. "But one of the drugs we picked up is an unknown. We're in the process of getting it tested, but Public Health and the provincial drug unit are on us about finding out who developed this drug and how. They're looking for information we don't have. The group we rounded up last month are not the chemical sciences type. Someone else made this drug, and we need to know who."

Marley swallowed and dared herself to speak. To show she had nothing to hide. "What about Randolph West?" she said. "I thought he was brought in for both production and distribution."

"That's correct. But he's all we've got. And there's nothing in West's history that suggests he has the knowledge to develop this kind of street drug." Crawford blew out a breath. "We're missing something."

Marley said nothing, still focused on not allowing her body or her expression to give away her nerves. She had not been front line on investigating this case. It had sat squarely in the hands of the drug unit right up until they'd needed the street cops to help on the day of the multi-site raid. That's when Marley had become involved. That's when she'd met Carla Slessinger and her granddaughter, Aimee West. Drug kingpin Randolph West's mother and his eight-year-old daughter.

Marley swallowed past that shaky feeling of a lie coming to the surface. "How can I help?"

"The notes indicate you were in charge of Randolph's daughter once she was brought to the station, is that right?"

"I was with Aimee from the moment she was escorted out of the Fleming Street house, actually. But since I wasn't on the first team, Miss West wasn't officially in my care until we got to the police station. Even then, I had no official capacity around her questioning or follow-up care. That was Constable Sheffield, I believe."

Crawford typed a few things into his phone, nodding along. Marley relaxed a little. A mistake.

"The notes also show you put in an official request and complaint to Constable Sheffield regarding Ms. Slessinger and her granddaughter. You objected to them being released to Family and Children's Services without further police protection."

Marley swallowed hard and, to her horror, began to cough. She reached for her water, feeling like every movement and silent moment was waving a red flag of guilt.

"I did," Marley said, once she soothed the dryness in her throat. "I had concerns that Ms. Slessinger, though wonderful, was not in a financial place to be able to take on her granddaughter. And Ms. Slessinger was concerned Randolph would come looking for his daughter. Or send someone. But no one else seemed worried."

"Because Randolph West is in jail."

"Ms. Slessinger says Randolph still has ties in Thunder Bay, which is where she lives."

Sgt. Crawford grunted and took notes. Marley had no idea if this was going well.

"You also had concerns about the child," Crawford said. He checked his notes, then pinned Marley down. "Eight-year-old Aimee West."

"Yes," Marley said. Aiming for calm and steady. And factual. This was all in the report. "No one knew how long she'd lived with her father."

"Or what she'd witnessed."

There it was, the heart of Crawford's questioning. Marley simply nodded her agreement.

"When was the last time you saw Ms. Slessinger and young Miss West?"

Marley's heart beat a strong, protective staccato in her chest. Before she could speak, she saw Devon in the doorway holding a cardboard tray full of hot beverages. Marley watched her pause, assess the scene, and pull back. Marley went back to Crawford.

"Family and Children's Services came late in the afternoon. I made my formal request to keep them in police protection when Sheffield said they were going to be released into F&CS care, likely passing them down the chain to Far North services, since Carla Slessinger's residence is in Thunder Bay." Marley took a deep breath, ready to complete her lie. "So, the last time I saw them was when they left with the intake worker."

Marley forced herself not to fidget as Crawford assessed her answer.

"Okay, thank you. I will follow up with the intake worker."

"Sounds good, sir. Is there anything else? I think I saw Devon back with the Timmy's, and it would be great to talk to her before I pass out again."

She was tired, that wasn't a lie. Though the adrenaline and stress humming through her body meant she wasn't ready for sleep.

"That's all for now, Marlowe. Rest and recover, and we'll see you when you're back on your feet. With a doctor's note to return to work, of course."

"Of course. You know me and rules."

Crawford looked at her sharply as he put his phone into his pocket. "Unfortunately, Marlowe, I do. Which is why I thought I'd remind you. Take good care of yourself."

Devon entered the room just then. "Coffee for the road, Sergeant

Crawford?" Devon said, pulling a cardboard cup from the tray and holding it out.

"Oh, I…yes, thank you. And thank you again from the Hamilton Police Force for looking after our officer."

Devon gave a solemn nod to the sergeant as he left. Marley let herself collapse against her pillows. She was drained but opened her eyes as Devon wheeled the tray table over to the bed and placed a Timmy's cup in front of her.

"Peppermint tea," Devon said, settling herself into the chair. "Your mother's orders."

Marley sighed and took the lid off, letting the fragrant steam escape. "Where is my mother, anyway?"

"She said she'd be back after lunch. She got a call while we were downstairs, something about a pastor locked out of the rectory?"

Marley grinned. "Father Zeke is incredibly forgetful. Mom rescues him at least once a week."

"A family of heroes," Devon murmured as she twisted her coffee in her hands.

Worry snaked through Marley's belly. She still wasn't sure she'd done the right thing with Carla and Aimee, taking them in, finding somewhere for them to live. They shouldn't have to be so dependent on her for shelter and food and news. And she hadn't anticipated being incapacitated, unable to care for them.

"You're tired," Devon said.

Marley picked up her cup and blew ripples onto the top of her tea. Still too hot.

"It's been a big morning," Marley said.

Devon nodded. "A walk and visitors. General consciousness." Marley answered Devon's small smile with her own. Then the smile faded. "Lying is also very tiring," she added gently.

Marley did not flinch away from Devon's words. It wasn't an accusation, more a gentle surfacing of fact, a calm acknowledgement. Marley's instincts had her responding before she'd even thought it through. Again.

"I need your help."

❖

Devon listened and sipped her coffee as Marley began her confession. She'd been in this position many times before, and she was comfortable slipping into this familiar role. Marley continued to amaze her. She was obviously exhausted from her morning, but the self-doubt of her actions and decisions were painted across her expression and her voice. Marley was worried about these two secret dependents.

"It happened too fast," Marley was saying, running the edge of the white hospital blanket through her fingers. "Carla is an amazing woman. She seems strong and capable, but she'd only met Aimee for the first time about six months ago. Randolph West had never mentioned a child, but when Carla found out, she insisted on coming down and meeting her granddaughter. Then she hears nothing until a social worker calls in the middle of the night saying she needs to get to Hamilton ASAP."

"Family and Children's Services wanted her to become Aimee's guardian?"

"I mean, it took two days of paperwork. They put Aimee in a foster home the first night because Carla had to travel down from Thunder Bay."

Devon gave a low whistle. "That's a hike. What's that, fifteen hours of driving?"

"Yeah, and she did half of it by bus," Marley said. "She's dedicated to that kid, I know she is. But she doesn't have a lot of resources. And she's scared of her son."

Devon heard anger and frustration mixed with worry in Marley's voice. This was a woman who wanted to do right. Always.

"And you tried to convince people to keep her here in police protection."

Marley nodded. "All the intake worker saw was a good fit for Aimee with Carla. I know their caseloads are huge, and a loving grandmother doesn't always magically show up for kids. I get that it seemed to everyone like a perfect fit."

"But not to you," Devon said.

"No," Marley said darkly. "They didn't *listen*. Not to Carla's fear about Randolph West or his reach even up into her northern community. When I tried to talk to the officer in charge, he said West was in jail, how much damage could he do?"

The question hung in the air between them, the sounds of the hospital playing out in the background.

"Tell me about Aimee."

Marley's eyes lit up. "She's smart and funny once she gets to know you and opens up a little. She doesn't talk. At all. We're still not sure if she can't or won't. She was medically cleared by a doctor when she was brought into custody. The doc suspects selective mutism, possibly caused by trauma." Marley's expression darkened again. "They handed Carla recommendations for counseling and some vitamins and sent them on their way."

Devon watched the anger play out on Marley's features. A tightening of her lips, narrowing of her eyes as she stared into her hands, as if she was constantly fighting a battle to right wrongs.

Devon fought her instinct for only a minute before she spoke.

"How can I help?"

Red flag words, Ash had called them. An indicator that circumstances had brought her to the edge of a cliff. You need to know your limits before you ask, Devon recalled Ash saying. Right now, she felt a little reckless using those words sitting in a hospital room with a cop who broke rules to help. But Devon's gut told her to be part of that help, to be part of whatever Marley was struggling with right now. Red flag words be damned.

"Groceries," Marley said. She tucked her dirty blond hair behind her ear and shifted to sit up straighter. "Carla's worried about Aimee being recognized by Randolph's guys, so they mostly stay in. I've got them in the East end because it's outside of West's known territory. But the Hammer's a small town city, really."

"Outside of West's territory but somewhere you aren't supposed to be? Somewhere they'd be safest and you'd be at the most risk."

Marley looked a little sheepish. "I maybe hadn't thought that all the way through."

Devon laughed, wondering how often those words were true for Marley. She was also wondering how much she wanted to stick around and find out.

"So, the stabbing had nothing to do with this case."

"No," Marley said firmly. "That was bad luck. Or bad planning."

Devon looked into Marley's earnest, repentant, worried eyes.

"Tell me what you need me to do."

Ten minutes later, Devon left the hospital with a list of groceries, an address, and a selfie of herself and Marley to prove to Carla she could be trusted. In the picture, Marley was holding up a piece of paper with the words "I'm OK. This is Devon. She's good people" scratched out in pen. Devon had laughed at the time, but as she wound her way down the back stairs of the hospital and out into the mid-July heat on her way to help this virtual stranger continue to break the rules, Devon wasn't so sure.

As Devon bought fresh fruit and vegetables, milk, pasta, and cheese crackers shaped like goldfish, she admitted to herself she'd turned off part of her brain. This was an instinct she needed to follow. And whether it was her instinct to protect or simply the pull of feeling useful after months of feeling alone and helpless, she wasn't sure.

The early afternoon sky had cleared from the hazy morning humidity to a searing spectrum of sunlight. Devon transferred the three grocery bags to one sweaty hand and checked the map on her phone. Marley had described the run-down neighbourhood, a mix of convenience stores, repair shops, and a few hole-in-the-wall restaurants. Gentrification was attempting to get a foothold here, but the neighbourhood resisted with its relatively high crime rate and utter refusal to open a halfway decent coffee shop or craft brewery. Marley had managed to rent a studio, listed originally as a possible art studio. Devon found the right entrance and pressed the buzzer for number two.

Devon heard a clattering of feet on stairs before an admonishing voice gave an indistinct command. She listened hard but couldn't hear anything for a long minute.

"My name is Devon Wolfe," she said through the door. "Your friend asked me to bring you some groceries."

A faint shuffling on the other side.

"I've got a picture with a message from Marley, if that helps."

Devon had forgotten to ask how Carla and Aimee referred to the cop. But right now shouting Marley's rank to the whole block seemed like a colossally bad idea.

The door clicked then opened a few inches. The woman inside was petite, with wavy dark hair and a suspicious expression. Carla.

Devon smiled but made no movement forward.

"I'm going to show you a picture from Marley," Devon said, swiping open her phone and opening the gallery app. She turned it toward the woman, who glanced at it before looking back to Devon.

"She okay?" Carla said, her voice raspy.

"She's okay," Devon said. "If you're comfortable, I can bring these groceries up and give you a quick update about what's happening. If not, I can leave the groceries here. It's totally up to you."

Carla swayed a little, as if she'd been pushed. She glanced down, then looked back at Devon.

"Yeah, okay. Come in."

Carla swung the door open, and Devon caught sight of a young girl stepping into her grandmother's shadow.

"This one's shy," Carla said, her expression no longer suspiciously hostile but not exactly warm. She put a hand behind her to her granddaughter, then indicated the stairs with her other hand. "First door on your right. I'll be right behind you, my knees don't love these stairs."

Devon climbed the stairs and entered the beautiful but sparse studio. Tall, thin windows that looked into the alley provided some natural light. Devon made out a floor lamp, two blow-up mattresses, a worn chair, and a bright purple beanbag chair as the only furniture. Some books and games were stacked neatly against one wall. There was a small kitchenette and a half-open door that Devon assumed led to the bathroom.

"These okay here?" Devon said, indicating the small counter beside the sink. "There are a few things that should go in the fridge."

"Yes, thanks," Carla said, lowering herself into the chair and rubbing at her knees. Aimee shadowed her grandmother, crouching beside the chair so Devon could see the top of her head. "How much do I owe you?"

Devon opened the fridge and added the fruit, vegetables, and milk. "Don't worry about it."

"I worry," Carla said sharply. Then, softening her tone a little, "I intend to pay Marley back. I won't live off charity. Never have."

Dignity was at risk here. Carla Slessinger was already sacrificing so much for her granddaughter.

"It was $28.41, I think," Devon said. "I wasn't sure what kind of milk you all liked, so I got two kinds."

"That's all right," Carla said. "This young one would drink milk all day long if I let her," she said, smiling. She placed a hand on her granddaughter's head. Most people didn't realize how much could be read by touch. The depth of warmth or subtlety of dominance. To Devon, Carla's touch was one of reassurance. *I'm here. You're okay. I'm here.* "Can you write that down, pet?" Carla said to Aimee.

A small hand reached up to grab a notebook and pen lying on the window ledge. As Devon watched, the hand tapped Carla on the arm twice. Then the hand disappeared, and she heard the pen tap sharply against the paper. Aimee could communicate, obviously.

Devon made her way slowly into the space, speaking quietly so as not to alarm Aimee.

"Looks like you've got some things in here to keep you entertained," she commented, looking around the studio and not at Aimee. She wanted her presence to be as non-threatening as possible.

"We're lucky," Carla said. "Marley found us a good space. Going outside more often would certainly be nice. But, well…It's temporary," Carla said firmly. She cleared her throat and sat a little straighter in her chair. "Sorry I don't have a seat to offer."

"That's okay, Carla," Devon said. Aimee was inching her way to the front of the chair, a quarter of her slight body now visible.

Carla reached down between the arm of the chair and the seat cushion and pulled out a pack of gum. She popped a piece in her mouth and then, after a double tap of that small hand, handed the pack to Aimee. Once Aimee returned it, Carla offered it to Devon, who declined.

"So," Carla said. "What trouble did Marley get into?" The tone sounded tough, but Devon read an undercurrent of worry and guilt. A lot was sitting on this woman's shoulders.

Marley and Devon had spoken about what to share with Carla, knowing Aimee would be present for the conversation.

"Marley was roughed up on Monday morning," Devon said, deliberately leaving out the fact that it had happened only a few blocks from here. "She ended up with an infection, which she's fighting, but it's going to be a few days until she's moving around freely. So, she told me a little of your story and asked me to step in and help."

Carla was clearly evaluating all the gaps in Devon's story, all the pieces she wasn't saying.

"I wish I had my morning paper," Carla said, snapping her gum with what seemed like annoyance. "Then I'd have some idea what was going on." She stared at Devon for a few minutes, chewing her gum vigorously. Between the gum and the smoker's rasp, Devon suspected the young grandmother had recently given up smoking. Maybe even once she took Aimee into her care. Another sacrifice. Another stressor. Carla Slessinger was riddled with them. But right now she seemed most concerned about Marley.

"You say she's okay? Recovering?"

"She is," Devon said. "Truly. She is going to be okay."

Carla gave a sharp nod. "She's an interesting one, that Marley. I've never met a cop quite like her." Devon silently agreed but allowed the woman to talk without interruption. "Don't get me wrong, she's tough. But soft in all the wrong places, somehow, too."

An excellent summary of the woman Devon was getting to know. Though she wasn't yet ready to place a value on her toughness or her softness.

Aimee reached up yet again and tapped her grandmother on the arm. Carla murmured to her granddaughter, who then held up the notebook. Carla scanned it, squinting, then looked back.

"You'll need to come out and ask yourself, my girl," Carla said, gesturing to Devon.

Aimee peered around the corner of her grandmother's chair. Devon smiled and sat on the floor.

"You're welcome to ask me anything you like, Aimee. And there's no hurry."

Curiosity soon won out over fear as Aimee emerged. Devon adjusted her original assessment of Aimee as slight. Aimee was small for her age and quite thin. She had her grandmother's wavy hair, though Aimee's was brown to Carla's dyed black. She also had Carla's wide eyes, but the rest of Aimee's features were hers alone. Devon had a moment to wonder about the mother before Aimee began to approach.

For all her initial hesitancy, Aimee now seemed almost defiant. She stopped in front of Devon and stared for a moment, then walked behind her and reached down, tapping twice on the phone tucked into Devon's back pocket.

Curious, Devon pulled out her phone, punched in her passcode, then held it flat on her palm. Aimee leaned in, frowning, as if looking for something. Then she pulled out her notebook and turned it to show Devon. *Marley?* was written in neat, child-like letters.

"Ah," Devon said. She opened her pictures and turned the phone toward Aimee. The girl hesitated, then with Devon's nod, she picked up the phone and held it carefully, seeming to study the picture.

Aimee dropped to the floor in a crouch, placing Devon's phone gently on the ground. Devon watched upside down as Aimee wrote *Devon* and *good people* in her notebook. Then she looked back up at Devon, obviously still unconvinced. She gestured at Devon then pointed to her name in the book.

"Devon," she said, pronouncing her somewhat unusual name.

Aimee drew her hands apart, as if she wanted more.

"Devon Wolfe."

An eye roll, and the young girl drew her hands even wider.

"Dr. Devon Rachelle Wolfe."

Aimee recorded this in her notebook and looked again at the picture of Devon and Marley. She tapped her fingers to her ears, then put one finger to her chest and took exaggerated breaths in and out, then pointed at Marley in the picture. She did it again when Devon didn't respond.

"I'm not sure what you're asking," Devon said, looking over her shoulder at Carla, who shrugged.

Aimee sighed and circled the word *doctor* in front of Devon's name then repeated the gesture to her ears and chest. She was miming a stethoscope.

"Ah, doctor. You're wondering if I'm Marley's doctor."

Aimee nodded.

"No, I just helped her out when she got hurt. A lot of my friends work at that hospital, though. They're taking good care of her."

Aimee cocked her head to the side and repeated the stethoscope gesture.

"No, I'm not that kind of doctor. I help people who are struggling with their feelings, when life is stressful and their heads and hearts make it hard for them to feel okay."

She always gave her friends' kids that answer when they asked about her job. She wondered if it would be enough for this intelligent little girl.

Aimee put a finger near her lips and held another finger out, then switched them back and forth a few times. Devon smiled at this sign for talking.

"Yes, I'm a talk doctor."

Aimee's eyes lit up brightly at Devon's quick understanding. Then she looked down at the picture again and pointed to Marley before tapping her forehead and then her chest.

"Are you asking how Marley's feeling? Her head and her heart?" The young girl gave a definitive nod.

"I don't really know," Devon said. "I just met her a few days ago. I know she's working hard at recovering, I know she has family taking good care of her, and I know she was worried about you and your grandmother." Devon paused, wanting to completely answer Aimee's question without adding any sort of burden. "Are you okay if I come by instead of Marley for a little while?"

Aimee took a long time with this question, looking once at the picture, then back to Devon. Then she nodded, gave Devon back her phone, and went back to sit in front of her grandmother's chair.

Carla placed her hand on her granddaughter's head, smoothing down the waves with a gentle motion.

"I think you've passed the Aimee test," Carla said.

Devon laughed. "Marley said she usually comes by a couple times a week, so I'll keep that up if it's okay with you."

"That's fine," Carla said. The edge in her voice made Devon think of helplessness, not anger.

"Is there anything else I can get you two? You mentioned missing the paper."

"I'd be grateful for a paper," Carla said. "Some books, maybe, for the little one."

Aimee gave a snort. She scribbled on her notepad, then crossed the room to give it to Devon.

"No horses, no princesses," Devon read. She folded the paper and put it in her pocket. She understood the pull of these two for Marley. They weren't case numbers or accidents or collateral from the drug raid. They were two people who needed some help.

She looked into the solemn brown eyes of Aimee West and silently committed herself to this cause. "I'll find you some good stories," Devon said. She held out her hand and Aimee shook it. "Promise."

# Chapter Four

*It was the stress, that's what Mikayla kept telling everyone. Her mom, her landlord, her best friend. Everything piled up. Not all at once, though. Mikayla was sure she would have asked for help if everything had piled on all at once. But it had been slow, and everyone had been so impressed with how she was raising her daughter on her own. Ava was in school now. Mikayla had two jobs. Her night shift at the House of Beer paid well, but her manager was a handsy asshole and Mikayla hated coming home so late to Ava, smelling like spilled beer and the touch of men. She never checked on her little angel until she'd showered. Even then, she worried she'd brought the evilness of the world into her daughter's pink and yellow bedroom.*

*Mikayla remembered the first time she'd wanted a hit of something, anything. To disappear like she used to in high school, sitting in someone's basement with bad music pumping through shitty speakers. Getting blissed out was what she and her friends used to call it. As if it was something they were seeking, not something they were escaping.*

*Ava had gotten an ear infection just before her first birthday, and she'd cried nonstop for a week. At first it had felt good to take care of her. Ava would quiet at Mikayla's touch, and she'd walk around the basement of her parents' house, bouncing her tiny baby. But soon nothing helped, and the wails of her infant daughter ripped through Mikayla's body, reverberated through her skull, and made her want to scream.*

*She hadn't used then. She'd survived. Moved into her own small apartment. She worked and watched* PAW Patrol *and tried to get her daughter to eat vegetables.*

*I was good,* Mikayla thought, *slumped in the front hallway of her apartment hours after Jaxon left.* I was good. *She thought maybe she whispered it this time to her empty apartment, afternoon sun blazing around the cheap blinds meant to keep the apartment cool. She didn't feel good now. Not at all. Whatever Jaxon had brought her hadn't made her feel blissed out, just blank, as if it removed hours of her day in one hazy chunk. Maybe that was good, though. Hours of not feeling stress or worry. Not feeling inadequate.*

*This sick feeling wasn't good, a hungry and nauseous sensation, as if a hole had been opened in her stomach. Mikayla slowly pulled herself up against the wall, tried to remember where she'd put her phone. Her relief at still having an hour until she had to pick up her daughter from daycare turned to self-loathing horror. She'd used again, fallen unconscious again. And she knew, because she knew herself, that soon she wouldn't only be using on her afternoons off. She was supposed to be dragging laundry up and down the apartment stairs, getting supper started, and paying her bills, not taking hits from the guy who'd been dealing drugs to her and her friends since the eighth grade.*

*Mikayla stood with her forehead pressed against the wall and felt tears gather and fall. It was the stress. There was just too much stress.*

Marley shifted her weight to try and ease some of the strain in her side as she looked down the eight steps to her basement apartment.

"Now will you change your mind and stay with me and your dad for a few days?"

Grace sounded like she was heading toward no-one-ever-listens-to-me mad. Marley needed to prove this was the right decision. She really, really wanted to be home.

But man, those were a lot of steps. And she was going to traverse them twice today. Grace didn't know about the second trip. Marley intended to keep it that way.

"Here we go," Marley said with false cheerfulness, and she took a step down. She sucked in a breath as her stitches stretched, but she took it slow and reached the bottom of the stairs, sweating and a little shaky. But she'd made it without any help.

Her mother opened the door with her key, and Marley followed her in with slow steps. Grace had already been in over the last few days, so her apartment was tidier than when she'd left. It gleamed a little bit, even in this dim light, as if actual cleaning had happened recently. Grace turned on every light, trying to chase the gloom away, but Marley liked the coziness of her basement apartment. It fit her budget and her temperament and was close enough to work that she could roll out of bed twenty-nine minutes before a morning shift, if necessary.

"I've stocked up your fridge and changed the sheets on your bed. That dryer in the laundry room is atrocious. I don't know why you can't get an apartment set. It would probably fit right here in the hall closet."

Marley lowered herself into her favourite grey chair and let Grace's mothering blur into a comforting backdrop of noise. She sighed and pulled the soft blue blanket around her shoulders, the slight chill of the basement and the smell of her own space pulling her eyelids down. Marley resisted for a moment as her mom bustled around the apartment, now talking about the need for Marley's kettle to be descaled. Then she stopped resisting.

It felt like she'd only nodded off for a few minutes because her mother was still talking, but her phone said she'd been sleeping for almost an hour. Grace couldn't have been talking for an hour. Then Marley heard another voice. Devon. Marley felt a warmth in her chest. She liked Devon being here. She was getting used to having her around.

Marley slowly stood up, noting every protesting muscle and reminding herself this was temporary. She would get her muscle mass back, and her body would eventually work the way she wanted it to. Marley shuffled into the kitchen. Her mother was leaning against the counter, and Devon sat at one of the barstools with a mug of something steaming. She looked more relaxed here than she ever had at the hospital, a softening of posture and expression that made Marley wonder how long Devon Wolfe had lived with her guard up.

"Hey," Marley said, her voice still a little gravelly with sleep. "Can I join the tea party?"

"Good morning," Devon said, smiling. "Happy release day."

Marley grunted as she levered herself onto the barstool next to Devon. "That phrase means something a little different to a cop," she joked, pleased when Devon laughed.

"I hadn't thought of that. Happy home day, then," Devon said.

"Tea?" Grace said, holding up a mug.

What Marley wanted was a coffee. Needed one, really, if she was going to get dressed, get to the precinct, and sit through a meeting that afternoon. The thought made Marley the smallest bit nauseous. So, maybe not a coffee.

"Tea would be great. Thanks, Mom."

Grace busied herself with making more tea, obviously having forgiven the state of Marley's kettle. Or more likely, having spent the last hour descaling it. Marley turned to Devon.

"How are you?" she said, wishing Grace wasn't there to overhear. She wanted to know about Carla and Aimee. Had they accepted Devon's help? Were they okay?

"I'm good," Devon said. "I went grocery shopping yesterday and hung out with some friends. Nothing too exciting."

Marley searched Devon's face for any sign of tension, but she seemed fine. Marley felt herself relaxing a little. Carla and Aimee were okay, and Devon would take care of them until Marley was back on her feet. But she still worried about their future.

"I like your apartment," Devon said, looking around.

Grace snorted as she pulled the whistling kettle off the stove.

"It's a bat cave. I raised Batman," Grace said.

Marley and Devon grinned at each other behind Grace's back, and Marley felt a moment of giddiness, a tilt back in time to sharing secrets with the girl from tenth grade algebra who was the object of Marley's every sweet and lustful thought.

"Thanks," Marley said to Devon. "I'm happy to be home."

"I can only imagine," Devon said.

Marley doctored the tea her mom put in front of her and listened to Devon humming under her breath, a habit that was all Devon. She smiled and raised an eyebrow at Devon.

"Sarah Harmer? 'Basement Apartment'?"

Devon laughed and looked a little sheepish.

"Yeah. You have to admit the song really fits this place."

Marley looked around her apartment, seeing it a little differently having been away. And having Devon here. Pictures of family and friends and trips were everywhere. Marley felt anchored by those photos, like she needed reminders of who she was. She turned back to Devon.

"You were humming in the hospital, too. I remember that, sort of. I was a little out of it."

Devon nodded solemnly. "You were. So, let's pretend I was not by your bedside humming Van Halen's 'Doctor, Doctor.' Agreed?"

Marley laughed, a real laugh that eased the tension in her chest and filled her head with a kind of light that felt familiar but distant. She could get used to this.

"All right," Grace said, straightening the tea towel on the handle of the oven. "I'm assuming you're settled and don't need me anymore, so I'm off to the grocery store to pick up a roast."

Marley itched at her side. "Dad's been looking up recipes again?"

Grace shook her head. "I wish that man had never found Pinterest. I've gained ten pounds on pork roast alone."

Marley smiled. "You're perfect, Mom. And thanks for everything."

Grace kissed her on the cheek on the way by. "Rest, Bridget." When Marley started to speak, to assure her in her most earnest tone that she promised to take it easy, Grace held her daughter's chin in her hand. "I mean it."

Parents knew when you were lying. They always knew.

"Yes, Mama," Marley said, swallowing her guilt.

Moments later, Marley and Devon were seated in her small living room. Marley checked the time. Under two hours until Superman came to get her.

"You're heading out somewhere?" Devon said.

"There's an update on the drug ring this afternoon. I want to hear it."

Marley waited for Devon's protest, but she didn't say anything. An awkward moment of silence stretched between them, and Marley realized she didn't really know this woman. Even though Devon had held her hand, held her blood, held her secrets.

"I told Carla and Aimee I'd stop by again tomorrow," Devon said. "If that's okay?"

Permission seemed like an odd thing to need to give. "Yes, of course. And thank you. I should be back on my feet soon."

"Don't worry about it," Devon said. "They're doing okay."

"I worry," Marley said as she rubbed her eyes. They were gritty and tired, and she knew a killer headache wasn't too far behind.

When she opened her eyes, Devon was looking at her like she had questions. Questions Marley likely couldn't answer about Carla and Aimee and breaking the rules and what exactly was Marley's plan. Marley didn't have a plan. Marley was hurting and very, very tired.

"I should go," Devon said, standing. "I'm guessing it would be nice to have some time by yourself in your own place."

Marley watched as Devon shoved her hands in her pockets and rocked on her feet. She seemed uncertain, and Marley was sure she'd contributed to that. Made Devon feel uncomfortable when all she'd done was help. And help and help.

"Don't get up," Devon said, as Marley began struggling to her feet. She smiled a crooked smile at Marley. "I can find my way out."

Marley sat back against the chair, breathing against the pain in her abdomen. "Yeah, okay. I'll text you tomorrow, if that's okay. To check in on Carla and Aimee."

Devon tilted her head. "Want to video chat with Aimee tomorrow while I'm there? I think she'd like that."

Marley grinned. "That could be entertaining."

Devon returned the smile, her eyes bright. "It really could. I'll let you know when I'm there."

"Thanks again, Devon," Marley said, wishing she could say more but not knowing how.

"You're welcome. Take your mom's advice, at least for a bit. Rest, Marley."

"I'll try," Marley said.

"I know."

And then Devon was gone and Marley was alone.

❖

The precinct was louder than Marley remembered. Or maybe that was the headache talking. She felt weird walking in without her uniform, her loose khakis and fitted T-shirt about as formal as she could get. Marley had worked hard the last six years to fit in and feel a sense of belonging, all the while wondering if she was really meant to be an enforcer of laws. She'd never been particularly good at following rules. Too often in her life, she had been odd person out. Marley had pushed and molded herself to be part of this. As she walked slowly through the halls, greeting her surprised coworkers, Marley wasn't sure she'd put her efforts in the right place. Now was likely not the place to unpack it. Especially because Sergeant Crawford was walking toward her, and he didn't look happy.

"Marlowe, I'm surprised to see you."

Clearly translated to *what the fuck are you doing here?*

"I thought there was some paperwork for me to sign?" Marley said, even though she knew full well it was being delivered to her apartment. "And then I heard there was an update on Fleming Street, and I thought I'd listen in, since I'm here."

Crawford nodded along like Marley was saying something reasonable. "Listen in," he echoed. "With the intention of…" He let the sentence hang. Marley began to sweat.

"I assume I'll be back on desk work before I'm back on active duty," Marley explained. "An investigation like this has hundreds of leads and thousands of pieces of information to sort through." She shrugged, like she hadn't been obsessing about this for days. "I figured I'd be useful there."

Crawford stared her down, and Marley felt a trickle of sweat in the small of her back despite the air conditioning in the precinct.

"You sit and listen, then you go home. Any usefulness out of you on this case will be directed by me when I have paperwork in my hand saying you are back from sick leave. Understood?"

"Understood, sir."

Crawford looked up and addressed the officers in the room, half of whom were pretending they hadn't been listening in to Marley and Crawford's conversation. "Two minutes, Fleming Street update in the IT Room."

Marley felt some of the tension leave her body as she followed the dozen other officers to the IT Room. The meeting room was the only space big enough to debrief most of the team in relative comfort. It had been painted in shades of brown for decades and, of course, had been dubbed the Shit Room. It had been an inoffensive light grey ever since Marley had worked here, but the name had stuck.

Marley slowly lowered herself into a chair near the back of the room, impossibly trying not to stick out. Injured, out of uniform, and one of only two women in the room. She was also one of very few out queer officers, a distinction which had become obvious last year when Marley had spoken out against how the police force had handled themselves at Pride the year before. She had voiced her opinion that it was their job to protect any people or community at risk of harm, regardless of how that community viewed the police. It hadn't helped her fitting in, and she still felt the sting of distance from many of her colleagues.

Marley pressed her thumbs against her eye sockets, trying to relieve some of the pain in her head. It didn't work, and she tried to focus on the front of the room as the drug investigation squad was giving an update.

"We initially considered this a pretty small operation," Constable Simms, the most senior of the drug squad, was saying. "A few of the high attain street drugs—speed, ketamine, Ecstasy—popular with the university crowd. Our intel showed they'd moved into production about six months ago, which is when we really started to target the place on Fleming Street."

"But we shut down Fleming Street," one of the young guys at the front of the room said, obviously uninterested in the history lesson. "Did we miss something?"

"Yes and no," Simms said, clearing his throat. Marley was pretty sure he was in his mid-fifties and was a serious, old-school type police officer. "Our take from Fleming Street included the three high attain street drugs, the equipment needed to manufacture at least one of those drugs, and a drug we had assumed to be an opioid, but we couldn't be sure so sent it off for analysis. We don't have the results back yet, but it looks like that substance is what's causing the problems."

Simms paused and looked at Sergeant Crawford, who walked to the front of the room.

"The substance is at the lab in Ottawa for analysis. The issue we've got right now is a red flag from Public Health." Crawford let the surprised chatter from the room die down before carrying on. With the onset of the opioid crisis across North America, the public health agencies had moved from tracking childhood disease and salmonella outbreaks to encompassing a generation of communities affected by instant drug addiction. For them to be involved this early meant something was up. "Since our takedown of Fleming Street and subsequent removal of Fleming Street's products off Hamilton streets, there has been an uptick in people seeking medical attention for a series of unexplained symptoms including vomiting, facial muscle paralysis, rash, and hallucinations."

"How many are we talking, Sarge?"

"Currently five."

"Not many," the cop said to the murmurs of agreement around him.

"Let me be clear," Crawford said, raising his voice a little over the din. "We have made no definitive link between the unknown Fleming substance and the uptick of hospital visits for these symptoms. But I'm not liking the coincidence of the timing, and if we've learned anything from fentanyl, it's to pay attention early. That means all of you on the front line are paying attention. You're listening to your sources and flagging members of the public who exhibit these symptoms." He paused for a moment and looked out over the assembled team. "We're all in this, not just the drug squad."

Marley raised her hand, pretending her body didn't protest the movement.

"Marlowe."

"Just so I'm clear, these symptoms weren't seen before the drugs were taken off the street? So it's a result of the detox, not an effect of the drug itself?"

"That seems to be the case. Our Public Health liaison will give us more information when they have it, but they're telling me they need to know what this drug is before they can comment on the side effects of the drug or the effects of detox."

"Any other jurisdictions seeing this, Sarge?" Superman said.

"I've spent the morning on the phone, and no. So far it's just us. Public Health and the OPP will be going through their sources as well, of course."

Marley felt a shift in the air at that information. This targeted but unknown threat aimed at their city became an enemy. The energy in the room swelled in response, the silent agreement to take on and eliminate the threat, no matter what. For some it was puffed-up arrogance, a superhero complex that had gotten them into uniform in the first place. For most, though, like Marley, it was simply a combination of instinct and oath to protect.

"Eyes and ears open, people," Crawford said. "That's all I'm asking. Simms is taking point, so leads and questions to him. Watch for memo updates, and I'll recall the team if we make any more definitive links."

Crawford looked around the room, and when no one said anything, he dismissed them with a short bark.

Marley let the team disperse around her, most heading to their desks or their patrol cars, their shifts delayed by this meeting. She got a few claps on the shoulder and a couple of sexist jokes about cute nurses at the hospital. Most officers barely spared her a glance. Superman sent her a questioning look on his way out, and Marley waved him off. She'd get a cab home. Lasagna and a nap in her own bed was sounding really good.

She was easing her way to standing and trying not to show how much it hurt when she heard her name being called. Crawford and Simms were walking toward her.

"Constable Marlowe," Simms said, shaking her hand. "I hear we're getting you as desk jockey when you're back on duty."

Marley glanced at Crawford, whose expression remained impassive.

"I should be back in a day or two," Marley said, basing her answer on want rather than fact.

"Good. Great," Simms said. "We've got a ton of intel to sort through and not enough eyes. We could use your help."

Before Marley could speak, Crawford jumped in. "Paperwork in my hands, Marlowe. Then you can report to Simms."

"Yes, Captain," Marley said and smiled a little when Crawford shook his head.

As Crawford and Simms walked away, Marley opened the taxi app on her phone and ordered a cab. She felt giddy as she shuffled back to the front desk. Exhausted, yes. In pain, absolutely. Her abdomen never seemed to stop itching or throbbing or generally reminding her that a blade had severed tissue and muscle less than a week ago. But she would be coming back to work, and she already had a role that would keep her close to the Fleming case and close to any information she could use to keep Carla and Aimee safe.

## CHAPTER FIVE

Devon had run on her treadmill, showered, eaten breakfast, and was grabbing her keys and phone to head out the door when the panic hit. The dual waves of anxiety and self-hate made the edges of her vision blur as she stood in her front hallway, legs trembling.

"Breathe," Devon said to herself through clenched teeth. "Can't fight if you don't breathe."

She breathed. A deliberate act, willing each inhalation and exhalation to allow the panic to leave her body and replace it with rational thought. It took so long that shame wormed its way in, and Devon almost let herself sink down and curl herself up against the wall.

*I can stay standing. I will stay standing.*

Small, attainable goals. One step. Focus on the present.

Devon endured the alternating waves of anxiety and shame, each one cresting in a sea of hurt until the waves lost some of their power, until she no longer felt pulled under. Until her legs felt solid, and the haze around her cleared. She emerged from the undertow. Shaken, but she emerged.

Devon left her keys and phone where they were and walked back to her kitchen for a glass of water. She added some ice and took a few moments to listen to the crack of each cube. The coolness of the water was soothing, the ice against her lips a spark of sensation.

Devon hadn't had a panic attack for weeks. Now that rationality had returned, Devon could begin to see the attack not so much as a regression but more a culmination of the last week, ever since finding Marley in the alley. Senses wide open now, Devon could feel the stiff cotton of Marley's rain-soaked shirt, the warmth of the blood mixed with the warmth of the rain. Grit beneath her knees and water dripping into her eyes. Marley's pain was a palpable sensation Devon allowed into her chest and breathed in with every beat of Marley's pulse against her fingertips.

Devon held the glass to her forehead and closed her eyes, letting the rawness of the encounter surface as it obviously had needed to do for the last week. She and Ash, her therapist, had talked about how that would happen. To accept it when it did. To try and see it as a gift of moving forward, even if it hurt.

It hurt.

Devon knew she should cry the tears that followed on the exodus of the panic. A few escaped and she trapped them with the cold, sweating glass of water against her cheeks. She breathed, she calmed, she opened her eyes.

Devon's phone chimed near the front door, and Devon went to check it out, grateful she felt steady. Marley had texted her saying good morning and wondering when they might be doing a video chat since she wanted to make sure she'd had coffee and put on pants.

Devon laughed out loud and reread the message. She took a moment before she replied, mentally replaying the steps of leaving the house, going to the grocery store, and making it to Carla and Aimee's hidden studio. She felt confident she could do it, her recent panic attack aside. Now she could do it.

*An hour maybe?* Devon texted. *Does that work?*

*Works for me. I'm just sitting here holding down the couch and building scar tissue.*

*Sleep okay last night?* Devon typed the question, then sent it before she could worry that it was too forward.

*12 hours. I'm reliving my toddler years.*

*You obviously needed it.*

*Suppose so. Your day okay? You don't mind an errand?*

Devon paused before she responded. It would be easiest to say yes, no problem. Everything was fine. It didn't feel right, though. Not with Marley.

*Tough morning. Errand will be good for me.*

Marley's response didn't come through right away, and Devon tried not to let her anxiety fill in the blanks.

*Come by and tell me about tough morning after errand? If you're up for it.*

Devon didn't hesitate. *I'd like that.*

They signed off, and with only a moment to remember the panic attack that had gripped her twenty minutes ago, Devon grabbed her keys and walked out the door.

The humidity was an oppressive weight Devon felt as soon as she walked outside. Southern Ontario in July usually saw weeks of heat and humidity, but this summer had been especially intense with storms that built and crested every few days but never seemed to disperse the heat. Devon put her sunglasses on against the glare of the morning sun, already sensing the afternoon storm that would darken the sky and flood the streets with rain.

The streets were busy, but the grocery store was quiet. Devon found the few items on her short list and was back in her car, air conditioning blasting, heading to the east end within twenty minutes. She felt a little raw from her morning, like an emotional workout that stretched her muscles and made her ache with the reminder of the exercise. Moving helped, purpose helped. Knowing she'd see Marley again helped.

When she arrived at the apartment, Aimee was waiting at the door, peering through the crack. Aimee swung the door wide as Devon approached and jumped and spun in silent excitement before racing up the stairs. Devon laughed and followed, first locking the door behind her.

"Hello again," Carla said, taking the bags from Devon as she hoisted a folding chair with the other.

"It's good to see you again," Devon said. "I hope you don't mind I brought a chair."

Carla waved her away, taking the bags to the kitchen.

"If I could get out for a bit, I was thinking of heading to a re-shop for a few things, chairs included. But..." Carla trailed off and looked at Aimee, who was standing by the window flipping through one of the books Devon had brought. "That's not in the cards right now."

Devon wanted to offer to stay with Aimee so Carla could go out. This wasn't good for either of them. Concern snaked in her stomach, and Devon acknowledged its presence. Before anything, Devon needed to talk to Marley.

"A paper," Carla said, looking through the bags. "Two!" Her eyes lit up, looking shockingly like her granddaughter. "Bless you."

Devon smiled. "It did sound like something you've been missing. It's amazing how the small things can make a tough situation seem normal."

Carla looked hard at Devon for a moment, and Devon wondered if she was searching for pity or condescension. She obviously didn't find it because she relaxed in the next breath.

"Tea or coffee?" Carla said. "I know it's warm out."

Aimee scrambled into the kitchen at the question and tugged on her grandmother's sleeve, then she opened the fridge door. She pulled out an orange juice container filled with brown liquid and held it up.

"Yes, of course. You can offer that to our guest."

Aimee looked up shyly, hugging the juice container to her chest.

"We made iced tea," Carla said. "Just some cold tea and lemonade, but the little chef here liked making it."

"I'd love some iced tea," Devon said to Aimee.

The young girl scrambled onto the counter, pulling down three plastic cups and filling them carefully, then distributing them around.

"Delicious," Devon said once they all had their drinks and were sitting down. "Perfect for this hot day."

Aimee grinned.

"We're lucky with the building," Carla said, resting her cup against the arm of her chair. "The brick stays cool on the alley side, so we're quite comfortable in here. Though I imagine it's another story in winter."

Carla sat back in her chair, looking defeated.

"Worry for another day," Devon said.

"I suppose it is," Carla said sharply. "Though this is not how I like to run my life. None of this is."

Aimee had begun shrinking down the wall until she was huddled on the floor. A look of distress passed over Carla's face.

"Ah, pet. It's okay. Grandma's got worries on her brain. But nothing is wrong."

Aimee clutched her drink and stared up at her grandmother.

"Say it with me?" Carla said. She put a hand to her forehead, and after a moment's hesitation, Aimee mimicked the gesture. "My thoughts are clear," Carla said as she moved her hand across her forehead. Aimee did the same, then they put their hands around their shoulders in the imitation of a hug. "My body is safe." Grandmother and child then placed hands on their chest. "My heart is healing."

The sweetness and heaviness of the moment hit Devon in her own chest. It chafed against her own recently unsafe thoughts, her own healing heart. She struggled for a moment to not let tears surface. Such a raw moment between these two. Devon cleared her throat.

"What a perfect mantra to get you through tough times," Devon said. "I'm going to remember that."

Carla looked pleased, and Aimee looked more relaxed.

"We have some tough days, don't we, pet?" Aimee nodded solemnly and drank her iced tea. "But we manage."

"More than manage," Devon said quietly. She didn't push, though, imagining Carla would be uncomfortable with acknowledgement of how well they were both handling an incredibly difficult situation. "I wondered how you would feel about Aimee doing a video chat with Marley this morning."

Aimee's eyes lit up, and she gulped the rest of her iced tea and slammed it on the floor and stood up and shimmied her excitement. Devon laughed, and Carla cracked a smile, then looked pointedly at the cup on the floor. Aimee rolled her eyes but picked up the cup and ran to the kitchen, tossing it in the sink before racing back.

Devon texted Marley asking if she was ready and received an instant reply: yes. Devon connected the call and handed Aimee the phone, pointing over her shoulder where the camera was and where Marley's face would pop up. It did a moment later, and Devon recognized Marley's living room and what she suspected was Marley's favourite chair.

"Squirt!" Marley said, and Devon heard a small, raspy, hiccupping sound. She realized it was Aimee laughing. Or maybe trying not to laugh. Interesting.

In moments, Aimee had taken Devon's phone and was showing Marley her new book. Marley kept up a line of chatter and questions, though Devon recognized that Marley allowed time and space for Aimee to communicate in her own way.

"This will be good for them both, I imagine," Carla said, watching her granddaughter race to the kitchen to show Marley the half-empty bottle of iced tea.

"Very much so," Devon said. She had so many questions for Carla about Aimee and her health and the evidence of trauma that marked her. She wasn't sure how to start the conversation or even if she had any right to.

"I worry about her," Carla said quietly. "Like I've never worried about anything in my life. And life has thrown me a fair few worries, but this little one…"

"What worries you most?" Devon said.

Carla gave her an assessing look Devon was coming to recognize.

"It's the things I don't know," Carla said. "I don't know what happened to this little girl while she was living with her father. An eight-year-old at the centre of an illegal drug ring." Carla shook her head, anger rising. "Who was she interacting with? What did she see every day? And the worst question…" Carla looked like she needed a moment to compose herself. "Why did my son want her in the first place? That man only looks out for himself, his only thought about others is how they can suit his needs. He's been like that his whole damn life." Carla looked at Devon and her eyes were angry and tortured. "So, what did he need from Aimee? When her mother died a year and a half ago, why did he take her in? He didn't even know her."

They both turned to look at a thumping sound. Aimee had dropped to the floor and was log rolling crazily across the hardwood, phone still in her hands. Marley's tinny laughter filled the room.

Devon turned back to Carla. "Hard questions."

Carla shook her head. "I can ask those. It's the hard answers I worry about."

Devon hesitated before asking her next question. Marley's boundaries be damned, Devon had an ethical obligation to this child. "Do you know some of the signs of trauma and abuse to look for?"

"Some," Carla said. "I guess the social worker ran a quick assessment before I arrived." Devon made a mental note to find out if she could see the results of that assessment. Not that this was her patient. Not that she was at work. Not that she was capable…

Devon swallowed. "Did they talk to you about the results?"

"Briefly. Something about no immediate and apparent problem areas, but they recommended counseling. Their biggest concern was her lack of speech, but they said it was outside their expertise and to follow up with a pediatrician, speech and language pathologist, and child psychologist." Carla snorted. "Like I've got those on my speed dial."

Devon recognized the obvious gap between services meant to help individuals in need and their capacity to follow through. The best practice/best intentions trap, as Devon's mentor had once called it.

"In psychology we talk about protective factors, things within and around a person that make it likely they will succeed and grow and thrive, despite their history. What are Aimee's protective factors, do you think?"

Carla's eyes lit up. "She's smart, that one. Curious, when it's safe to be curious. She loves to laugh, though sometimes I catch her looking worried. Like at any moment that laughter is going to get her in trouble. But it's at the core of her, that laughter."

"And you," Devon said. "You are a critical protective factor in her life."

Carla was silent, her eyes far away.

"It's the strangest thing. It feels like I've known her since she was born, even though I haven't. I met her for the first time six months ago when my son let it slip his daughter was living with him. Eventually I didn't give him a choice and just came down to see her. We got on like a house on fire, us two." She looked up at Devon. "I'm going to try and be good for her. And hope I'm not too late."

At that moment, Aimee came running over and handed Devon her phone, then she took off again. Devon juggled the phone and saw the video chat was still connected.

"Hey," she said to Marley. "How was that?"

"Dizzying," Marley said, laughing. "That was a wild Aimee ride."

Devon laughed and Carla did, too. "You still good if I stop by?"

"Definitely," Marley said. "I wouldn't say no to a Mountain Dew Slurpee if you happened to have one in your back pocket."

Devon shook her head. "I'll see what I can do. See you in half an hour?"

"Eleven hundred hours, yes ma'am." Marley gave a lazy salute and signed off.

Devon pushed her phone into her back pocket.

"She's a good one, that Marley," Carla said. Devon nodded her agreement, and Carla seemed to take this as invitation to say more. "She's the only one who listened to me. Everyone else was giving me things. Information and instructions. Warnings. Reassurances. Marley brought me a coffee and found some sandwiches for me and Aimee and just…listened. When I asked her if my son would know I was being made Aimee's legal guardian, she told me he would likely find out. And when I said he would use whatever influence he had to make sure Aimee was not with me, she heard me. She went to a supervisor or someone. Everyone else told me not to worry. They told me to focus on Aimee and not to worry about any of that." Carla fiddled with the cup in her hand. "Out of everyone, I should know to worry about Randolph West."

Devon looked across the room to where Aimee seemed absorbed in her book again. She sensed Carla wanted to open up about her son, but it absolutely could not happen in front of Aimee. The look they shared confirmed that.

"Enough about that," Carla said, hoisting herself out of the chair. Devon drained her iced tea and followed Carla into the kitchen. "We found some baking soda and vinegar in a cleaning cupboard downstairs, so Aimee and I are going to do some science experiments today."

Devon laughed. "Sounds messy. And fun."

Aimee trailed into the kitchen and started poking around in the bags Devon had brought.

"Anything you want next time I come?" Devon said.

"Girl's going to get spoiled," Carla said, as Aimee ran off and returned with her notebook and a pen.

They waited as Aimee wrote her note, ripped it out, and handed it to Devon.

"Grandma gum, coffee creamer, berries," Devon read out, impressed there was only one spelling mistake. She looked up at the beaming little girl. "It's good you take care of your grandma."

Carla pulled her granddaughter tight in a one-armed hug. "We take care of each other."

Ten minutes later, Devon was back in her car, heading to Marley's. She was deeply absorbed in her own thoughts about Carla and Aimee and how she was going to bring up her concerns to Marley. She was almost to Marley's apartment when she remembered the Slurpee. Finally, with sticky takeout cup in hand and a bank of grey clouds following her, Devon knocked on Marley's door.

"You're the gayest angel I've seen today," Marley said when she opened the door.

Devon laughed and acknowledged the heat in her belly at the words as she handed the sticky cup to Marley. Devon went to wash her hands in the sink as Marley slurped her drink. Marley was wearing a sleeveless T-shirt and cut-off track pants and looked comfortable for the first time since Devon had met her. Devon also noticed the definition in Marley's arms, and the blood pounded a little harder in her veins.

"Feeling okay today?" Devon said, refocusing.

"Stronger, yeah," Marley said. "No nausea, moving around better." Marley made a face. "You don't want a patient update. It's boring. Tell me about Carla and Aimee."

Devon steadied her breath and leaned forward, her elbows resting on her thighs and her hands clasped together. Marley cocked her head to the side, looking curious.

"Is there something wrong?"

"No," Devon said. "Carla and Aimee are good."

"Okay," Marley said. "You got a really serious look on your face, that's all."

"I have some concerns about them living there long term. It's not a good environment for Aimee, and it's a real stressor on Carla. They're okay for now, but I'm not sure how long that will be true."

Devon watched annoyance flicker in Marley's grey eyes, quickly replaced by consideration.

"I suppose this is what happens when you ask a psychologist to deliver groceries," Marley said. Devon gave a half-smile, acknowledging Marley's attempt to ease the sudden tension in the room. "And it's not long term. It was never intended to be long term, anyway."

"I understand that," Devon said. "But Aimee needs somewhere to settle. She needs to be in school and seeing a therapist. She needs to be able to leave the apartment."

"I know that," Marley said sharply, sitting up in her chair. Then she drew in a sharp breath and closed her eyes.

Devon's heart ached at the sight. She hated adding this to Marley's plate right now. But she couldn't ignore her concerns about Carla and Aimee. Marley opened her eyes.

"How long will you give me?" Marley said.

"What do you mean?"

Marley took a breath and pressed her hand lightly against her side. "I know I need a plan for Carla and Aimee. I've been working on that. Carla is afraid to go back to Thunder Bay because Randolph still has too many connections there, and it would be too easy for him to track her down."

"Even from prison?"

"Yes, even from prison. It takes one phone call. And besides, he's only being held on bail right now. He could be out any time."

Devon leaned back in her seat. "I didn't know that," she said. There was a lot she didn't know. And she was beginning to recognize Marley was carrying most of it on her shoulders.

"So, this whole time I've been trying to figure out if I should help Carla set up somewhere brand new where she has no connections."

"Which is good and bad."

"Yes, exactly. Or should I keep them here? Randolph hopefully wouldn't look for them because the paperwork says they left weeks ago. And at least here I can look after them."

"And me," Devon said. Whatever compulsion she had to help, to fix, to make better, was now a commitment.

"I guess what I'm asking is how long until you are no longer comfortable with Carla and Aimee's current living situation? Until your instinct or your ethics won't allow you to support this, and you feel the need to report me."

"What?" Devon said, startled. She leaned toward Marley, who remained very still. "No, that's not what I—"

"You already know Sergeant Crawford. He would be the best person to contact with your concerns."

"Marley, stop." Devon said. "Please just give me a second."

They sat in silence. Devon felt a faint rumbling through the walls and floor—a truck on the upper road, maybe, or the storm that had been following her all morning. "I don't need to report you. I know you're trying to balance the risk to Carla and Aimee with their well-being. I trust that."

Marley nodded without saying anything, and Devon gave an inward sigh. She'd blown this, taken the wrong approach and alienated Marley.

"I'd like to help," Devon said. "Not just do you a favour while you're recovering but really be part of this. Which means I need to be able to bring up my own concerns. That's all this is. It's not judgment or a threat. I want us to work together."

Marley's eyes softened, her guarded look replaced by speculation. Devon relaxed as well. Obviously, she'd said something right.

"You're not good at breaking rules, are you?" Marley said, eyes twinkling.

Devon let out a short laugh and ran a hand through her hair. "No, not particularly. But I always want the rules to make sense."

"In my experience, rules almost never make sense," Marley said.

"Interesting perspective for someone tasked with upholding the law," Devon said. She moved through this conversation tentatively, aware of their now loose connection.

Marley shrugged. "I want things to be right, but I'm fully aware I'm not always the holder of right. I'm comfortable with not always having the answer. I'm uncomfortable sticking to rules or laws that have the potential to hurt."

"Which is why you gave me permission to tattle to your supervisor?"

Marley laughed and held her side with her hand. "I used to make my little brother, Caleb, be ready to tell on me to an adult. Whenever I was about to do something stupid, I'd make him list two adults he could go to if he felt something was wrong." Marley smiled and shook her head at the memory. "He almost never did. He usually just stood back and watched and cried as I jumped off the garage or stole raspberries from the neighbours. Probably traumatized the poor guy. No wonder he went into academia."

Devon laughed along with Marley, happy they seemed to be building a bridge over their disagreement and happier still they seemed to be building a foundation. Of what, she wasn't sure. Right now, it didn't matter. Devon felt connected and happy.

"You've got an interesting approach to the world, Constable Marlowe," Devon said. "I've never met anyone quite like you."

Marley kept a straight face and, maintaining eye contact with Devon, picked up her Slurpee and took a long, loud slurp. Devon leaned her head back and laughed.

"Okay, enough about me," Marley said. "You were going to tell me about your morning."

Devon felt herself go still, felt the immediate resistance to being the subject of the conversation. She fought it for a moment, as she'd fought the impulse to curl up and not move this morning. "A panic attack," Devon said, before she could talk herself out of it. "As I was leaving the house. I haven't had one in a few weeks."

"You used to get them more often?" Devon was relieved Marley's expression hadn't changed.

"Not all the time, but frequently enough that it began to impact my life." Devon took a breath. "I've been on medical leave from work for the past few months. The day…you were hurt, I was on my way to meet with HR about extending my leave and making a back-to-work plan."

"You needed a break," Marley said. "These jobs are hard on the soul."

*Exactly. And I couldn't stand up to it.*

"It just overwhelmed me," she said. "Everything seemed to get away from me, and I was completely overwhelmed. I couldn't get above it."

"It feels that way sometimes, doesn't it?"

Devon noticed the slight correction in Marley's statement, moving Devon away from being self-critical and blaming. Marley opened up the circle and Devon heard the unspoken "me, too." *Us, too.* Marley was effortlessly empathetic.

"So, I took a leave. I'm seeing a therapist. And only occasionally struggling to leave the house, like this morning."

"Sounds like a tough way to start your day. Was it okay once you were out?"

"I think it helped to have somewhere I needed to be," Devon said. "Once I could think again, it helped pull me out of the hole more quickly than before." Devon shrugged, forcing herself to look into Marley's eyes. She wondered if Marley understood how hard this was, how little experience she had in formulating words about herself.

"But being out isn't easy for you yet," Marley said. It was part statement, part question but all gentleness.

Devon leaned back a little, needing distance because she didn't know what to do with needing closeness.

"Not yet," Devon said. She let the silence stretch, then opened up the vulnerability wide. "Was it that obvious?"

"Obvious? No, not at all. Remember, I've had nothing better to do this last week than watch the people around me."

"And grow scar tissue," Devon said with a smile.

Marley gave a small laugh but kept talking. Devon hadn't really expected to distract her. "I notice you always arrive tense, then relax, then get tense again when you're leaving. Like you're constantly putting on and taking off armour."

"Yes. That's how it feels."

"Sounds exhausting," Marley said quietly.

"It is." Devon felt something in her chest, the smallest of vibrations as she looked into Marley's eyes and saw happiness and fear and worry and connection.

Silence filled the space between them, and Devon could hear the sound of rain pattering against the window in the kitchen.

"I'm glad you're here," Marley said.

She could interpret those words in so many ways with the light in Marley's eyes and the tone of her voice. Devon smiled back.

"I am, too."

## Chapter Six

*M*ikayla had stopped for three weeks. She'd been proud of herself because she'd done it on her own. Her parents still helped out so much with Ava, but this she had kept to herself and done on her own. She was a little shaky. It didn't feel great knowing she didn't have the drugs to fall back on if she had a tough day. Just keep going, she told herself. And she did.

It wasn't stress that sent her back. It was celebration. The victory of a good month, feeling on track, feeling like a good mom and an adult. Feeling like she deserved something to relax. She thought about finding time to go out with friends, meet up at a bar or dance all night or sit and smoke pot in someone's backyard. But her friends were either stuck in the grind of surviving like she was or were still partying like it was high school. They didn't have a clue what Mikayla was dealing with in her life.

Mikayla felt bad she had no one she wanted to celebrate with. So, she texted Jaxon. He said he'd missed her, and she told him she was feeling good and wanted something that could make her feel a bit better. It felt like a confession, an offering of her worth as a mom and a productive member of society, as her dad always said. But Jaxon seemed to understand, even told her she was a good mom and she was doing great. He told her taking a break was allowed, and he had something new she might like to try. A great high, he said. Smooth and lasted a long time. More expensive, but worth it.

Worth it, Mikayla repeated it over and over, as the smoke hit her lungs and her fingertips tingled and her legs went soft and her head *felt like a pillow and her body succumbed to weightlessness, even as it dragged her down, down, down, to the floor.*

❖

Marley clutched her beat-up silver travel mug full of coffee and tried to keep her expression flat. The office buzzed around her in a chaos of noise as she sat at her desk, everything feeling painful and wrong as she absorbed the news from Sergeant Crawford.

"He made bail?" Marley repeated.

"Yesterday," Sergeant Crawford said in his deep voice. "He already checked in with his parole officer this morning. He's playing the game for now."

Randolph West had made bail and was now free—or as free as you could be while on parole and awaiting trial—to wander the streets of Hamilton. Hopefully nowhere near Carla and Aimee. Marley felt cold, but she suppressed a shiver. She couldn't look weak in front of her sergeant, not as he scrutinized the letter from her doctor she had submitted to HR the day before.

"Constable Simms has taken over the back boardroom, you can go ahead and check in with him."

"Thank you, sir."

"You're on desk duty, Marlowe. No street work, no ride-alongs. Nothing. You're sitting at a desk, and you're going to like it."

Marley straightened carefully, still conscious of the ripped layers of tissue in her side.

"No, sir," she said with a straight face. "I'm going to love it."

Sergeant Crawford walked away shaking his head, and Marley went back to the boardroom, tucked away in an inconvenient but quiet corner at the back of the building. Her work pants felt loose, her plain leather belt almost inadequate to hold them up over her hips. Maybe it was the lack of utility belt—she didn't need any of the holstered weapons or tools to ride a desk—but more likely it was the weight loss from her hospital stay. Either way, nothing felt right about the way she moved or felt. None of that mattered, she reminded herself as she entered the boardroom. She was back at work, and Randolph West was out on bail.

"Marlowe, good to see you on your feet," Simms said, greeting

Marley with a welcoming but distracted smile. Marley liked Simms, though she didn't know him well. She'd heard the rumours of his impending burnout. Bets were on for Simms to transfer to a school safety officer any day, an easy slip into retirement. But he was here today, focused.

"Where should I start, Constable?"

"Simms is fine," the officer said, waving Marley to a seat. "You want to start with paper copies or computer files?"

"I may have been born in the 80s, but I can handle paper."

He gave a short laugh. "You're a funny kid. We don't get a lot of funny in the drug squad."

Simms brought her an evidence box from a small pile stacked along one wall. Marley recognized the excitement in her belly. She was a community officer, spending most of her time in a cruiser, on the streets, or writing reports at her desk. She rarely had the chance to be part of an ongoing investigation.

"Paper evidence from the house on Fleming Street. There wasn't a lot of it, surprisingly. We're finding more evidence stored on phones, tablets, and laptops these days."

Marley started to take the lid off the box but stopped when Simms slid a piece of paper, a pen, gloves, and a surgical type mask in front of her. Marley looked questioningly at Simms.

"Drugs were rampant in that house," Simms said. "And we've still got an unknown substance waiting to be identified. Anyone handling evidence from the site wears gloves and a mask."

Marley sighed but picked up the mask and slipped it over her face.

"Didn't tell me about wearing a mask before you asked me paper or computer files," Marley grumbled. It already felt hot and moist.

"Guess I failed to mention that part," Simms said with a grin. He pointed at the paper. "Evidence log. You can input it into an e-document later."

A little of the excitement had died down now that Marley was facing the reality of sifting through evidence. But she lifted the lid of the box, after Simms had put on his own mask.

"Am I looking for anything in particular?"

"This is a combination of logging the individual pieces of evidence and labeling each one as a receipt, personal note, communication, or whatever. But we want you to keep an eye out for anything that stands out as significant, particularly around drug manufacturing."

"Chemical compositions, science notes, compounds, codes—that kind of thing?"

"You got it." Simms grabbed his laptop and headed to the door. "Evidence doesn't leave the room, and the room is never left unlocked. No food or drink in here, either. Call me if you need me."

"Yeah, sure," Marley said.

Marley pulled the first piece of paper off the top of the pile. A crumpled receipt from Canadian Tire, the ubiquitous hardware store. Marley noted the relevant information on the evidence sheet as well as a list of items: garden hose, seven BBQ lighters, two X-ACTO knives, a tub of tile adhesive, and chocolate covered almonds. She bagged the receipt, labeled it with a marker, and grabbed the next piece of paper.

Two hours in and Marley had filed twenty-seven pieces of evidence, including receipts, municipal garbage schedules, three-for-one pizza flyers with a series of numbers written in pen across the garlic bread section. She was feeling pretty good about the work, but her body was giving her signals she'd had enough. Her side was throbbing, and her back was stiff from trying to hold herself up without using her abdominal muscles. Marley thought about the painkiller she had in her pocket. Might not be a bad idea.

She looked up at a tapping on the meeting room door. Simms leaned his head in, holding up a bottle of water.

"Come on out. Take a quick break."

Marley eased her way to a standing position, satisfied her legs felt solid, even if the rest of her body felt like a disaster. She joined Simms out in the hall and gratefully took the offered water bottle.

"Anything interesting?"

"Mostly garbage, I think," Marley said after she'd gulped some water. "I did notice a waste pick-up schedule and two receipts for the municipal landfill, though."

"How old are the receipts?"

"One about six months ago, the other a few weeks. End of June, I think."

"Huh, yeah. We might try to follow up on that," Simms said.

"Tough place to find evidence," Marley said as she pulled a pill out of her pocket and swallowed it with another gulp of water.

"We'll take any lead on evidence," Simms said. He jerked his chin at Marley. "You're good to keep going?"

"No problem," Marley said, her body already protesting her answer.

"Good enough."

Marley launched her empty bottle at a nearby recycling container, then headed back in the room. She was glad she was alone in the room as she carefully lowered herself back into the chair. Another ten minutes and the pain meds would kick in.

Masked and gloved, Marley reached into the box and pulled out three pieces of paper stapled together. Marley recognized Aimee's handwriting even before she noticed the neatly printed name in the upper right hand corner. It looked like a school assignment, the life cycle of a frog, coloured and labeled with pencil crayons. Marley scanned each page for any other information, but the grade school assignment yielded nothing interesting for the investigation. Still, once Marley had documented the stats on the evidence log, she stared at Aimee's handwriting.

She thought about the conversation with Devon three days before. Marley had tried and failed not to feel the judgement in Devon's worry. She tried not to admit it had doubled the burden of guilt she'd been carrying around, so afraid she was not doing right by these two vulnerable people. That, once again, Bridget Marlowe had taken a misstep and was charging headlong down the wrong path, all along believing she was doing right.

It wouldn't be the first time and certainly not the last, Marley thought, the voice in her head sounding like her mother.

Marley shook her head and labeled the bag of evidence before reaching for the next paper.

Over the next half hour, Marley found more of Aimee's handwriting and schoolwork sprinkled amongst the receipts, flyers, and takeout menus. She wondered if the layers represented time. Marley desperately wanted to look up Aimee's file to see if she could sort through the confusing timeline, but she knew the system would flag her. Still, she wished she knew how long Aimee had been with her father in this run-down drug lab of a house.

An idea surfaced, and Marley pushed back on her wheelie chair until she could reach the phone. She stripped off her gloves and lowered her mask, punching in the extension for Simms once she'd navigated the internal directory.

"Simms."

"Hey, it's Marlowe."

"Find anything?" Marley couldn't help but hear the hope in the constable's voice.

"Not yet. But I was wondering if I could have access to the scene photos?"

She heard Simms typing on his laptop. "Yeah, I can do that. Any particular reason?"

"I guess I'm getting a sense of where this information was picked up, how it relates to the scene." She shrugged, even though the gesture was lost over the phone. But she felt foolish. "I don't know, I thought maybe it could give some context."

"Works for me," Simms said. "I've given you access, so you should be able to call it up in the meeting room now."

Marlowe hung up the phone and wheeled herself over to the beat-up laptop in the corner. She logged in and turned on the projector. As she sorted through the files, Marley wished she had more water. Or lunch. Or her bed. She was starting to sweat, even though the air conditioner kept the office cool.

Huge images flashed up on the screen, and it took Marley a moment to orient herself to the layout of the two-story townhouse she'd only seen from outside. The walls were builder's beige, shiny with unwashed handprints. A picture showed the front entrance, a pile of shoes with one pair of purple rain boots. Marley swallowed hard, her blood pressure pounding more with every image. A living room filled with video game consoles, overflowing ashtrays, and garbage. The kitchen was a lab, with one small table and a blue and green plastic chair covered in half-peeled stickers in the corner. Image after image. Marley's nausea grew so intense, she thought she might throw up. Instead, she clicked off the slideshow, logged off the system, and sat with her eyes closed. She needed to get out.

With effort, her hands betraying the lightest tremor, Marley signed and dated the evidence log sheet, filed away the logged and unlogged evidence, and left the room. She pulled the mask off her face with relief, the cool air on her face making her feel the smallest bit better.

Marley double-checked the room was locked, then she shuffled to her desk and grabbed her bag, waving away the concerned look of her colleagues. She texted her sister asking for a ride, then sent a short email to Simms saying where she'd left off and that she'd be back tomorrow.

By the time Audrey arrived in her shiny Lexus SUV, Marley's tremor was more like full body shakes.

"No wonder you called me instead of Mom," Audrey said, grabbing Marley's elbow as they navigated the steps to the parking lot.

"Might have pushed it a little," Marley mumbled. She pulled herself into her sister's car, felt the sun-warmed leather seats and the blasting air conditioner and thought vaguely that being at work on painkillers was not going to work.

"Need to stop anywhere?" Audrey said, pulling back onto the street. "Or just home?"

"Just home, please," Marley said, her nausea spiking with the movement of the car. She really did not want to throw up in her sister's car.

Audrey was blessedly silent as she drove, and Marley focused on keeping her nausea at bay. Images flashed behind her eyelids: Aimee's boots, Devon kneeling in the alley, a child's drawing, Randolph West's mug shot, rain soaking into her jeans, IV in her hand, a soft, reassuring voice.

"We're here."

Marley surfaced from her half dream. Audrey had pulled up outside her apartment.

"Thanks, sis," Marley said.

"I can help you in," Audrey said, opening the door.

Marley waved her off. "No, I'm good. Really. Go back to work and tell Mom I'll call her later for a lecture."

"You sure?" Audrey looked worried.

Marley eased herself out of the car and turned to her sister. She was so tired of everyone looking worried.

"Twenty-nine steps between me and my chair." She smiled weakly. "I got this."

"Text me when you're safely inside," Audrey said, returning Marley's strained smile with one of her own. "Or, you know, when you collapse in the stairwell. Either one."

Marley laughed and pushed the door closed and waved from the sidewalk as Audrey pulled away.

There were so many steps into Marley's apartment, into the bathroom and then the bedroom to change her clothes, the kitchen for a drink of water and a few crackers before collapsing into her chair, the soft blue blanket covering her shoulders. With her eyes once again closed, the tremors making quiet, disconcerting waves through her body, Marley focused on her breathing and finally slept.

❖

Devon hadn't heard from Marley in three days. She paced and fretted, worked out and chopped vegetables for salad while watching a cooking show. Nothing eased the feeling that something wasn't quite right.

She picked up her phone, but the only message was from her dad, asking if she had any strong feelings about brands of plumber's glue. Devon put the phone back down, not prepared to deal with the minutiae of her leaky kitchen sink in the face of crisis.

Not a crisis, Devon thought as she poured olive oil into an old jam jar and added some red wine vinegar. Not a crisis, not her job, not her decision. This was the same litany she'd laid out to her counselor yesterday, after giving a very general version of what had been happening the last week or so. Ash had nodded thoughtfully, following Devon's agitated list spewing with a question.

"What are you mad about?"

"I'm not mad."

"Describe what you are."

Devon had needed to take a moment to pull air deep into her lungs and centre herself before she'd lashed out at her counselor and proven her right.

"Tense, worried, stressed, anxious." Devon started off with the easy ones. "Lost," she added. She took a breath. "Attempting to dictate circumstances beyond my control."

"What's fueling all that?"

*Blood-soaked cotton. Marley's hurt grey eyes through a blur of rain. Evidence of bruises, on the surface and buried deep. Aimee's silent chuckle, Carla's guttural laugh.*

Devon's shoulders had slumped. "I want to open myself up to all of it. I've got this deep drive to be there and just…"

"And just…" Ash said, waiting. But Devon could only shake her head. "Just fix it?"

"No, not fix it. Be there. Acknowledge what they've been through, what they're going through. Leaving them alone with it feels so wrong." She'd looked up at Ash then, as she'd registered how closely this fit with what had brought her to Ash in the first place, leaving front-line workers alone with the heaviness of what they faced every day. She hadn't seen the burden shift until she'd fallen under its weight.

"And absorb it," Ash had added.

"Yes. And I can't. Not anymore."

"You're wrong, Devon. You're recovering from absorbing too much and losing yourself in the process. But you're not broken."

Devon listened, trying not to be frustrated that she needed to hear this truth again and again.

"Describe what you are doing. What is your job right now?"

"Recover, refocus, relearn." Those were the goals they'd come up with months ago when Devon had finally acknowledged she couldn't do it anymore. She couldn't go back to the hospital, not for one more day.

Devon zoned back to the present as the oven beeped, declaring it had come to temperature. Sunlight broke through the clouds and slanted through the kitchen window, highlighting the flour particles in the air from the scones she was making.

Devon scored the dough in front of her, making almost even triangles out of the sticky mass. Then she popped the baking sheet into the oven and set the timer.

Relearn didn't mean changing her life completely. It didn't mean becoming a hermit, hiding herself from people, never engaging with hurt. It meant learning how to handle the emotions of others while recognizing her own vulnerability and treating it with equal care.

She'd missed caring these last few months. Longer, if she thought about life outside of work, which had been her singular focus for so long now.

Devon looked at her phone where it sat on the counter. She picked it up and sent Marley a text. Then she waited for her scones to rise, the weather to change, and Marley to respond.

❖

Marley stared at her phone, blinked back tears, and wondered when she'd become such an emotional disaster. "I'm blaming the antibiotics. Gut rotting, life-saving motherfuckers," she mumbled. Then she read the text from Devon again and wiped at the fresh tears on her face with the sleeve of her hoodie.

It was only a few words. Simple, really.

*Checking in. Wondering how your heart is doing.*

No pressure for an answer, not even a real question. Just the gentlest reminder that she wasn't alone. Pretty much exactly what she'd needed to hear when she'd woken from her body-drained nap to feel the full enormity of the last week.

What had she done to deserve Devon in her life so unexpectedly?

*Thanks for check-in. Today you are a cherry-flavoured Life Saver.*

Marley scanned the text. It seemed flirty, though it was hard to tell since she wasn't very good at flirty. She sent it anyway, followed by another text asking how Devon was doing.

*Restless but good*, Devon replied.

Marley tapped her phone against her thigh, wondering if asking Devon for another favour was too much.

*How do you feel about playing chauffeur? Great idea or terrible idea?*

*Definitely a great idea.*

Marley smiled to herself. She texted back she needed time to shower, and then she eased her body out of her comfy chair. The nap had been a good idea. She wasn't shaking anymore, just sore and a bit weak.

Half an hour later, wet hair tucked behind her ears and half a sandwich in one hand, Marley answered the knock at her door.

"Hey."

Marley had no idea why her body chose that moment to react to Devon's presence. She was beautiful in her casual androgyny, simply dressed in grey denim and a fitted blue T-shirt. Her short, dark hair had curled a little in the heat. But Devon's eyes and her sweet, almost uncertain smile had Marley's stomach going into free fall.

"Antibiotics," Marley mumbled.

"Sorry?"

"Nothing. Come on in, let me grab my wallet and phone."

Devon stood inside the door as Marley collected what she needed.

"You hungry?" Marley said, hearing her mother's voice in her head admonishing her to offer her guest something to eat. "Want the other half of my sandwich?"

Devon peered at the half-eaten sandwich in Marley's hand.

"What kind is it?"

Marley hesitated. This felt like a critical moment in their friendship, beautiful eyes and butterflies or not.

"Peanut butter, bacon, and lettuce."

Devon looked curious, and Marley felt a moment of hope. Curiosity was better than disgust, the typical reaction to her sandwich concoctions.

"I'm not particularly hungry, but can I try a bite?"

Marley handed over the other half of the sandwich and watched as Devon took a bite. Devon's expression remained neutral at first. But then she saw the delicious sweet-salty combination of Marley's favourite sandwich really hit home.

"Good, right?" Marley said.

Devon nodded as she chewed and swallowed. Marley wondered if it was weird that she found this moment sexier than any romance movie.

"So good," Devon said, brushing a crumb from her fingers after handing back the sandwich. "Amazing."

"Yeah," Marley said. "Amazing." She meant the heat in her belly, the tingle up her spine, and the insistent beat of her pulse.

"Shall we go?"

"Let's go," Marley said.

They walked up the stairs and out onto the street. The day was still warm but grey, and a dry, chaotic wind pushed and pulled them to Devon's car. Through the wind, Marley could hear the sky quietly rumble a petulant warning.

"Looks like another storm," Marley said as they climbed into Devon's Subaru.

"A whole summer of storms, it seems," Devon said. "Where to?"

"Oh, right. Carla and Aimee's. We could stop for some food, maybe."

"I stopped by yesterday, so they should be okay," Devon said. She tilted her head toward the back seat. "I've got some books and science stuff for Aimee."

Guilt, awe, and worry mixed uncomfortably in Marley's gut. She could not be more grateful Devon had stepped in when Marley was down, but the guilt and worry dragged at her, exhausting her again.

"You okay?" Devon said.

"Yeah." Marley rubbed at her eyes then let out a short, frustrated breath. "No. Randolph West is out on bail. I spent my morning going through evidence of Aimee's living conditions in a drug lab. I keep lying to my boss about knowing where Carla and Aimee are living, and I'm having a hard time continuing to justify that. I'm utterly dependent on other people. And I've dragged you into this and probably turned your life upside down. And my fucking body still isn't working right."

Devon signaled and pulled into a left turn lane, stopping at a red light. Marley felt shaky from her outburst and regret threatened to surface when Devon turned to look at her. Her brown eyes were understanding, and her whole demeanor exuded calm. God, she must be good at her job. When it wasn't draining the life out of her.

"What's worrying you most?"

"Carla and Aimee," Marley said immediately. "Then you. Lying to my boss. My fucking body."

Devon gave her a quick grin before focusing back on the road. "I like that you prioritized," she said, laughing a little.

Marley felt her heart get a bit lighter with the easing of a shared burden. She ate more of her sandwich, recognizing her body's need for energy, especially given the conversation she needed to have with Carla.

"I need to talk to Carla today about Randolph and what she sees as the best plan moving forward."

"Want me to distract Aimee while you're doing that?"

"Yes, please. It's hard to have a real conversation with Carla. Aimee's smart and she listens."

"I've noticed. I'll keep her busy with the science kit I brought. Maybe listen to some music so you and Carla can have a chance to talk."

"Thanks," Marley said, finishing off the last of her sandwich and wiping her fingers on the napkin she brought. The word seemed inadequate, but burdening Devon with her guilt seemed unfair.

Devon pulled into a spot in front of a run-down Bible Mission store, about a block from Carla and Aimee's. Marley wasn't sure, but it sounded like Devon was humming a song from *The Blues Brothers.*

"This okay?" Devon said. "I could get closer."

"As long as we're not running, I should be good."

It was late afternoon, and the neighbourhood felt summer busy with kids on bikes and people sitting on their front porches trying to escape the heat of the summer. A few air conditioning units sagged out of windows, rattling in the July heat.

That all changed once they turned down the back street. These streets were nearly empty, and the smell of garbage and waste was soaked into the pavement and the bricks. Marley remembered the morning she was last here. The memory itched, an annoyance more than fear.

Devon stopped abruptly before they turned toward Carla and Aimee's studio. She stepped in close to Marley, blocking her view of the alley.

"You're safe here? I should have checked earlier. There's no one looking for you? No one is going to recognize you?"

Marley had never had a protector before. The women she'd had relationships with were fun and independent; they'd blended daily lives and shared good times. They had cared about her, Marley knew. But they'd never wanted to carry her burdens.

Devon was standing close, shielding her, Marley realized. Marley touched Devon's arm, feeling the tension in the muscles, her heated skin.

"I'm safe," Marley said, looking Devon in the eye. "There's no risk to me being here." Devon didn't move. She seemed to be searching for lies and truth. Marley slid her hand down Devon's arm, fingers resting against her wrist. "I promise."

Devon turned her hand and their fingers slid together. Devon squeezed lightly, and Marley returned the pressure before they both let go.

They turned toward the door of the studio, walking close but not quite touching. Everything about having Devon here felt reassuring.

Everything about it felt right. Marley swallowed the enormity of the thought and knocked.

After a few moments, Carla cracked open the door. She smiled when she saw Marley.

"I hope you're really back on your feet, Marley," Carla said gruffly, opening the door wide. "Aimee is going to be happy to see you."

"I'm back on my feet," Marley said. "And it's good to see you."

Carla shooed them upstairs with a wave, though Marley could see the brightness in her eyes.

They could hear Aimee before they could see her, thumping feet and hands, like she was cartwheeling around the apartment. She probably was. As Marley pushed open the door, Aimee zoomed past in a blur, a pillowcase tucked into the back of her shirt like a cape. She leapt into the air and slid across the floor sideways, arms outstretched in a superhero pose. Marley laughed, delighted to see her joy.

At Marley's laugh, Aimee whipped her head around, then immediately ran to the front door. She stopped in front of Marley and Devon, hopping and bouncing, her face beaming. She raised both her hands for a high ten, and Marley clapped them with hers, laughing as Aimee jumped higher and higher, finally gripping Marley's hands.

"So good to see you again, Squirt," Marley said.

Aimee's only response was to begin dragging Marley across the floor, clearly intent on showing her something.

"Take it easy with Marley," Carla said to her granddaughter as she headed into the kitchenette. "Remember she's still recovering."

Aimee immediately dropped Marley's hand and looked ashamed, eyes darting around the small space, stopping to check the expression of each person before landing back on Marley. Her body was very still, uncertain.

Marley glanced at Devon, who had obviously noted the same odd behaviour. Marley made a mental note to ask Devon about it later.

"I'm okay, Squirt." She lifted up her T-shirt to show the unassuming and hopefully not too scary bandage on her side. "Almost better. I just have to move a little slower."

Aimee took a step closer and stared at the bandage before looking back up at Marley. She pointed at the bandage and then made a face, like she was wincing.

"It hurts a bit, but not much anymore. I'm trying to be careful."

Aimee nodded seriously. She carefully grabbed Marley by the elbow and walked her over to the window. As Aimee showed Marley her books, towers made out of cardboard, and her many drawings, Marley snuck a look at Devon, who was standing in the kitchen talking with Carla. Marley appreciated the easiness between them. She got the sense Carla didn't trust easily. Now they seemed to be discussing a book Devon had brought. Of course Devon would be just as concerned for Carla as she was for Aimee.

After Aimee had shown Marley every scrap of paper, every new gymnastics move, and her new ability to climb the inside of the bathroom doorway, Devon came over with the cloth bag, snagging Aimee's attention. Marley eased away and sat near Carla, who was already ensconced in her favourite chair.

"You're on the mend?" Carla said as they both watched Aimee rip into the science kit Devon had brought.

"I am," Marley said. "Though my body recovered much quicker when I did something stupid at fourteen rather than thirty-four."

Carla grunted a laugh. "Amen to that."

Devon glanced up at Marley, who gave her a slight nod. Devon pulled out her phone, and Marley heard her telling Aimee all good scientists and doctors worked to music. After a few moments of intense searching, with Aimee giving Devon a dark look when she suggested "Baby Shark," the studio filled with the soft beat of current radio hits.

Marley took a breath and turned to Carla.

"I already know about Randolph," Carla said, before Marley had a chance to say anything. "Devon's been good about bringing me the paper."

"I'm sorry I wasn't able to bring you the news myself," Marley said.

Carla waved away the apology. "I've been thinking about where we could go. Somewhere Randolph wouldn't think to look, if he is looking." Her eyes bored into Marley. "Do you have any reason to think he's looking for us?"

Marley blew out a breath. "No, nothing to suggest he is." It was an incomplete answer, and Carla deserved to hear it all. "It's my gut telling me Aimee was there for a reason. She's part of this."

Carla nodded. "Exactly. So, we're laying low for now."

"And this is no longer the best place for you to hide," Marley said, a question and a statement.

"No. It's been what we needed when we needed it, and I'm grateful to you and Devon. But I can't raise Aimee here."

Guilt writhed like a live thing in Marley's belly. Devon looked up as if she sensed Marley's discomfort and upset. Marley gave her a small smile, and Devon nodded her encouragement. Then she pulled on a second set of child-sized goggles and Marley laughed. Devon grinned before becoming absorbed with Aimee again.

"How can I help?" Marley said, turning her attention back to Carla.

"I've been thinking maybe I could connect in with a few people. Back home for sure but also other family and friends. People will tell me if Randolph or his guys have been asking around. Give me some ideas where not to go."

"That makes sense," Marley said neutrally. She couldn't tell if the anxiety welling up in her chest was from guilt or her instinct telling her moving was a bad idea. But Marley's idea was not working. Everyone agreed. But letting Carla and Aimee drift somewhere new and disappear…

"A city centre, for sure," Carla was saying when Marley tuned back in. "I don't have my car, so I'll need busses to get us around."

"Yes, of course."

Marley kept listening as Carla laid out the bare bones of her plan, even as warning signals blared in the background.

"Is that possible?" Carla said, and Marley realized she had no idea what the question was referring to.

"Sorry, Carla. Is what possible?"

"Is there some way to use a phone without the person knowing where I'm calling from? A number block? No good announcing I'm still in Hamilton."

Marley pulled out her phone and googled it. She showed Carla what to punch in before the number.

"I'm going to call a few people now out on the landing while you two are here to keep Miss Aimee occupied. That okay?"

"Not a problem," Marley said.

Carla eased herself out of her chair and shuffled out of the studio. After a moment, Marley joined Devon and Aimee in the kitchen.

"What are you two doing?" she said, forcing a lightness she did not feel into her voice.

Aimee pointed to the two brightly coloured bowls filled with different coloured powder. Then she tapped the box to show Marley the picture.

"You're making a gummy brain?" Marley said and Aimee nodded, grinning.

"We're creating a model of the left and right hemispheres of the human brain," Devon said with mock seriousness. "It's very scientific."

"And potentially delicious," Marley said, and Aimee made the hiccupping sound that Marley recognized as laughter. "Don't let me interrupt scientific discovery."

Marley watched as Aimee measured water into a small cup and poured it into one of the bowls of powder. Devon handed Aimee a wooden popsicle stick.

"Here's your stirrer, Dr. Aimee."

Aimee began methodically mixing the sticky-looking substance together. Music filtered through the studio, though Marley could still hear the occasional gusts of wind outside and the distant sound of Carla talking on the phone. Marley thought she heard the front door bang, maybe with the wind. She didn't blame Carla for wanting to take a moment to step outside. Being cooped up in a small studio with an energetic and voraciously smart eight-year-old would be exhausting.

Marley was about to speak when a noise outside the studio door caught her attention. Voices. More than Carla's. A man's voice, definitely, and now Marley could hear the hiss of Carla's angry words. Then footsteps on the stairs, more than one set.

"Marley?"

Devon and Aimee both looked to Marley for direction, the experiment forgotten.

"I'll go see what's happening. You two stay here."

Devon nodded, and Marley saw her ease Aimee over to the far side of the counter, putting herself between Aimee and the door. Marley approached the studio door and Carla's voice became clearer.

"Not like this, Randolph. This is the wrong way to approach her and you know it."

Marley's stomach dropped. She had nothing—no badge, no weapon, no backup if things with Randolph went badly. But she wasn't alone. Marley pulled out her phone and opened the door.

Randolph West shared his mother's and daughter's dark wavy hair, but he was bulkier. He had a barrel chest under a black T-shirt that boasted a UFC fight from two years ago. His eyes were flat, calm, and mean. And obviously surprised to see someone standing in the doorway of the studio.

"You must be Carla's son, Randolph," Marley said, aiming for a manufactured calm.

"And who are you?" Randolph said, folding his arms over his chest as he tried to look over Marley's shoulder into the apartment. Marley didn't think Devon and Aimee were in his line of sight. She hoped.

"I'm Constable Bridget Marlowe."

Marley could almost see him switching gears. Carla, her eyes spitting fire, pushed her way past him and stood next to Marley. Randolph didn't even glance at her.

"You must be the cop who got caught by the Warren brothers. You gotta be slow to get nabbed by those idiots."

Marley smiled and kept eye contact with Randolph. "It wasn't one of my finest moments."

Randolph's laugh was cruel and cold. Rage began filling Marley's chest, and she fought to control it. She needed to stay focused on Randolph. She needed to get him out of here.

"I want to see my kid," Randolph said.

"No," Carla said, her voice icy and calm. "That's not going to happen."

Randolph's dark eyes snapped, but his voice didn't waver. "Aimee's mine. You can't keep her from me."

"I'm her guardian, and I say it's not good for her."

Randolph uncrossed his arms, and Marley read the intention in his body before he'd taken a step.

"Don't, Randolph," she said, stepping between them. "Call your parole officer, ask for visitation, go through proper channels."

"I have to ask for permission to talk to my own fucking kid?" he shouted.

"You raised her in a goddamn drug lab, Randolph," Carla shouted back, peering around Marley to yell at her son. "You lost all rights!"

Marley held up a hand between them as Randolph was about to shout his reply. She stepped to the side, pushing Carla gently back with her shoulder.

"Okay, okay, let's all just take a moment here," Marley said. Carla muttered something under her breath and walked into the studio.

"Bitch," Randolph grunted.

Marley chose to ignore it, needing this situation calm and resolved.

"Go through the right channels, Randolph. It's the only way to see your daughter."

There was not a hope in hell Marley was going to allow him anywhere near Aimee. Almost as if reading the truth of it, Randolph's eyes went cold again. Calculating.

"She's here, isn't she? I heard she was here, living with my bitch of a mother. That won't look too good to the social workers, will it?"

Marley said nothing, waiting. They stared at each other, the implied threats hanging between them.

"Why do you want to see Aimee so badly?"

"Because she's my kid," Randolph said, again trying to peer over Marley's shoulder. He raised his voice when he spoke again. "And sometimes kids need reminding to only tell the truth, not some made-up shit."

Anger, cold and focused, dropped like an anchor through Marley's stomach.

"Are you threatening an eight-year-old, West?" Marley's voice was very, very calm.

Randolph focused back on Marley. "Definitely not."

They stared at each other.

"You should go now."

"I'm looking forward to meeting you again, Constable Marlowe."

Marley didn't move. But after a moment, he took two steps back, turned around, and walked down the stairs. Marley listened as he thumped his way down each step and slammed the front door. She approached the top of the landing, making sure he'd left the building.

As quickly as she was able, her stitches pulling with every step, Marley followed his path and locked the front door. It took longer going back up, and she took a long breath in and out to calm her racing heart before entering the studio, closing and locking the door behind her.

"He's gone," she said.

The apartment was quiet; the music had stopped. Marley followed the sound of low voices to find Aimee huddled on the floor between Devon and Carla. Aimee was curled in a tight ball, her head on her knees, long hair falling around her face. Carla sat next to her, rubbing her back and speaking in a soft, reassuring tone. Devon sat on Aimee's other side, looking worried.

Marley sat down, completing the small, tense circle.

"He's gone," she repeated quietly.

Carla looked at Marley, still circling her hand gently on Aimee's back.

"I don't know how he found us."

"It doesn't matter now," Marley said, though she had her suspicions. The Warren brothers had likely talked.

"This changes things," Carla said, her eyes hard.

"Yes." They couldn't stay here anymore. "We'll make a plan."

Aimee curled more tightly into herself and leaned further into her grandmother. Marley could smell urine, noticing the small wet puddle Aimee was sitting in. Her heart ached.

"It's okay, pet," Carla said. "I know you're scared. Nothing is going to happen to you. You have me and Marley and Devon. All you need in life is some good people who will look out for you."

Marley looked at Devon a beat and then longer. *All you need in life.*

Aimee shifted and lifted her head. Her eyes, usually full of joy and intensity, were sorrowful. She looked around at the three of them, then dropped her head again.

"We're here, Aimee," Devon said.

"We're right here," Marley added.

Aimee didn't look up, her small body swaying with the motion of her grandmother's hand on her back.

"Come on, pet," Carla said, her voice gaining some of the no-nonsense tone. "Let's try the mantra, see if that moves us out of the scared."

Aimee didn't react, but Carla started anyway, using her free hand to complete the actions.

"My thoughts are clear, my body is safe, my heart is healing."

When Carla started going through the mantra a second time, Devon and Marley both joined. They touched their foreheads, hugged their shoulders, and placed a hand on their hearts. It was a prayer and a promise.

Aimee looked up, but she didn't look reassured. She sliced her hand through the air, then slapped at her shoulders in an angry imitation of the hug. Devon picked it up first.

"You don't feel safe," Devon said.

Aimee then pointed at her grandma and sliced her hand through the air, slapped her shoulders. Not safe. Then Marley. Not safe. Devon. Not safe.

The apartment was silent. Marley didn't know what to say. All her training, her oath to serve and protect. And she didn't know what to say.

"You're right, pet," Carla said. "Let's take a step anyway. How about you help me up off the floor, we'll get you cleaned up, and we'll start making a plan. All of us."

Aimee sniffled and wiped her nose on her forearm. She looked around the circle and nodded. Then she stood up and started pulling on Carla's arms. With Marley and Devon's help, they got Carla up off the floor, and Aimee, looking defeated and ashamed, followed her to the bathroom.

Marley found a stack of old takeout napkins and started wiping up the floor, heart aching and mind racing. Devon rummaged in the small cupboard under the kitchen sink.

"I've got a two bedroom townhouse," Devon said, handing Marley a half-empty bottle of all-purpose cleaner. "They can stay with me for a few days."

Marley swallowed her immediate dismissal, inhaling the sharp scent of the cleaner as she sprayed some on the floor. She finished wiping up and tossed the handful of napkins in the can under the sink. Still needing a moment, she washed her hands before turning to look up. Devon managed to exude both calmness and intensity. Marley had never met anyone who could be so *present*.

"I don't know," Marley finally said.

"You think it's not safe enough or you're worried about putting a burden on me?"

Marley sighed and closed her eyes. Maybe dating a psychologist was not a good idea. Not dating, Marley corrected herself. Why was she so tired? Marley opened her eyes.

"Both," she said. "The safety worry is a bit of a stretch, I'll admit."

"There's nothing that links me to this."

Marley knew she was right. The brief mention in the paper of Marley getting injured had not identified Devon as the helpful bystander. Her name only showed up in official reports, and Marley trusted her department enough to not suspect a leak.

"I agree," she said reluctantly.

"That leaves your worry about whether or not I can handle this."

Marley tried to read her expression. Hurt or nervous? Doubts?

"It's a lot to ask."

"I know. And I'm offering."

Before Marley could formulate a response or even evaluate which way she was leaning, Carla and Aimee emerged from the bathroom. Aimee was wearing blue leggings and a sweatshirt with the hood pulled up. She wasn't crying and she didn't look angry, but she was very subdued.

"Hey, Aimee," Devon said. "Can I show you something?"

Aimee looked up at Devon, almost suspicious, then nodded.

Devon pulled their completed but not yet set brain Jell-O mold closer to the edge of the counter. She turned it around, the colourful liquid sloshing in its plastic casing. She pointed at the base.

"Humans all have an animal part of the brain. It takes over when we're scared, and it tells us not to think, just act. This part of the brain," she tapped the plastic case, "is only worried about keeping us safe. So, sometimes our bodies do things out of our control because our brain is doing exactly what it needs to do."

Aimee seemed to be considering Devon's words, then she glanced over to where she had been sitting on the floor. Her cheeks reddened, and she ducked her head.

"Your brain was doing exactly what it was designed to do," Devon repeated. She moved the brain again to the side and tapped the casing. Aimee looked up at the sound. Curious. "This is where shame lives in the brain. Shame tells us we've done something wrong." Devon tapped her hand to her chest. "Shame lives right here, too."

Aimee glanced at the model of the brain on the counter, then back to Devon. She tapped the side of her head and then her chest.

"You did nothing wrong, Aimee. No shame."

Aimee didn't look entirely convinced, but she stepped in beside her grandma and leaned into her.

Carla hugged her and looked at Devon and Marley.

"I can find somewhere for us to go, but it will take a few days."

Devon looked at Marley, eyebrows raised in a silent question. Marley appreciated she hadn't overstepped, letting Marley evaluate what was best. She sighed.

"Devon has offered for you two to stay at her place until we can find something more permanent."

Carla looked at Devon. "That's good of you. Are you sure?"

"I'm positive. I'd be happy to have you two."

Carla looked down at her granddaughter, then back up at Devon and Marley.

"Okay," she said. "Let's pack."

# Chapter Seven

Devon woke to the unfamiliar sound of voices in her house. She smiled to herself, listening to the thump of Aimee's feet as she flitted into the living room, careering off walls, followed quickly by Carla's whispers to be quiet. Aimee had been subdued the whole time they were packing up Devon's car with their bags of clothes, toys, books, and food. Devon thought she was turtling, pulling back into protective silence, trying to keep herself safe in a world that kept changing. It was a good sign she had some life back in her this morning.

Devon stretched and got up, pulling on a pair of sweatpants. In her ensuite bathroom, she splashed water on her face and looked in the mirror, pushing her hand through her hair. She thought back to the night before. The four of them had carried everything into Devon's apartment and then sat around eating pizza, Aimee entranced by a nature documentary Devon found on Netflix. By the time Carla had gone to put Aimee to bed, Marley looked utterly exhausted and alarmingly pale.

Devon had said she should either crash early like Aimee, or head home. Marley had agreed, ordering an Uber as they went outside to wait on Devon's front porch, a body-warm wind enveloping them. They didn't talk, but after a moment, Marley had looked up at Devon, given her an exhausted, grateful smile, and slipped her arms around Devon's waist. Devon had pulled her in close and they stood there, swaying a little with the wind and their own intimate rhythm. Then the car pulled up, Marley kissed her cheek, and was gone.

Devon smiled to herself in the mirror. So much of her life had been disrupted since meeting Marley. Her daily routines were thrown off, the order of her thoughts thrown into chaos. She also hadn't smiled this much or laughed or felt connected in so long. Marley was tugging her back from aloneness with her easy smile, her humour, and her understanding. Marley seemed to get it, where Devon had been and where she was now. She even seemed to understand where Devon was trying to go, even though Devon herself wasn't always sure. Devon grinned at herself in the mirror. And she made a kick-ass sandwich.

Feeling lightness in her chest, Devon followed the sounds of life to the kitchen. Aimee was spinning herself around on one of the barstools, giggling and looking a little dizzy. Carla looked up from where she was rifling through cupboards. She'd found the mugs but not the coffee.

"Good morning," Devon said.

"I hope we didn't wake you up," Carla said, grimacing.

"Not at all." Devon reached into the cupboard above the toaster and pulled out the silver canister of coffee. "I should have showed you where everything was last night. Or at least the coffee."

Carla leaned back against the counter as Devon began assembling the coffee.

"It's good of you to put us up," Carla said.

Devon glanced at Carla as she measured grounds into the filter. Carla looked tired today, her spirit somewhat dimmed.

"You are both welcome here as long as you need a place to stay," Devon said. "I'm happy to have you."

Carla said nothing, watching Aimee inspect the glinting bits of quartz in Devon's granite countertops.

"Are you okay this morning, Carla? Did you sleep alright?"

Carla snorted. "This one is an octopus when she sleeps. I swear she grows limbs at night so she can toss them around."

Aimee looked up from tracing patterns through the countertop and waved her arms in the air, making Carla and Devon laugh. Once Aimee was occupied again and the coffeemaker was burbling, Devon tried again.

"You seem worried this morning."

It was an invitation, and Devon wasn't sure if Carla would accept it. They were quiet, the only sound the coffee maker behind them and a light rain on the windows.

"I've always hated feeling like I'm indebted to someone," Carla said. "Always. But I can't find any way around it right now. I'm totally dependent on your kindness, you and Marley." She cleared her throat and looked at Devon. "I appreciate it, don't get me wrong. It's just…" Carla trailed off, looking more defeated than before.

"It just eats at your soul a little."

Carla looked surprised. "Exactly. Add on what happened yesterday and worried about this one's reaction—" Carla cut herself off, seeming to get choked up.

Devon didn't know the best way to offer her comfort. She knew she could not offer reassurance about her son or her granddaughter and the future, so she sat with her in the silence as Carla cleared her throat again and tried to pull herself together.

They both watched as Aimee ran to the large window by the kitchen table. She clambered up into the frame, bracing her arms against the sides.

"Aimee," Carla started to say.

"It's okay, really," Devon said.

Aimee looked back at them and grinned, then used her nose to chase raindrops as they dripped down the outside of the window.

Carla sighed. "That's going to dirty up your windows real fast."

Devon laughed and looked at Carla. She still seemed worried; the heaviness was still there.

"Nose prints on the window might be the very least of our worries, I think," Devon said, smiling.

Carla gave a short laugh, but her eyes glimmered with a spark. Devon wanted to keep that spark alive.

"How about some coffee and breakfast and then a short, rainy walk to the corner store to get the paper?"

Carla looked surprised and a little like she was trying not to get excited. "I was thinking that was okay, being where we are now. But I wasn't sure."

Carla's uncertainty tugged at Devon. Not being able to make decisions, take care of Aimee, or even make herself coffee in the morning was killing her.

"I hope this feels less like a prison," Devon said softly. "And I checked with Marley. She thinks you guys should be able to have a little more freedom in this neighbourhood."

They'd discussed it the night before. Devon's little enclave of townhouses was a good distance from Randolph's area and the east end.

"A walk would be welcome," Carla said. "I don't think I have a raincoat for Aimee, though."

Devon grinned. "We'll improvise."

Carla smiled back. "You know, a walk in the rain to get the paper sounds a little like heaven today."

"I couldn't agree more."

❖

Marley had been staring at the paper for more than ten minutes. She'd stare and look away, glance back, and then away again. Ten minutes of this dance, her blood pressure skyrocketing whenever she looked at the list of addresses in Aimee's neat printing. Marley was frozen. She needed to take this to Simms. She needed to talk to Crawford.

The investigation had stalled. Their leads were turning up almost nothing that could help answer the uptick in hospitalizations or the odd symptoms of withdrawal. Everything pointed to this being a run-of-the-mill drug manufacturing and distribution business. Not a small one, for sure. But nothing that could give Public Health the information they were looking for.

Marley glanced back at the paper. Three addresses written on a page of French spelling test words. Marley glanced at the careful numbering one to twenty on the left side of the page. Aimee had spelled all the words but *printemps* correctly. Spring. Aimee had forgotten the *s* at the end of the word and had copied it out six times at the bottom of the page.

She looked at the three addresses and her blood pressure rose again. There could be other explanations as to why Aimee had written down addresses. Play dates, maybe. Another school assignment. She shook her head and rubbed at her nose under the itchy mask. Marley knew what she was looking at. Evidence that Randolph West had involved his eight-year-old daughter in the drug trade.

A knock at the seminar room door made Marley jump. Superman opened the door and leaned his head in.

"You're not supposed to be in here," Marley said.

"Only my perfect hair follicles are in the room. Hardly counts. And you're supposed to check your texts."

Marley pulled her phone toward her, wondering what she'd missed.

"Your annual review with Crawford. Five minutes."

"Well, shit," Marley said, reading the three texts from Superman and one from Crawford. She also had two texts from Devon, and one was a picture.

"Let me log this last piece. Tell Crawford I'll be two minutes?"

Superman gave her a lazy salute. "Will do. But hurry up, it takes you ten minutes just to walk down the hall."

Marley resisted giving him the finger, but he laughed anyway as he closed the door.

Without allowing herself to think, Marley logged the French test with the addresses as evidence, put the lid on the boxes, and left the seminar room, locking it behind her.

She went down the hallway faster than she had a few days ago but still pretty slow. The rawness of the injury had faded, but the ache of stitched-together muscle remained, making it hard to feel comfortable in her skin.

Also uncomfortable was her yearly review. Marley wasn't nervous, not entirely. But it was awkward to sit there while her boss went through her record, bringing up any complaints from colleagues or the public as well as commendations. Marley usually had a secret, ridiculous fear her boss would lean on the desk between them with his serious stare and tell her there had been some mistake. She was never meant to be a cop and maybe it was time for Marley to find a new career.

It had never happened, of course. Would never happen, but the childlike anxiety lingered.

Crawford was on the phone in his office and he held up a finger, asking Marley to wait. She sat on the chair outside his office and pulled out her phone, not wanting to talk to anyone walking by. She pulled up the texts from Devon. The picture was of Aimee, though taken from behind so Marley couldn't see her face, about to jump into a giant puddle. Marley grinned at the photo. Aimee was wearing an adult-sized blue and turquoise raincoat with the sleeves rolled up and something to tie it around her waist. It still hit Aimee at the knees and was comical in its largeness. Devon's text read: *Rainy walk to get the paper. I checked with both re: sending a photo. Hope it's okay.*

Marley was about to text a reply when she heard Crawford calling her in. She tucked her phone in her back pocket, greeted her boss, and sat across from him at his desk. He had a file open and began with the annual review preamble. Marley barely listened. She was with Devon and Carla and Aimee on their walk. She was confronting Randolph West in the studio. She was staring at Aimee's purple boots she'd seen in the scene photos, wondering if she'd worn those boots to deliver drugs.

"Constable Marlowe?"

Marley blinked as Crawford's face came into focus, worried and annoyed. Definitely more annoyed.

"I need to tell you something."

Crawford put down the paper he'd been referencing and folded his hands. "I'm listening."

"I helped Randolph West's mother, Carla Slessinger, and his daughter, Aimee West, secure housing in the city after they were released." She checked Crawford's expression. It hadn't changed. Not a good sign. "Carla was fearful her son would track her and Aimee down if she went back up north, and she had nowhere else to go."

"Where are they now?"

"Staying with a friend." Crawford's absolute silence asked the question for him. Marley sighed. She couldn't keep Devon out of this. "Dr. Devon Wolfe offered to take them in when Randolph West tracked them down at the apartment I'd found for them."

More silence and a very long, unblinking stare from her superior. Marley struggled not to squirm. She lifted her chin a fraction, ready to take on the consequences.

"Let me see if I have this straight. You registered a concern when Ms. Slessinger and her granddaughter were being released into the care of Family and Children's Services. You were told to leave it alone. You ignored that directive and secured housing for the two, out of concern for their well-being." He paused here and allowed Marley to nod. "And let me guess, this housing was in the east end, possibly very near where you were stabbed by the Warren brothers." Another nod from Marley. "And you lied when I asked you directly if you knew where they were, since F&CS had no record of them ever showing back up in Thunder Bay." He paused here, seeming to want Marley to say something.

"I did. The investigation had moved on, no one was taking Carla's concerns seriously."

"That wasn't your call to make, Constable Marlowe." He wasn't angry.

"I know."

He paused. She didn't say any more, and he went on.

"And now you're saying Randolph West did track down his mother and daughter within days of being released on bail." Marley nodded, wishing this was over. The pause stretched, but Marley refused to blink. "Your concerns were validated."

It was a trap. "It doesn't excuse my breach of protocol."

"You are correct. And that will be addressed." Crawford picked up Marley's annual review report again, then very deliberately moved it to the side. "I'm putting this review on hold for now, in light of current events."

"I found some evidence," Marley blurted out before he could finish his sentence. "Just now. It links Aimee to Randolph's drug business."

Crawford barely blinked at Marley's revelation. "Tell me what you're thinking."

Marley described the homework she'd found. "I think Aimee was an active participant in the drug trade, not just a kid living on the periphery. Carla's been worried about why Randolph would have taken Aimee in. She's always suspected he used her in some way." The thought made her sick. She remembered Aimee's fear and shame yesterday at the sound of her father's voice. But she held on to the image of Aimee jumping in a puddle today. She was okay.

"And Randolph making the effort to track her down supports the idea that Aimee has information he doesn't want anyone else to have, doesn't it?"

"Yes, sir," Marley said, grateful he'd arrived at that conclusion on his own.

Crawford picked up the phone on his desk and punched in an extension. "Simms, meet me and Marlowe in the seminar room."

Marley felt tired as she traced her route back to the seminar room. She hung back as Crawford updated Simms, glossing over the fact that Marley had known where Aimee was this whole time. Simms's eyes grew wide, and his expression went from confusion to excitement.

"Sweet Jesus, we've needed this lead," Simms said. He pulled the French test out of the box and glanced at the addresses. He frowned. "I don't recognize these addresses, but I'll get on it right away." He looked up at Crawford. "It would be good to talk to the kid. Let's get all the information we can get."

Marley felt her hackles rise, the worry in her stomach changing instantly to protection on a wave of acid and adrenaline. Crawford didn't even look at her when he spoke.

"Marlowe and I will follow up regarding Randolph's daughter. You focus on the addresses for now, and then we'll reconvene."

Simms looked surprised. Crawford was never actively involved in investigations. But he said nothing, just glanced at Marley and said, "Good find. We'll stay in touch, keep each other in the loop." And then he was gone.

The seminar room felt ominously silent as Crawford looked at the log sheet, running his finger down the long list as if trying to glean if anything had been missed. After a few minutes, he seemed satisfied and looked up at Marley.

"Disobeying a directive in an investigation is problematic, Constable Marlowe."

"Yes, sir."

"It will need to be addressed."

"I understand, sir."

He paused. "We'll address it in your annual review. After this investigation."

A temporary reprieve, but Marley would take it. "Thank you, sir."

"Dr. Wolfe is a trained psychologist, is she not?"

Marley blinked at the sudden change in topic. "Yes, sir. She works with the trauma unit at the hospital."

"And she already has a rapport built with young Miss West?"

"Yes." Marley felt a cold sweat on her back, even though she knew this was coming. Even though she knew it needed to happen. Aimee would have to be questioned, and Devon's involvement would have to be made permanent in the official record.

For the first time since landing in his office, Crawford's expression softened a fraction. There was an understanding in his eyes, of knowing how hard this was, how much it was going to hurt. Then it disappeared.

"The girl will need to be questioned," he said. He waited for Marley to nod. "I'll make the call to F&CS myself, and I will get in touch with one of the psych people on our roll." He paused again. "I'll leave it up to you to discuss what's coming next with Ms. Slessinger and Miss West. Why don't you take the afternoon and do that while I arrange for questioning?"

"Yes, I can do that."

"All information comes through me, Marlowe. I'm not suspending you from the investigation, but you have lost the right and privilege to make decisions on your own moving forward. All evidence, all information, any suspicion you have will come directly to me. Have I made myself clear?"

Marley had to clear her throat before she answered. "Perfectly clear, sir."

Marley gripped the back of a chair, feeling suddenly exhausted as Crawford walked to the door. He paused, though, before he opened it and turned back to Marley.

"I've always admired the care you take with people, Constable Marlowe. Colleagues, citizens, suspects. It's your strength in this job, but don't let it become a weakness."

And then he left. Marley collapsed into the chair, putting her head in her hands. She didn't know if what she'd heard was a compliment or an admonishment. All she knew was that her worry was heavy and she was so very tired.

Devon glanced at the short text conversation on her phone for the fifth time. Marley had texted half an hour ago.

*Updates. Okay if I come over?*

*Of course. What updates? Need a ride?*

*Have my car today. See you in half an hour.*

It didn't escape Devon that Marley had ignored the question about updates. Maybe some kind of police protocol, though Marley had never seemed too worried. Which meant maybe now they had something to worry about.

Devon stood from where she was sitting in the living room,

Carla and Aimee both reading on the couch, though Carla seemed to be napping more than reading. Unable to sit still, Devon walked back into the kitchen where she could see onto the street while she started dinner. The chicken was already marinating in the fridge, so Devon began cutting peppers, onions, and zucchini for the skewers. She heard the splash of tires through puddles and looked up to see a dark blue SUV pull up outside her house. A moment later, Marley appeared and headed toward the house.

Devon met her at the front door. Marley looked pale again, tired. And distant.

"Hey," Marley said. She pushed a strand of wet hair off her face and tucked it behind her ear.

"Hey, yourself. I'm just getting dinner started."

Devon began walking back to the kitchen, then stopped when she realized Marley wasn't following her. In fact, she wasn't even moving.

"You okay?"

Marley stared for a moment, and Devon wondered if she was going to answer the question.

"I can't get my boots off."

Devon glanced down at Marley's lace-up work boots. "Hurts to bend over?"

"I wanted to drive today, so I didn't take my pain meds."

Devon walked back, then knelt in front of Marley and began untying her laces. Marley held still, not even a self-deprecating joke to ease the slight tension of the moment. Devon touched the back of Marley's calf as she loosened the laces as best she could. She looked up.

"Can you pull them off yourself?"

Marley began toeing off her now-loosened boots. She grunted softly with the effort, and Devon held out an arm. Marley gripped it and finally succeeded in taking her boots off. She sighed and dropped Devon's arm.

"Did you want to take a pain pill? I can drive you home."

Marley shook her head. "They make me loopy. I need my head clear."

"For updates," Devon said.

"Yes," Marley said.

She seemed so distant, it made Devon uncomfortable. She didn't want to push. She understood needing barriers and guards. But she needed to make sure Marley was okay.

"We're in this together, okay? Remember that."

Marley closed her eyes and seemed to take a steadying breath. Her expression had softened a little when she opened her eyes.

"It's about to get messy."

Devon smiled a little. "We always knew it would."

Marley returned the smile. It was a tired smile, a hurt smile, a worried smile. But it was Marley's. "Yeah, I guess we did."

This time Marley followed her back to the kitchen where Devon washed her hands and finished cutting the vegetables. Marley considered the high barstools against the counter before lowering herself into a dining room chair at the table near the window.

"You guys had a good day?" Marley said.

"A good day," Devon confirmed. "Aimee found all the puddles between here and Cambridge Street. Carla got three newspapers and actually had some time to read them, so she was happy."

"They seem okay after yesterday?" Marley said.

"Aimee had some definite moments of quiet, where she disappeared inside herself for a while. But nothing overly worrying."

"And you?"

Devon glanced up from coating the vegetables with olive oil and spices. "Me?"

"Unexpected house guests, tangled up in a police investigation, bad guys showing up." Marley seemed to swallow. "Taking care of me. How are you?"

Such a simple question, Devon thought. And such an odd sensation to have someone sitting in her kitchen asking it. Expecting an honest answer. An in-depth answer. Devon had no idea if she was capable of giving one.

"I'm good," she said, looking back down at her task. "I like being useful. It feels like a long time since I've been useful. And I enjoy these two. They're fun to have around."

Marley smiled. "They are." She seemed to be waiting for more.

"I'm worried. About them and about you. Whatever updates you're bringing. But I feel solid."

She swallowed the unease as the words left her mouth. It felt like a burden she was passing off, this acknowledgement that sometimes she wasn't solid. That some days were hard. The anxiety in her chest mounted until she took a breath and glanced at Marley. She didn't look burdened. She didn't look concerned. In fact, she smiled.

"In this together, remember?" Marley said.

Devon blew out a breath and gave a short laugh. "Yes, I remember."

A moment later, they heard voices and Aimee's thumping, running feet as she flew into the kitchen. Carla followed, moving much more slowly than her grandchild.

"Hey, Squirt," Marley said.

Aimee waved and jumped up on one of the barstools, spinning herself in circles.

"It's her favourite feature of the house," Carla told Marley drily before turning to Devon. "Can I help with dinner?"

"Maybe you can make some rice while I cook the skewers in a bit? Everything is marinating, so there's nothing that needs to be done right now."

Devon looked at Marley, who gave a slight nod.

"I have something I need to talk to you all about," Marley said. Aimee stopped spinning and Carla looked curious. "I was wondering if we could have a family meeting."

Carla put her hand on the back of Aimee's neck on her way to the table. "Come on, child. Family meeting means everyone needs to listen."

Devon wiped her hands and picked up a pad of paper and pen on the way to join them at her dining room table. It seemed crowded, so many bodies in the space she usually occupied alone. She put the paper and pen in front of Aimee, who immediately started doodling.

"I talked to my boss today at work," Marley started. Devon could tell she was choosing her words carefully. "I told him you guys were staying here with Devon for a little while until you decided where the best place to settle down with the Squirt urchin would be."

Aimee stuck out her tongue.

Carla cleared her throat. "Your boss wasn't..." She glanced at Aimee, who was still doodling. "He didn't seem concerned we hadn't gone back up north?"

Marley tilted her head back and forth. "His concerns have to do with me and how I'm sharing information. His concern for you and Aimee is that you are safe and taken care of."

"I don't want to get you into trouble," Carla said, her voice gruff. She glanced at Devon. "Either of you."

Aimee had stopped doodling and was looking around at the adults.

"We're good, Carla," Devon said. "We're going to talk and eat supper and make a plan. No one is going to get into trouble."

"Agreed," Marley said. "Okay?"

Carla waved her hand for them to continue, concern evident in her annoyance. "Carry on."

"Aimee, do you remember the day I met you at the police station?" Marley said.

Aimee nodded, her little body tense.

"Do you remember someone asked you some questions about how you were feeling and about your dad and where you lived?"

Aimee nodded again.

"We need to ask you some more questions."

Devon appreciated Marley taking this slow, allowing Aimee time to process. Not because Aimee was slow, but because she needed time to absorb the impact.

Aimee turned the page on the pad of paper and drew a large question mark and turned it to Marley.

"Are you asking what kinds of questions?" Carla said to her granddaughter.

Aimee nodded, her eyes never leaving Marley.

"Questions about where you lived, what you did at your dad's house, jobs you had, who you talked to."

Aimee gripped her pen and held very still.

"Aimee?" Devon said and waited until the girl had turned toward her. "Can you tell me people you feel safe with? People you know will look out for you and worry about making sure your head and heart are okay."

Aimee pulled the paper back toward her and began writing. Devon looked up at Marley. She seemed pale and worried. Devon tried to give her a reassuring smile before Aimee pushed the paper into the centre of the table.

Marley read out the list. "Grandma, Marley, Devon, Miss K, Mrs. Townsend." Marley pointed at the last two names. "Are those teachers?"

Aimee nodded.

"My grade three teacher was one of my favourite people in the whole world. Mrs. Cunningham. She volunteers at the library now. Maybe we can go visit her there sometime."

A light briefly surfaced in Aimee's eyes. Then it dimmed and she flipped back to the page with the big question mark. She tapped it and looked at Marley.

"How do you feel about someone asking you questions?" Marley said. "Possibly someone who isn't on your list of people who make you feel safe."

Aimee shrugged. She seemed lost for a minute, like she disappeared inside her head, something she'd been doing on and off all day. Then she looked around the table and drew the pad of paper toward her. She drew out the letters of what she wanted to say very slowly this time. When she turned it around, Devon felt her heart drop into her stomach.

*Randolph is gone?*

Devon noted she referred to her dad by his first name.

Marley shook her head. "No, buddy. Randolph isn't gone. We're..." Marley trailed off, clearly unsure what she should say. Devon didn't know either, but Carla jumped in, pushing Aimee's chair so they were facing each other.

"Remember we talked about how your dad made bad decisions and hurt some people? He broke the law." Aimee looked scared. "He knows better, and the police are there to make sure he won't do it again. And that means they have to investigate and make sure they have all the information. I'm guessing you might have some information because you lived there with him."

"You won't get in trouble, Squirt," Marley said softly. "Not for anything you say, not for anything you've seen, not for anything you've done. I promise."

Aimee looked at Marley with such hurt, and Devon felt sadness surface before she pushed it back down.

Marley stretched her hand across the table toward Aimee and left it there. After a moment, Aimee put her small hand in Marley's. Aimee glanced around the table and gestured at Devon and Carla.

Carla laughed and put her hand in as well, and Devon covered the three with her own hand. Then she felt as Aimee lifted all their hands in the air, like a team cheer. They all laughed, a smile finally surfacing on Aimee's face. Then Aimee flipped to the question mark page of her paper, pushed it toward Marley, and nodded. Then she tapped her chest, hugged her shoulders, and leapt out of the chair and back on to the barstool, spinning madly.

"Guess our family meeting is adjourned," Carla said in her rough voice, but Devon thought she looked more relaxed.

"I think that's the cue to start cooking," Devon said.

"I'll help," Carla said, pushing herself out of her chair.

"And I'll...sit here and try not to fall asleep on your table?" Marley said.

Devon thought Marley looked drained. She was pushing herself too hard.

"How about I find something comfier for you to wear? And maybe you can take a pain pill?"

"I've got my car here."

"We'll figure that out later," Devon said. "One thing at a time."

"Yeah," Marley said. "One thing at a time."

Dinner was a team effort. Marley, in a soft pair of Devon's sweatpants and a T-shirt, kept Carla company in the kitchen while Aimee held an umbrella for Devon, who barbecued the chicken and vegetables skewers in the rain. Having Aimee outside meant Marley and Carla could talk more openly and more specifically about Randolph and the investigation. They all met at the dining room table again, passing food and commenting about the weather system moving in. Aimee demonstrated her best puddle splashes from their earlier walk to Marley, who laughed.

By ten o'clock, dishes were done, Aimee was bathed and in bed, and Carla had retired to read in their shared room. When Devon returned from starting up the dishwasher, Marley was leaning sideways on the couch, a pillow across her abdomen, half asleep. Devon watched her for a moment, feeling a combination of protection and connection and somehow a sense of rightness with Marley here, curled up on her couch.

"Hey," Marley said, opening her eyes. "Come join me."

Devon sat on the opposite end of the couch, and Marley shifted her feet to make room. Devon took the invitation and pulled her feet up on the couch as well, their legs resting lightly against each other. The touch felt good, warmth that enveloped them both.

"Pain meds worked?" Devon said.

"Yeah. Loopy now."

"You can sleep here tonight, if you like."

"Don't have a choice. I am one with your couch," Marley said, smiling. She held out her hand to Devon, and without thinking, Devon took it. "Thank you. For everything."

Devon smiled in response. She ran her fingers over Marley's knuckles. When Marley hummed happily and closed her eyes, Devon began tracing Marley's fingers with the lightest touch. She stroked the folds of Marley's skin, the pads of her fingers, the lines of her palms, and the bones of her wrist. Warmth in Devon's core turned to heat.

"That feels so nice," Marley said. "I wish I wasn't half asleep."

Devon laughed. "I think you're more than half asleep, Constable Marlowe."

Marley opened her eyes, and Devon saw the heat she felt mirrored in Marley's expression.

"True. And if I wasn't more than half asleep, I'd kiss you."

Devon's heart pounded in her chest. It had been so long since she'd really wanted to kiss anyone, to be this close. And she wasn't sure she'd ever wanted to kiss anyone this badly.

"Might be the pain meds talking," Devon said, feeling her bravery slip away.

Marley gave a half smile and closed her eyes again. "No, definitely not. But I'd like to be more awake when I kiss you."

Devon squeezed Marley's hand and whispered, "Me, too."

After a few moments, Devon carefully stood from the couch and found an extra pillow and blanket for Marley. She helped Marley ease down onto the couch, finding a more comfortable position to spend the night. Then Devon covered her with the blanket and knelt down in front of her.

"I'm just down the hall if you need anything," Devon said. "I hope you sleep well."

Marley mumbled out a quiet thank you. Devon listened to her soft breathing for a moment longer, then leaned in and brushed a soft goodnight kiss across Marley's cheek.

## CHAPTER EIGHT

Marley walked into the precinct at seven thirty the next morning. It was quiet in the back room, the energy of the day yet to disrupt the working space of Hamilton's city police force. Marley was always conflicted about coming in this time of day, when no one was there to say hi or stop her with a question. No one she matched in their dark blue uniforms, who looked at her like she was a cop. Like she belonged. But also no one here to ignore her, to remind her she'd crossed an invisible line by daring to find fault.

"Just focus on the job," Marley muttered to herself.

"Marlowe?"

Marley looked up as Simms wound his way around cubicles, desks, and a whiteboard on wheels.

"Hey, Simms. You're in early."

"We found a lead on those addresses yesterday," Simms said. "Windsor. We knew West lived in Windsor, but he had no criminal history other than keeping a broken-down car registered to his name parked on the street for a month."

"Aimee lived in Windsor?"

Simms looked momentarily confused. "The kid? Yeah, I guess so. If you want to follow up on that, go for it. I know it's sort of your... thing."

Right, because only female cops cared about kids. Marley wanted to roll her eyes. That probably wasn't how he meant it. Simms was a good guy, a good cop. And a dad.

"I'll do that," she said. "Find out if she was registered at school or had a babysitter. Someone who could comment on what she did while she lived there."

"Done. Excellent. I'm heading to Windsor. One of the addresses got the precinct there all stirred up. Known drug activity with a suspected link to one of their kingpins."

"Right along the border, Jesus," Marley said. "That can't be easy to police."

Simms shrugged. He looked more excited than anything. "I've got to go. I'm picking up Salik from Public Health, who wants to liaise with the guys from their health teams over there. See if there are any similarities to what we've got."

Layers upon layers. "Anything new on that front?"

"Suspicious opioid overdose in the east end early this morning. One of our guys flagged it on the call. The exact symptoms we talked about the other day, but mega worse." Simms checked his watch. "I gotta go. Keep in touch, Marlowe."

Simms almost jogged out of the work area, taking his fast-talking, excited energy with him. Marley felt somehow more drained, as if Simms's thrill in the chase highlighted her own indifference. She loved being a community officer. She loved making connections and the power that the position gave her to intervene, but she could never suspend her understanding of the stories long enough to love the hunt, the takedown, the raids, the arrest.

None of that mattered now. Marley picked up the unfamiliar travel mug and took a sip of coffee. The slight sweetness of hazelnut made her smile. She'd woken this morning to Devon moving quietly around the kitchen. Her sleep on the couch had been comfortable enough, pulled down by pain meds that gave her bizarre dreams of endless ladders to climb, starving dogs, and the feeling that she wasn't going to make it on time. Seeing Devon in the kitchen in gym shorts and a faded McMaster University Faculty of Science T-shirt chased the nastiness of her dreams away. Having Devon smile at her in the early morning light, remembering the sweetness of Devon's good-night kiss that had followed her into sleep, made something chaotic in Marley finally settle.

Marley brought herself back to the present. She had work to do before Devon brought Carla and Aimee in at ten. She needed to check in with Crawford to try and convince him to let her and Devon interview

Aimee with Carla present. Gripping the travel mug Devon had handed her on the way out the door that morning, Marley went to hunt down her supervisor.

By 9:47, Marley had drawn out a line of questioning for Aimee with Crawford, who hadn't needed any convincing to let her and Devon take the lead on questioning. She had also met with the psychologist who often did contract work with the RCMP to get a better understanding of how to get to the most information with the least intrusive methods, smoothed things over with the disgruntled F&CS worker, and made sure every person who might be interacting with Aimee today had a solid understanding of her history and her needs. She had just sent Devon a series of pictures to show to Aimee—where they would be coming into the precinct, the hallway, and the room where they would be talking. The intake worker had recommended it to try and at least get Aimee prepared for the space. She was wondering if she had time to run to the grocery store down the street and grab some of Aimee's favourite snacks when Devon texted to say they were coming in.

Marley went to the front to meet them and spotted them right away. Aimee walked between Devon and Carla, a notebook and pen in her hand. Her face was blank with none of the animated expressions and smiles she showed when she was calm and comfortable. When she felt safe. Marley swallowed the ache and the guilt of having to put Aimee in this situation. She tried to control her surge of anger at Randolph West. None of that was helpful to Aimee right now.

Marley looked at Devon, trying to anchor herself in the calmness she exuded.

"Hi, guys," Marley said. She tried not to be overly cheerful. Pretending this was a fun little outing was an insult to Aimee. She gave Aimee a half-smile. "This might be a little bit shitty, kid. I'm not going to lie."

Aimee's eyes brightened, and she put a hand to her mouth to cover a smile before glancing up at her grandmother.

"We were just talking about that in the car," Carla said. Marley noticed she was chewing gum, a definite sign she was nervous as well. But the hand she placed on her granddaughter's unruly waves was steady.

"Though we managed to say it without the curse words, Constable Marlowe," Devon added, smiling.

Aimee's smile disappeared again as someone approached. Marley turned to see Crawford, who had stopped short of the small group. They had agreed Aimee would have to interact with as few people as possible.

"Room is ready, Constable."

"Thanks. Ready for this?" she said to Aimee, who had lost all glimmer of her smile. "It's only going to be us in there, promise."

Aimee blinked and leaned into her grandmother. Marley waited, a quick glance at Devon telling her it was okay. After a moment, Aimee stood straighter and nodded.

The interrogation room was bland and unassuming, with a laminate wood oval table and a few office chairs. The only distinguishing features were the audio and video recorder mounted in the ceiling and the one-way mirror on one wall, behind which Crawford and the psychologist planned to watch the interview.

Marley began once they were all seated, Aimee kneeling on a chair so she could lean her elbows on the table.

"I'm going to start with some official things because that's part of the job, and then I'm going to ask you some questions." She waited for Aimee to nod her understanding before continuing. "Our talk is going to be recorded so we can remember what gets said and we don't have to take notes." Aimee followed as she pointed to the video camera. She seemed unconcerned. "If you write out something, I'm going to repeat it so it gets picked up by the microphone. You can stop anytime you want. If you're unsure about a question, that's okay. And I want you to try and remember you will not get into trouble for any of your answers. Not at all, not even a little, no matter what you tell us. Okay?"

Aimee grabbed her pen and wrote something down. She pushed it across to Marley.

"Dad in trouble?" Marley read out loud. She glanced at Aimee. "He is," Marley said. "Remember how we talked about your dad making some not great decisions about illegal drugs? Those drugs are making people sick, so we're asking a lot of people a lot of questions about that to try and get all the information."

Aimee scrunched up her face as if unsatisfied with the answer.

"Can I ask a question?" Devon said to Marley. "To see if I can clarify what Aimee might be asking."

"Go ahead," Marley said.

"Are you asking if your answers will get your dad in trouble?" Devon said.

Aimee nodded at Devon, then glanced back at Marley.

Marley took a moment with the question before she tried to answer. "Your dad's actions are his responsibility, not yours. Anything he has done or anything he has asked you or other people to do *for* him, that's all his responsibility. We are going to ask questions of you and a lot of other people. But at the end of the day, your dad has to answer for his own decisions and actions."

Marley held Aimee's gaze, though she desperately wanted to check in with Devon to make sure she'd said the right thing. After a moment, Aimee pulled back her notebook and waved her hand in Marley's direction, a move that made her look just like her grandmother. She was ready.

"How many houses did you live at with your dad?"

Aimee held up two fingers.

"Were they both in this city, in Hamilton?"

Aimee shook her head.

"Do you know the name of the other city?"

Aimee shook her head again, but then wrote something down.

"St. Agatha's," Marley read, then looked up at Aimee. "The name of your school in the other city?"

Aimee nodded. Then wrote again. "Miss K."

Marley smiled after reading the note out loud. "Miss K was your teacher at St. Agatha's." Marley decided to use this avenue to steer them toward some of the tougher questions. "How did you get to school every day?"

Aimee walked two fingers across the surface of the table.

"You walked by yourself?"

Aimee shrugged, like it wasn't a big deal. Marley sensed Carla's tension at this answer. She hoped Carla could keep it together. Aimee was a sensitive soul, very in tune to the people around her. If Carla got angry about the way Randolph treated her, Aimee might begin to shut down, unwilling to upset her grandmother.

Devon obviously noticed, too. She leaned back in her chair so she was out of Aimee's line of sight. Devon caught Carla's eye and tapped her chest, reminding her of her own mantra. Carla closed her eyes briefly and nodded her understanding to Devon.

"Did you have homework at St. Agatha's?" Marley said.

Aimee tilted her head back and forth.

"Sometimes, right? Did you have jobs in your classroom? I remember we had jobs in the third grade. I loved cleaning the chalkboard best."

Aimee excitedly wrote down a list.

"Recycling, putting up chairs, sweeper." Marley smiled as she read it out loud. "Did you have jobs at your house with Randolph?"

Aimee's smile disappeared. She hesitated, then grabbed the paper.

"Breakfast, lunch, visits," Marley read out loud. Her heart rate spiked for a moment, but she took a steadying breath. "Who did you visit?"

Aimee shrugged and didn't meet Marley's eyes.

"Did you visit by yourself?"

Aimee nodded but offered nothing more.

"How did you know where to visit?"

Aimee wrote a short note.

"Randolph list," Marley read. "He gave you a list?"

Another nod.

Marley swallowed her frustration at herself. This was important, but she wasn't getting anywhere.

"May I try?" Devon said.

"Please."

"Aimee, we're going to make a bit of a movie. You have a whole picture in your head of what these visits look like, but we don't. So, let's make a movie so we can all see it, okay?"

Aimee looked curious.

"So, in a movie we need to know the setting. Where is the star of our movie, Aimee West?"

Aimee's eyes sparked with life and she wrote a note, which Devon read out loud. "Outside Randolph's apartment. Good. And what time of day is it?"

Another note.

"After school. Excellent. What does the star of our movie have with her?"

A pause.

"A list, a map, and your backpack. This is good, I can see all of this movie," Devon said encouragingly. She glanced at Marley, who took the cue.

"What's in your backpack in this movie?" Marley said.

A slight hesitation, then Aimee wrote a short note. She crossed it out and wrote it again before huffing out a breath and pushing it across to Marley.

"Envelopes," Marley read. It was the first word she'd spelled wrong, and she'd tried a few times. That seemed to frustrate Aimee. "Did Randolph give you the envelopes?"

Aimee nodded.

"Okay, so in our movie, Aimee West is outside her apartment after school with envelopes in her backpack. Then what happens?"

She repeated the walking with her fingers.

"You walked. How did you know where to go?"

Aimee found the note from earlier and tapped the word *map*.

"Oh, right. Randolph gave you a map. The kind you can buy with all the colours?"

She shook her head and mimed sketching.

"Do you mean Randolph drew you a map of where to go?"

Aimee nodded.

"So, our camera is following Aimee West as she walks down the street with her map. Then what happens?"

Aimee wrote a longer note. "Addresses on map. Knock on door. Give envelope." She still looked frustrated at that word, her face scrunched in anger.

"Did the people who answered the door give you anything?"

Aimee shook her head, still staring at the word.

"Did you ever go into their houses?"

A harder shake of her head, vehement. Marley relaxed a little.

"Do you know what was in the envelopes?"

Aimee shrugged and shook her head.

"You think you know what was in the envelopes?"

Aimee looked up at Marley. Her eyes seemed a little wild and very angry. The joyful Aimee was nowhere to be seen. Marley was about to remind Aimee she didn't have to answer the question when Aimee gripped her pen and began writing. The letters were bigger, all capitals, each stroke a sign of Aimee's agitation. She filled a page with the giant, angry words and slapped it on the desk and kept writing.

Marley picked it up and read it out loud. "DRUGS. AIMEE WEST CARRIED DRUGS. AIMEE WEST CARRIED DRUGS IN HER BACKPACK." Marley fought to control her voice. She barely had time to glance up to see Carla's pale face and Devon's shocked expression before Aimee pounded the notepad with a small fist, an awful strangled sound escaping from her throat as she angrily scratched out a word.

Marley didn't know how to calm this angry child. Devon pulled her chair closer to Aimee, their shoulders just touching, reading the words Aimee was struggling with. Then she grabbed a pen and used one of the used papers to write out the word *envelopes* and put it in front of Aimee without saying a word. Aimee looked at the note, then copied the word in giant letters, even as angry tears surfaced and spilled down her cheeks. She pushed the notepad to Marley, then collapsed sideways into Carla's arms.

Marley lifted the note up with shaking hands. *Aimee West carried envelopes of drugs in her backpack.* Marley couldn't bring herself to read it out loud. She listened as Carla murmured into the top of her granddaughter's head, rubbing her back, trying to soothe the distraught child. The strangled, coughing sounds of Aimee's crying began to subside. Marley's guilt didn't.

Devon leaned forward in her chair, looking at Marley for a few beats. Marley drew strength from the reassurance in her brown eyes, then she cleared her throat.

"This is Constable Bridget Marlowe, suspending the questioning session at 10:57."

Marley went to the other side of the desk and crouched down by Carla's chair. She grimaced as her stitches protested this new position but smoothed her expression as Aimee peeked out from her grandmother's hug.

"Hey, Squirt," Marley said quietly.

Aimee blinked, her eyes sad, ashamed, and swollen with tears.

"That was kind of shitty, wasn't it?"

Aimee nodded.

"I'm sorry, kid," Marley said, trying very hard to control the tremor in her voice. "I'm sorry that was so hard on your heart. But I'm glad you told us. That's a heavy thing to carry around with you."

Aimee leaned her head back against her grandmother's chest. She looked spent. Marley glanced up at Carla, protection and love in her expression along with an angry fire as she held her granddaughter fiercely.

"Can we take her home?" Carla said.

"Yes. We're done for today."

Carla's eyes sparked at that, but Marley thought now wasn't the time to explain that there would likely be more questions for Aimee.

Aimee lifted herself up and rubbed at her eyes. She glanced at the pile of papers Marley had collected, but her expression didn't change. Instead, she reached over and tugged Devon's hand.

"You're ready to head out of here? Sounds good to me," Devon said. "You can decide what berries we get at the pop-up market on the way, okay?"

Aimee unfolded herself from her chair and jumped down. She clung to Carla's hand and stuck close to her hip as Marley led them out of the interrogation room.

The ride home in Devon's car was quiet. Carla sat in the back with Aimee, who stared blankly out the window. Devon took a bit of a longer route back to her place, stopping at the pop-up farmer's market that had just finished setting up the tables and tents. She said she'd be right back, but a minute later she heard the car doors slam and smiled as Aimee's small hand slipped into hers, her head leaning tight against Devon's arm.

Aimee pointed at her favourite berries, and her eyes lit up when she saw cherries. They were Devon's favourites, too, so a large container went into the bag. Aimee looked confused at the pile of corn until Devon showed her how to pull down the top of the green leaves and separate the strands of cornsilk to get a look at the corn underneath. Aimee blinked in surprise and smiled, and a few minutes later they were back in the car with half a dozen ears of corn and a bag full of berries.

As Carla told Aimee a funny story about a girl who ate too many berries and turned purple, Devon let her mind wander to Marley. Devon had desperately wanted to touch her, draw her into a hug, tuck her head into the curve of her neck and tell her to let it all go for a minute. She wanted to remind her to breathe, take her pain meds, find something to eat, and ignore the thoughts in her head telling her she'd messed up. But Marley had work to do, information she needed to follow up on, a boss who required an update. All Devon could do was send her a text, let her know that she was thinking about her, and invite her to dinner.

Devon pulled into her driveway, still distracted by thoughts of Marley and their morning. Aimee clambered out of the car and bounced up the stairs, an excellent sign she was starting to feel better. Devon unlocked the door and Aimee ran ahead into the kitchen, clutching the bag of berries. Carla and Devon both laughed and exchanged a relieved look. The girl was going to be okay.

A thump in the kitchen made Devon pause. Then she registered a man's soft voice in the kitchen, and Aimee running back toward them, her eyes full of fear. The pieces fell into place for Devon almost immediately. The voice was her father's, and only now did she register the familiar truck parked across the street from her house.

"Hey, Dad," Devon called, cursing at herself as Aimee hid behind her grandmother's legs.

Her dad popped his head around the corner, rubbing his hands on a rag, his eyes full of concern and confusion.

"Hey, sweetheart. Sorry, I didn't know…"

Devon held up a hand to stop him. "Can you give us a minute?"

"Of course," he said, and he disappeared back into the kitchen.

Devon sat down on the floor and waited for Aimee to peer out.

"That's my dad," Devon said. "I didn't know he'd be here, or I would have given you a heads-up."

Aimee stared at Devon for a moment, then blinked.

"I think he's here to fix my sink. You know how I have that bucket underneath because it drips?" Aimee liked taking the coffee can of water out to the back porch to water the hanging baskets of flowers. "I forgot my dad said he'd come fix it for me."

Aimee sent another nervous glance toward the kitchen but stepped out from behind Carla.

"Two options, kiddo," Devon said. "We can go into the kitchen and meet him or I can ask him to come back another time. It's been a big day for you already, so you decide what your heart can handle today."

Aimee touched her heart briefly and glanced at the kitchen again. Then she wrapped her arms around her shoulders and looked at Devon with a question in her eyes.

"He's the safest person I know," Devon said. "Did you want to go meet him?" A brief hesitation, then a nod, and Aimee took her grandmother's hand.

Devon stood up and looked at Carla. "Is this okay? I didn't know he'd be here."

"It's fine with me," Carla said. She looked like she wanted to say more, but then she snapped her mouth shut.

Devon walked back into the kitchen, where her dad was washing his hands in the sink. His expression was curious and his demeanor relaxed. He'd had enough years in his own psychology practice to be neutral and open in the face of the unexpected.

"Hey, Dad," Devon said, giving him a quick hug. "Sorry I haven't been responding to your texts."

"Not a problem. Sorry I showed up unannounced. Just thought I'd get that leaky drain fixed for you."

Devon turned to include her guests. "Dad, these are my friends Carla and Aimee. They're staying with me for a bit."

"It's great to meet you," her dad said, shaking Carla's hand. He smiled at Aimee but stepped back out of her personal space. "I'm Andrew, Devon's dad."

They talked a little about the weather and Devon's leaky drain, casual words adults exchange as they test the social waters of a situation. Carla seemed relaxed, and Aimee poked her head out curiously. Andrew smiled at her.

"I see you picked up some berries, Aimee," Andrew said, indicating the bag on the kitchen counter. "How about I get this sink fixed and then you can rinse them?"

Aimee nodded but didn't move from her grandmother's side.

Devon made herself comfortable on the floor as her dad knelt down and stuck his head under the sink. He had everything he needed laid out, and he called for various tools using the silly names they'd come up with when Devon was a child.

After a few moments, Devon heard something behind her and turned to see Aimee approaching and crouching down behind Devon, peering over her shoulder.

"I couldn't remember which tool was which when I was a kid, so I gave them names."

Aimee pointed at a small wrench.

"That's little Mary," Devon said.

Aimee pointed at a ratchet.

"That's Colin. That flathead screwdriver is Anne."

Aimee pointed again.

"Misty. James. Old Yeller."

Aimee made a small laughing sound at that one.

"Could you pass me a Colin?" her dad said, his voice muffled as half his torso was now wedged into the small cupboard under the sink.

Devon passed him the tool he needed. "I mostly named them after characters in books," she said to Aimee. "I read a lot when I was a kid."

"Now there's an understatement," her dad said, laughing. "We barely saw your face."

Aimee tapped Devon's shoulder, then pointed at her chest.

"I know you're a big reader as well," Devon said. "That's one of the reasons we get along so well."

Aimee smiled, then flinched as Andrew pulled himself out from under the sink. She seemed to catch herself and she gripped Devon's shoulder but didn't back away.

"Okay, I think that's it. I'm going to turn on the tap. Can you two watch for drips?"

Aimee looked very serious as she clambered over Devon until she was half sitting in her lap, peering into the space under the sink.

The water came on and Aimee stared intently. Devon smiled up at her dad, who winked.

"Anything?"

Aimee shook her head.

"Grab a dry rag there," Andrew said. "Give the pipes a little wipe down, see if there are any sneaky drips we can't see."

Aimee hesitated slightly, then grabbed the rag and wedged herself under the sink. A moment later, her arm emerged, waving the dry rag. Then her head popped out, followed by the rest of her.

"Should have had you fix the leaky pipe, Aimee," Andrew said. "You fit there much better than I do."

Aimee scrambled out and helped clean up the tools, pointing to each one and having Andrew name them again as they were put away. Devon stood and stretched her back, pleased but unsurprised her dad had gained even a small measure of trust with Aimee in such a short time. Carla was still sitting at the table. She had a paper in her hands, but she was staring out the window.

"Can I make you some tea, Carla?"

"That would be just the thing, I think," Carla said. She looked tired, weighed down.

"I've got Aimee if you want to lie down for a bit," Devon said.

"Better to keep busy, I think. Keeps the dark thoughts at bay."

Devon saw Andrew glance up at this, but then he looked back at Aimee fitting all the pieces of his old red toolbox together.

"I usually stress cook or stress bake," Devon said to Carla, smiling. "Do you have any recipes that go with berries?"

Carla's eyes brightened, and she looked so much like her granddaughter in that moment.

"My grandmother always made biscuits and cream to go with berries," Carla said. "It's not exactly a dessert…"

"It's perfect."

Marley arrived while the biscuits were baking, the corn was boiling ripe and yellow on the stove, and Aimee and Andrew were playing a loud game of Go Fish at the kitchen table. Devon had sent a text inviting her for dinner and giving her a heads-up as to what she was walking into. Marley, still looking more exhausted than Devon thought she should, chatted with her dad like they were old friends. Devon mentally stepped back from the scene playing out before her in her own kitchen. She was so used to this space being one of quiet and contemplation, a sanctuary after stressful and heart-sore days at the hospital. But it had become a place to hide over the last few months. The energy and life in her now very full kitchen made her smile.

"I always liked having a full kitchen," Carla said, seeming to read Devon's mind. She was drying a mixing bowl with a kitchen towel. "Whatever else was going on, it always felt like I was doing something right with my life."

"I'm starting to see that," Devon said, watching as Aimee brought her dad a stack of papers so he could show her how to make paper airplanes. "It's a good feeling."

"And we haven't had a lot of those today," Carla said.

"That's true."

Carla glanced up and gave Devon a tired but true smile. "Then we'll take what we can get, won't we?"

"Yes," Devon said, looking out over her busy kitchen. "We'll take it while it's here."

## Chapter Nine

Marley pressed the phone more closely to her ear and tried to block out the sound of conversation around her. Annoyance crept up the back of her neck as she strained to hear.

"I'm sorry," Marley said. "It's a busy office."

The elementary school principal on the other end of the line, Priya Anand, laughed. "My office is regularly filled with crying four-year-olds, so I have some idea what you're dealing with."

Marley had spent the morning tracking down the principal of St. Agatha's school in Windsor, Ontario. Not an easy feat given it was three hours away and school was out for the summer. But she'd connected through the school district's main office, faxed the appropriate paperwork to confirm, and was thrilled when the principal called her back within a few hours, rather than the days the mildly grumpy office administrator had warned her about.

"I appreciate you taking the time to connect with me today. I know you're on your summer vacation."

"It's not a problem," Priya said. "The paperwork said you wanted to talk about a former student, Aimee West?"

"Yes. What can you tell me about her?"

"Not a whole lot, I'm afraid," Priya said. "She was a student with us from November until mid-April, when her father said he was moving to Hamilton for work."

"Did you meet Randolph West?"

"Only once, when he came in to register his daughter."

"And what kind of student was Aimee? I know she had a good connection to Miss K?"

Priya laughed. "Yes, Eva Karagalis. She really took Aimee under her wing, knowing it's hard to start at a school partway through. Aimee was hesitant when she started with us, very careful, and very quiet. But it didn't take much effort to see she was a bright star. As Miss K said, once Aimee started talking, you were never going to get the genie back in the bottle. She encouraged it, though. Aimee thrived when her curiosity was fed and she was given an opportunity to use her voice."

Marley stared at the jot notes she was taking, trying to process what she was hearing. "Aimee talked while she was at St. Agatha's?"

"Yes," Priya said, seeming confused. Then she seemed to hesitate. "You sound surprised, Constable Marlowe."

"Aimee hasn't spoken since April," Marley said, trying to keep her intonation professional and factual.

"I see."

"There was no indication of trauma or illness or mutism when Aimee attended your school?"

"No, nothing like that."

Marley cleared her throat, needing to shift gears. "Is there anything else you can think of that you might want to tell me about Aimee or her father?"

Priya took a moment with the question. "We have a pretty high-needs population around here, a lot of families dealing with poverty, new Canadians, families in transit. Other than Aimee's obvious intelligence and love of school, her story didn't seem that different, I'm afraid."

"That's okay, you've been very helpful today."

"Did you want to speak to Miss K? She could tell you more about Aimee's day-to-day."

"I have everything I need right now, but if you could send me her contact information and maybe fill her in on why I might be calling, that would also be helpful."

Marley listened as Priya made herself a note. "Done."

"Thank you again for your time," Marley said. "I appreciate all your information and insights."

"You are most welcome," Priya said. "Aimee is a wonderful kid. We are glad to have known her and hope very much she is going to be okay."

"Yes," Marley said, hearing the professional tone slip a little. "We are hopeful as well."

Marley signed off and hung up the phone. She stared at her notes, wishing she had a more complete story about Aimee's recent history but also wishing she didn't have to uncover any more evidence of Aimee's hurt.

"Anything useful?"

Marley looked up as Superman made himself at home on the corner of her desk.

"More info about Aimee's background, but nothing that helps the investigation."

"Did Simms find anything in Windsor?"

"No idea." Marley checked her phone for the time. "But there's an update in ten minutes. You coming?"

Superman stood up. "Nope, I'm out on patrol. In fact, you never saw me."

"It's like you don't even exist," Marley said, waving a hand in front of his face. He slapped it away, and Marley laughed.

"Don't get too comfortable over there, Marlowe," Superman said, wagging a finger in Marley's face obnoxiously. She grabbed for it, but he moved it out of the way too quickly.

"Whatever," Marley said, annoyed and laughing.

"All I'm saying is you're a street cop, one of Hamilton's best and shiniest community officers."

Marley knew that wasn't true. But she didn't fit on the drug squad, either. "You're only saying that because I get you free coffee from the place down on Main and Sixth."

Superman flashed Marley his trademark dimpled smile. "That's because the owner has a crush on you."

Marley threw a pen at Superman. He ducked, and it went sailing over his head, landing in the middle of the aisle. An officer walking down the aisle picked it up. It was Simms. He completely ignored Superman and approached Marley, dropping the pen on her desk.

"Question. Did you ever come across the name Mace or a reference to Mace in any of your evidence searches?"

Superman rolled his eyes behind Simms's shoulder and took off.

"Mace? No, I don't think I've come across that name."

"Has the kid ever mentioned anything about a Mace?"

Marley swallowed her irritation. "No."

"It was a long shot, but I thought I'd check."

"Is this coming out of your visit to Windsor yesterday?" Marley said.

"Got some good information from the precinct down there. Looks like West initially set up shop down there, possibly with this Mace guy, whoever he is. West was picked up for small time possession with intent to sell. He's actually waiting out a court date in Windsor and isn't supposed to have left the county. But they've got all the same issues we do. Court systems back up, and we don't have enough parole officers to keep track of everyone."

"And of course our jurisdictions don't speak to each other, so he's got a parole officer in Windsor and one in Hamilton, and neither of them know it."

Simms pointed a finger at Marley. "Exactly. He's a dude who knows how to play the system."

"So where does the Mace guy fit in?"

"I don't know. The Windsor guys said that name was coming up in another drug case. Someone trying to cut a deal offered to spill on the Windsor drug scene as long as they kept him out of gen pop. This guy said West and Mace were on to something new that was really shifting the underground drug scene, and people were noticing. Then last fall, they both seemed to disappear."

"And West set up here," Marley said.

"Right. Lucky us, we got West and the new street drug."

And Aimee got moved again. To something better? Away from something worse? There was no evidence Aimee was involved in the drug scene in Hamilton. She'd confessed only to her time in Windsor. What had happened to Aimee between the time her mother had died and when Carla showed up to become her legal guardian?

"Marlowe, can you ask her?"

"Who?"

"The kid. Aimee," Simms said impatiently. "Can you ask her about someone named Mace?"

"Yes, I can," Marley said, trying to keep the reluctance out of her voice. Aimee was a resilient kid, but Marley didn't want to keep testing it.

"Good. And you up for field work yet?"

"Depends," said Marley, shifting in her chair. She was officially off pain meds other than Advil. She wasn't sleeping well, but she didn't think that had anything to do with her injury. "What are you thinking?"

"Maybe heading down to knock on some doors, ask some questions."

"Yeah, Simms. I'm up for that. Let me know."

Marley's phone chimed and vibrated on her desk. Marley ignored it for now.

"Could be this afternoon, could be tomorrow. I'll text you."

"Sounds good," Marley said, wanting him to disappear.

When he did, Marley flipped her phone over to check the notification. It was Devon.

*Aimee cut her forehead. I think someone needs to look at it.*

Marley's heart sank. Poor kid. *She okay?*

*A little freaked out but okay.*

Of course she was. This was Aimee West. *Walk-in clinic?*

*Thinking my ER, Centennial. Wait times probably same but thought she might be happier in a place I know.*

Marley considered that. Walk-in clinics were potentially quieter, with no urgent cases, though likely they were the same time sitting and waiting to get seen. But Devon would know the staff at the ER. Maybe even find a quiet corner for Aimee if she was overwhelmed or upset. She was just typing that back when Devon sent another text.

*Stupid idea?*

Marley deleted her original text and tried again. *Not at all. Want me to come?*

*Why don't Carla and I start and we'll see how it goes?*

*Done. Keep me posted, Dr. Wolfe.*

*Will do, Constable Marlowe.*

Marley put down her phone and stared at her desk. She knew Aimee was fine. She didn't know what to do with the fact that she would rather be with Devon and Carla and Aimee right now. She'd rather be seeing them through this rough time than sorting through the chain reaction of this drug bust. It was becoming one hazy blur of human sadness.

Marley shifted in her seat, stretching to adjust her belt away from her wound. Devon was more than capable of supporting Carla and Aimee, and she always seemed to know the balance of checking in with Carla without patronizing. And Aimee loved Devon. They were safe and cared for. Marley was here now, this was her job. This was an opportunity to help Carla and Aimee in a way Devon couldn't. She could help collect the evidence against Randolph West and piece together Aimee's trauma so maybe, just maybe, some day she could put it to rest.

She pulled out a piece of paper, a useless memo with directions on how to change your voice mail on one side. A little embarrassed, Marley listed questions down the left side. Who, what, when, where, how, why?

She started with who. Randolph West and the three associates arrested with him. She added the name Mace with a question mark. Marley held her pen against Aimee's name. She could list the relationship between Aimee and her father, between Aimee and his three associates. She tapped the name Mace, then circled it.

Next, what. Drugs. What kind? Marley turned on her computer and accessed the files she was looking for, thankful Simms had opened it up to her. She scrolled down to the still-incomplete report on the drugs. Suspected opioid, a variation of the addictive substance. Marley jotted a few notes about the drugs, then looked at her two filled-in columns. Something wasn't quite right, something incomplete. She added drug users to the who list. Then added *drug distributor* beside the name of West's associates and *drug developer* with a question mark beside West himself and the still unknown Mace. Marley circled the drug users. She needed to ask Simms if anyone had questioned any of the drug users.

The when, where, and how went pretty quickly, as it was the bulk of the evidence they had: the details of locations and drug paraphernalia, distribution routes, and cash. It was the information that Marley cared about least and Simms cared about most. *Possibly why I'm a terrible cop*, Marley thought.

Marley shook her head and looked at the last empty column. Why. Why does anyone do what they do? What motivates them to break the law, to harm others, to harm themselves? What stories do they tell themselves so they can give themselves permission to hurt in any given moment? Continuously hurt. And not care.

She wrote down the names from the who column in the why column. West and his associates seemed easy. Why? Money. She hesitated with Aimee's name, then wrote *lack of power, agency, fear.* Mace was still a question mark. Drug users? Marley considered what she knew about why people used drugs. Trauma, poverty, lack of power, agency, untreated mental health issues. The similarity to Aimee's list wasn't difficult to see, and Marley felt a hard resolve anchor itself in her chest. This wouldn't be Aimee's future. It couldn't be.

"I've got an update, Marlowe."

Marley had been absorbed in her list and hadn't seen Simms arriving. She'd been blocking out the sound of the office pretty effectively for the last half hour.

"What is it, Simms?"

Simms put a paper on her desk and tapped it with one finger.

"Chemical analysis of West's drug."

Marley scanned the page, recognizing the chemical compound jargon but not understanding any of it. She scanned until she saw a summary.

"Chemical compound mimics fentanyl," Marley read. She looked up at Simms. "But we're not seeing the overdose numbers like with fentanyl."

"You got it. Farther down, it explains that. When I talked to the lab guy on the phone, the one who did the final report, he said this was a pretty sophisticated formula and not something he's seen in a lot of street drugs in Canada."

"Sophisticated," Marley said, considering the word.

"He called it 'elegant and creative', I believe," Simms said.

Marley blinked. These words were strange here, jarring even. She glanced at her list. Where did sophisticated, elegant, and creative fit in?

"Whatcha got there?"

Marley hesitated, then showed him her list. "Don't laugh," she said. "I was trying to wrap my head around the whole picture."

Simms scanned the list and grunted, though Marley wasn't sure how to interpret that. "You can add to the 'what' list. We've got a better idea what this drug is. We're calling it opioid Z for now." He put the paper down but kept looking at it.

Marley hesitated, then leaned forward and pointed at the who. "I'm more curious about who, to be honest with you. I don't see anyone on this list who has the knowledge for sophisticated chemical compound composition. Let alone elegance and creativity."

Simms stared at her for a moment, then looked at the list. He tapped it again.

"You're thinking Mace?" he said.

"I'm thinking we've got a big fat question mark around Mace."

"And I think we should do something about it. Let's go talk to some people."

Marley checked her phone. No updates from Devon. They were good, they were fine. This was how Marley could help Aimee.

Marley looked back up at Simms.

"Let's go."

Devon could feel the bones in her hand crunching together as Aimee held her hand tighter and tighter and tighter. Carla was filling out paperwork, a long process since she only had a temporary health card for Aimee and a letter from Family and Children's Services. Aimee's birth certificate and health card hadn't yet shown up in the piles of evidence from Fleming Street. Or maybe it was lost in transition between agencies. Aimee's whole life seemed currently lost in transition.

The whoosh of the automatic doors made Aimee cringe, and she tucked her bandaged head into Devon's shoulder.

"That door opens and closes about a thousand times in a day, I bet," Devon said conversationally. "It allows the medical staff to go back and forth between the waiting area and the treatment rooms without having to touch a door handle."

Aimee didn't say anything, but she peeked over Devon's shoulder at the door before settling again.

Aimee had been spinning on the barstool in the kitchen while Devon and Carla were chatting after breakfast. Her foot had caught as she was climbing down, and she'd fallen into the stool next to it, slicing her head on an exposed wood staple. It wasn't too deep, but it was deep enough.

"Can I get your finger, honey?" the triage nurse said to Aimee. "I'm going to put this clip on it."

Aimee looked at the pulse-ox monitor, with its glowing red button. She extended her hand, still leaning into Devon.

"There you go," the nurse said. She was kind and efficient. "Next up, a thermometer. This one goes in your ear."

Aimee held still through all the prodding and questions, but Devon could feel her agitation. When they were released from triage and sent back to the waiting area, Devon carried Aimee in her arms. She walked to the main desk and waited, knowing interrupting a nurse was one of the very best ways to get your head bitten off, chewed up, and spat out. Devon was relieved to see Gloria on shift. She was bright and efficient and always made things work.

Gloria shoved a pen into the side pocket of her blue and purple scrubs and turned around, her eyes lighting up when she saw Devon.

"Well, if it isn't the Zen Tiger." She glanced at Aimee, who was still hiding her face. "With a babe in arms even."

"It's good to see you, Gloria," Devon said, relieved the sentiment wasn't forced. "How mad would you be if I waited with this one in the alcove? She's a little overwhelmed."

Gloria came around the other side of the desk, pulling on a pair of gloves from a box on the wall. Devon had almost forgotten these fluid movements, the dance and interplay of muscle memory repeating a motion again and again, seeking out answers to the unknown.

"Who do we have here?"

"This is Aimee and her grandmother Carla. Aimee's got a cut to the head from a fall off a stool in my kitchen."

"Hey, Aimee. I'm Gloria, I'm a nurse. Sometimes they call me Glorious, but that's because every now and then I bake cannolis."

Aimee turned her head just enough to see Gloria.

"Mind if I touch your forehead, honey? Will only take a sec."

Aimee nodded and sat through another short exam.

"It's not too bad. You go sit with her in the alcove, and I'll tell Bryson where to find you when he's got a minute. Could be a while."

"Thanks, Gloria," Devon said.

The nurse squeezed Devon's bicep. "It's good to see you. You are missed."

Then Gloria was gone, swept up in the never-ending movement of the emergency department.

Devon swallowed a lump in her throat and indicated with a quick jerk of her chin to Carla which way they were going. The alcove was an odd space outside the staff room, with two chairs tucked behind the tall wheelie shelves of blankets and sheets. It didn't diminish the sound of the busy hospital much, but it felt calmer, a respite from the constant energy.

Carla sat in one of the chairs and held her arms up. "Here, let me take her. Your arms must be tired by now."

Devon leaned down, and Aimee awkwardly clambered from her arms to her grandmother's. Devon shook out her arms, muscles aching.

"You guys okay here for a bit?" Devon said to Carla. "I'm going to double-check Bryson knows we're back here."

"We're good," Carla said, rocking Aimee a little in her arms. "Thanks for finding us a quiet spot. I know how busy these places can get."

"Not a problem. I'd offer to bring you some tea or coffee, but I know how gruesome it is here."

Carla laughed. "Let's not risk it," she said.

Devon walked back through the busy, familiar halls, looking for the doctor. She felt conspicuous now without Aimee in her arms, a tangible, easily explained reason why she was here back in the ER. But it was okay, Devon realized. There was concern in her body, awareness of others, apprehension at having to repeat why she was here and where she had been. But no panic, no overriding sense of wrongness. No voice in her head blaring the siren of *you can't do this*.

"Devon! Hey, I was just coming to look for you."

Doug Bryson hadn't been a med student for twenty years, but it was hard to tell. His light beard did very little to cover his baby face. Bryson was a good doctor and had been one of Devon's best allies in the beginning, as she tried to integrate mental health practices into the busy trauma unit.

"Looking good, Bryson. I like the beard."

Bryson stroked his beard dramatically. "This puppy took me a month. I'm quite proud of it. You're looking good, kid. You running a lot?"

"Thanks and yeah. Most days, if I can avoid these storms. Hey, thanks for your texts over the last little while. It's meant a lot." Devon swallowed, making space for the feeling of vulnerability and gratitude.

Bryson cuffed her on the shoulder. "Team takes care of team. You taught us that."

Devon hoped that was true.

"I hear you've got a kid with you needing some stitches?"

"Aimee and her grandmother are staying with me for a bit and Aimee, she's eight, took a fall off one of my spinning barstools."

Bryson nodded. "Give me about fifteen minutes—which means half an hour—and I'll take a look. Hopefully we can use some epoxy and not make the kid suffer through stitches."

"You've got the best hands on the floor, Bryson. That's why Gloria put you on the case."

"Ah, flattery," Bryson said, grinning. "I do like flattery. Fifteen minutes."

"Perfect. And just a heads-up that Aimee doesn't talk. She gestures and writes to communicate."

"Okay," Bryson said, looking curious. "We'll make it work."

Bryson waved as he walked off and Devon leaned back into the wall, out of the way of the busiest of the traffic flow. She pulled out her phone, responding to a message from her dad. She hesitated before sending a message to Marley, not wanting to interrupt her day. Marley was back to work, focused on uncovering what exactly Randolph West had released onto the street. Devon thought a quick check-in message would be okay, giving an update without requiring a response.

As she was tapping out the message on her phone, a commotion by one of the curtained-off beds caught Devon's attention. She saw the curtain yanked and heard a voice hiss. She also heard the sound of crying, gulping, and sniffing and the cracking voice of someone trying to hold it together. Another cycle of blame and regret and guilt. Histories played out in the emergency room, relationships cut to their core in these moments of pain and stress.

A moment later, Gloria pushed back the curtain, closing it halfway as she left. Devon recognized the nurse's professional mask, the armour that front line workers put on every day. When she caught sight of Devon, Gloria let the mask slip, shaking her head a little. Devon thought the annoyance on the nurse's face looked awfully close to defeat.

"Family drama?" Devon guessed, talking quietly.

"Big time," Gloria said. "Daughter OD'd and Mom is choosing this moment to announce she's taking away her four-year-old grandchild."

Pain on pain, Devon thought. She could see the young woman in the hospital bed. She looked to be in her early twenties, hair in a fallen ponytail over her shoulder, shredding a tissue into small pieces on the sheet over her lap. Devon's heart ached to see the hopelessness and self-loathing in her expression. Self-hatred was a deep and dark pit. This young woman had a tough climb ahead of her.

"Calling social services for sure," Gloria said. "Medically she's fine, though I need the doc to check out that rash." Gloria sighed. "Patch 'em up, see if we can get her some help, and make space for the next one."

Devon raised her eyebrow at the nurse. Gloria snorted and rolled her eyes.

"You're really going to make me reframe? No free passes?"

"You can do it in your head if you like," Devon said mildly, smiling at Gloria's resistance to the process they'd practiced as a unit over and over.

Another eye roll as Gloria tapped sharply on the keyboard recessed into the wall. Devon said nothing, just continued looking around the ward, feeling the familiar rhythms and finding a sense of peace.

"Fine," Gloria said, shoving the keyboard back into the wall. She crossed her arms over her chest and stared Devon down. Devon could see the glint in her eye, though, the acceptance that she needed to shift the negative thoughts. "I was here today to take care of the patient. I provided care. I made things as betterer as I could." That hint of laughter, a defense mechanism Devon had always encouraged. "I can make up words, right?"

"Totally."

"I made things betterer as I could. And I'll do it again because care is what I can give and care is what they need."

Devon smiled. "Yeah, that's a good one. Feel any better?"

Gloria shrugged. "Maybe? Proof is if I show up tomorrow." She winked when Devon laughed. "Catch you later, Tiger."

*Maybe I'm ready to come back*, Devon thought after Gloria had left to see another patient. Something to think about, when she wasn't worrying about Marley and Aimee and Carla.

Devon looked up as a woman in her mid-forties pushed the curtain back all the way. Her hair was puffed around her head in an oddly deliberate cloud. She stormed out of the treatment area and down the hall. Devon glanced at the young woman, who stretched out for the box of tissue, tears streaming down her face. She couldn't reach it from the bed, tethered by the IV pole. With a glance behind her to see if Gloria was around, Devon crossed the distance to the small treatment area, grabbed the box, and handed it to the young woman.

"Thanks," the woman mumbled.

"You're welcome," Devon said. "Anything else I can get you?"

The young woman looked up, her eyes red and puffy from crying. Devon could see the rash Gloria had mentioned, an angry red that covered one half of her face and neck and disappeared under her T-shirt.

"You work here?" The woman said.

"Sort of. I know where to find the juice stash, anyway."

"No, thanks," she said, taking a tissue and dabbing at her eyes. "I just need to see the doctor and get out of here."

"Okay. I'm Devon, by the way."

The woman looked up again. "Mikayla," she said.

"I hope your day gets better, Mikayla."

Mikayla looked down at her hands and said nothing. Devon stood there a moment longer, noticing the way Mikayla's one hand twitched spasmodically, like a tremor. It could be the effects of the drug, the overdose, or maybe even the opioid reversal used to bring this young woman back. Either way, she was in a world of hurt.

"Take care of yourself," Devon said, leaving the young woman to herself.

When she approached the alcove, Bryson was standing at the entrance, talking to Carla.

"Perfect timing," Bryson said. "I was wondering if Ms. Aimee here would be more comfortable in a treatment room."

Devon peeked into the alcove. Aimee was standing now and leaning into Carla.

"Might be easier to see your cut," Devon said. "And have my friend Dr. Bryson treat it so we can get out of here. What do you think?"

Aimee nodded and hid her face. Carla followed Devon and Bryson down the hallway with Aimee glued to her side, her eyes squeezed shut.

"All right," Dr. Bryson said. "First let's find out what happened."

"She likes spinning on the stools at Devon's place," Carla said. "Her foot got caught, and she hit her forehead on the stool next to her. Started bleeding pretty good."

"Did she lose consciousness at all?"

Carla shook her head.

"Complaints of head or neck hurting? Dizziness?"

Carla shook her head for all.

"Okay, I'm going to do some tests with your eyes, and I'd like to check your neck." He turned around to show Aimee his own neck. "See these bumps? Those are your cervical vertebrae, and I want to check that nothing got jostled when you fell."

Aimee looked curious at this, and Devon and Carla shared a relieved smile. Devon hung back as Bryson continued his questioning and his examination. Not only did he have great hands, he was amazing with kids. When Devon had asked him one day why he didn't go into pediatrics, all he said was "the parents".

Devon's phone vibrated in her back pocket. A call from Marley. She stepped out of the treatment area and picked up the call.

"Marley, hey. Aimee is seeing a doctor now."

"Good," Marley said. "Where are you?"

"At the hospital," Devon said, confused. She thought it sounded like Marley was walking. "Are you here?"

"Uh…yeah." Marley sounded sheepish. "Bad idea?"

"Good idea. I'll come and get you and let you through the doors."

Devon waved through the window to indicate to Carla she'd be right back. Bryson had the bandage off now and was inspecting the wound. God, she hoped it was something simple. As if anything in Aimee's life could be simple.

Devon could see Marley through the glass portion of the locked doors. She always looked bigger in uniform, her posture and the protective vest making her look imposing, threatening. Devon knew Marley had fire. And strength. But she'd also seen Marley curled up in her favourite chair with a cup of tea, laughing. There was gentleness in this woman, too.

She pushed open the locked doors. Fire and laughter, strength and gentleness. Devon knew she was drawn to every part of Marley.

"Hey," Devon said, needing to clear her throat. "How has your day been?"

"Weird," Marley said. Devon glanced back but Marley was already busy looking around the room.

It was hard to talk, dodging people and equipment. They stepped to the side as an ambulance crew pushed a stretcher down the hall, trundling through like a freighter in a narrow channel.

Devon took the opportunity to really look at Marley. She seemed pale and her posture was tense. One hand gripped her utility belt, and the other was at her side. Devon sensed an aura of readiness about her.

"Come here for a minute," Devon said, touching the short sleeve of Marley's uniform.

Devon made sure Marley was following as they ducked down a hallway. She opened the staff room door part way and made sure no one was using it as a place to catch a nap. It was empty, the smell of coffee and someone's microwaved lunch leftovers filtering through the dim space.

Devon faced Marley, who was looking around the room. "Tell me about your weird day?"

"Yeah, definitely weird."

Devon waited but Marley still hadn't focused. Devon took a step closer until she was inside Marley's personal space.

"Hey, Marley," Devon said quietly.

Marley's eyes cleared a little, and she looked at Devon.

"Hey, Devon," Marley said, just as quietly.

The moment was a hungry one. Starved for words and empty of touch. For now though, this was enough.

"Tell me about your day?" Devon tried again.

"I think I'm in the wrong profession," Marley said. She didn't sound upset, more speculative. "We spent the afternoon talking to people with known drug connections. Everyone from a guy who'd spent time in jail for possession and distribution to a teenager just released from rehab to a woman who lives on the street and can tell you the chemical compound of every street drug. Every one."

Marley lost focus again for a minute, her gaze traveling away from Devon.

"Sounds like you're carrying stories," Devon said.

Marley's focus snapped back to Devon. "Yes," she said, her voice stronger. "That's what it feels like. Simms, the drug enforcement team lead who I was working with, is out there sorting through what they're saying, pulling out the evidence, finding connections and leads. He knows what's relevant and what's not. He takes the nuggets of evidence and then…" Marley shook her head, struggling. "Then he walks away from the rest. He can strip people down to their usefulness and it's… horrifying. And absolutely necessary."

"What were you thinking about as you were talking to people today?"

"Aimee, mostly. I'm collecting evidence to find out what her living situation has been like the last year. And I keep looking at these people and wondering where was their Carla when they were eight? Who was their Miss K?"

A familiar ache of compassion and connection rose in Devon's chest, and she ran her hand down Marley's bare arm, touching the bones of her wrist, then she smoothed her thumb across Marley's knuckles and entwined their fingers.

"You're not less of a police officer because you see the people you're talking to. And you're not alone in not always knowing how to carry stories."

Marley looked down at their joined hands. "My supervisor said the same thing recently," she said. "And I know it's one of the primary stressors on front-line workers." She gave Devon a small, crooked grin. "I've read the articles."

Devon laughed. "We've probably read the same ones."

"And you probably wrote a few."

Devon shook her head, still smiling. "Only one."

Marley's smile slipped and she leaned back, loosening her grip. "I shouldn't put this on you. You've told me this is why you're off work. And all I've done is heap burden after burden on you."

"Stop," Devon said, the sharp edge to her tone cutting through Marley's babble. "Enough. I need you to trust that I know what I can handle. I may not have been that great at it the last few years, but I'm working on it, and you believing I can do it is important to me."

Marley looked stunned and Devon felt the vulnerability of the moment acutely. She also felt hope as Marley squeezed her hand.

"Message received, Dr. Wolfe," Marley said.

Devon smiled. She squeezed Marley's hand then eased away. "Let's go find Aimee."

When they walked into the treatment area, Aimee had a fresh, bright white bandage on her forehead, and Bryson was instructing her how to use the otoscope to look into Carla's ear.

"Gross, right?" Bryson said and Aimee nodded and made a face.

"All good in here?" Devon said.

Aimee's eyes lit up when she saw Marley, and she ran over and tugged until Marley knelt down so Aimee could look in her ear.

"No stitches, and Aimee was a complete champ," Bryson said. "We'll grab some instructions about wound care and signs of infection, and you guys are good to go." Bryson pulled his gloves off and threw them in the garbage. "Another life saved."

"Thanks, Bryson," Devon said, clapping him on the shoulder. "You made this way easier."

"That's what I'm here for."

Aimee handed back his otoscope reluctantly but waved at Dr. Bryson when he said goodbye.

"Can I talk to you for a minute?" Marley asked Devon once Bryson had left. Aimee continued to try and see inside her grandmother's ear. Carla was rolling her eyes but held still.

"Sure."

Devon followed Marley back into the hall. Marley sighed and rubbed her forehead.

"I need to ask Aimee about a person of interest. Someone she might have come in contact with," Marley said.

"You need to ask her today?"

"I know," Marley said, obviously having heard some judgement in Devon's voice. "Not great timing. Is she up for it?"

Devon felt irritation and protectiveness shift uncomfortably in her chest. Aimee wasn't her child, wasn't her patient. She couldn't be the only one making these assessments and judgment calls. Devon took a breath, feeling the bite of the words as they were about to leave her mouth. She let the breath out slowly and tried again.

"I don't know," Devon said. "She's doing really well, but maybe check with Carla."

"Okay," Marley said. She looked contrite. Then curious. "Why do I get the feeling you just stopped yourself from biting my head off?"

Devon let out a short laugh. "Because that's almost what happened."

"Impressive level of self-control, Dr. Wolfe."

Devon caught Marley's eye then, a mix of warmth, worry, and fatigue.

"You need some sleep," Devon said without thinking.

"I need to wrap up this case and get Carla and Aimee settled," Marley said. "That's what I need."

"No," Devon said gently. "That's what *they* need. *You* need some sleep."

Marley shook her head. "According to my boss, *I* need to stay out of trouble and help break open the case. Preferably starting with some actual information about what this drug is and why we're seeing such weird side effects after it's off the street."

"Side effects?"

"Tremors, rash, and hallucinations, according to the admittedly little information from Public Health."

Devon blinked. "I saw someone like that. With those symptoms."

"Here?"

"Yeah, a young woman. Early twenties, maybe. I was with her earlier."

"Do you know if anyone has called Public Health? A memo went out to regional hospitals, walk-in clinics, and doctor's offices a few days ago about calling Public Health immediately for anyone with those symptoms."

"I know which nurse she was working with."

"Would you mind introducing me to her? Then I could talk with her without compromising patient privacy."

"Give me a minute."

Devon searched the hallways of the ER, eventually finding Gloria chewing on a protein bar while sticking a label on an orange-lidded urine sample bottle. Joys of the emergency room.

"You got a minute, Gloria?"

"For you, peanut? Yes."

Gloria put the urine sample on a cart and gave Devon her full attention.

"I've got someone I'd like you to meet."

Gloria's eyes lit up, and Devon considered how it sounded. She blushed. "I don't mean like that." Wasn't it like that? "I mean…"

Gloria laughed. "You never trip over your words, Tiger. So, I think it's definitely like that."

Another blush. "Okay, yes. But that's not why I want you to meet

Marley. Constable Marlowe. She's working on a case that involves Public Health and some odd symptoms from drug use."

Gloria expression shifted to serious. "Public Health, yes. We had a stand-up staff meeting about it." Her gaze shifted inward, as if replaying the moment. Then she looked up at Devon. "You're thinking about the young woman from earlier. Curtain four. With the angry mom." Gloria's shoulder slumped. "Shit, I almost missed that."

"It's not all on you," Devon said.

Gloria closed her eyes for the briefest moment before she straightened, grabbed the last bite of protein bar, and shoved it in her mouth before tossing the wrapper and wiping her hands together.

"Let's meet this Constable Marlowe of yours."

## Chapter Ten

Mikayla Roy was twenty-one years old and lived in a world of hurt. Marley sat by her hospital bed and took down her age and address, drug history, and family history.

"Can you remember what time it was when you used last?"

Mikayla blinked a few times rapidly. "Yesterday around four."

Marley wrote it down, then closed her notebook.

"How are you feeling?"

"Weird. Tired. Sick." More rapid blinks, like she was struggling to see. "Have you heard from Family and Children's Services? Are they taking Ava? She can stay with my parents."

Marley grabbed another tissue from the box on the bedside table and handed it to Mikayla. Her eyes were watering again. Tears streaked down her face, and she didn't seem to notice.

"I believe your worker is with your mom right now. But I'm not here about that, Mikayla, okay? Remember I explained I'm here about the new drug you took, the one that made you so sick."

"Blissed," Mikayla said, her lips barely forming over the word. "Jaxon said 'blissed'."

Mikayla had mentioned her dealer, Jaxon, more than once. Marley guessed he was known to Simms and his drug team, but she'd have to check.

"How many times have you taken it?"

"Third time. Unlucky."

Mikayla looked up at the lights and squinted, her head moving side to side, like she was following movement. Marley glanced up as well but didn't see anything. Then Mikayla slumped back against her pillow.

"I need to sleep."

"Okay, Mikayla. Someone might be coming by to talk to you later."

Mikayla mumbled an answer, her hands twitching spasmodically on her lap, her head cranked at a weird angle. Marley considered trying to make her more comfortable, then decided to let her be.

She left the small enclosure, pulling the curtain around Mikayla's bed. Gloria was in the hallway with Dr. Li, the doctor who had admitted Mikayla earlier in the day. Marley checked her phone while she waited for them to finish talking. Devon had left with Carla and Aimee over an hour ago and had texted briefly to say they were home and settled. Marley looked at the message again, reading the short phrase over and over. Home and settled. Home. Settled.

"Did you get everything you need?" It was Dr. Li, a woman with serious posture and a warm smile.

"I did, thanks. Mikayla is resting now, says she's not feeling great. She was starting to act oddly near the end. I'm wondering if the hallucinations have started."

"We'll keep an eye on her. I've got a long list of symptoms to look out for and symptoms to document from Public Health."

Marley winced. "Sounds like I added to your busy night."

"No, no," Dr. Li said. "That wasn't a complaint. Well," she grinned, "not much of a complaint."

Marley smiled. "Call me if anything comes up. Not sure I'll be a huge help but…" She shrugged.

"The offer is appreciated," Li said. "It's good to know we're not the only ones on the front line with this. Devon helped us see that." She grinned again. "Forced us, really. Very gently forced us."

Marley hesitated. Asking about Devon in her workplace seemed like an invasion of privacy.

"She's good at that, I imagine," Marley said.

"Good at making a team of front line medical staff agree that we're a bunch of stubborn assholes who won't admit to needing help even when every single piece of evidence suggests we're drowning and screaming for help?" She snorted and shook her head. "Dr. Devon

Wolfe is a savior disguised as a psychologist. I'd elect her for sainthood if I could."

Marley laughed. "I think knighthood would suit her better."

"Sir Devon," Li said, eyes flashing. "I like it." Li looked over her shoulder when someone called her name. "Gotta go. I'm sure I'll see you again, Constable Marlowe."

Marley stood in the hallway for a moment, wondering if she should go home and sleep or go to the office to write up the report. She was leaning toward sleep when her phone rang, Simms's name on her screen.

"Marlowe? I need you down at the precinct. We've got a lead on Mace."

It was dinner by the time Marley arrived back at the station. She was already dragging. She went to the staff room and rummaged until she found a package of microwave popcorn. Leaning against the chipped laminate counter, she stared at the whirring bag with a tired blankness until the popping and beeping startled her into full consciousness. Tearing the package open as she walked, delicious hot steam escaping from the top, Marley went to find Simms.

"I like an officer who shows up with snacks," Simms said, looking up from his desk.

"Dinner, actually," Marley said around a mouthful of popcorn, extending the bag towards Simms. He grabbed a handful and launched into his update.

"Mace shows up in a bunch of police databases, all dark internet shit I don't understand."

"So Mace is a username?"

"I guess. We've got no real name at this point. He pops up on RCMP radar for chat groups dealing in homemade chemical bombs, biological warfare, and—this is my favourite—an underground art movement using..." Simms looked down and read directly from his notes, "'reactive chemical art installations as an act of social disruption'."

"I heard about that, I think. They were responsible for turning the waterfall feature outside Vancouver City Hall into a putrid cess-pool."

"You got it. Mace's name comes up in that investigation."

"So, we've found our chemist. Sort of."

Simms rubbed at his eyes. "And 'sort of' is a problem."

"Vancouver is a long way from here. We don't even know if we're trying to find an actual living, breathing person stirring up shit in Hamilton. We could be chasing a very intelligent ghost."

Simms pointed at Marley. "My first thoughts exactly. But in the other investigations where Mace comes up, someone on the ground with chemical or biological know-how was there to put together whatever sick prank or 'art installation' they had cooked up. We don't have that. So, I'm wondering if in our case, Mace is the brains *and* the brawn."

"Lucky us," Marley mumbled, shoving another handful of popcorn in her mouth.

The phone on Simms's desk rang, startling them both. Simms picked it up.

"Simms…Yes, put him through." Simms pressed a series of buttons, then put the phone back in its cradle. "Salik, I've got you on speaker phone. Constable Marlowe is with me, we're working this case together."

"Constable Marlowe, hello." Ben Salik, their contact at Public Health, spoke with traffic sounds in the background. "I'm actually at the hospital, I just finished speaking to Mikayla Roy."

"Does she fit the profile? Symptoms and time of last drug use?"

"She does. It's a solid data point."

A person, Marley thought. A person in pain, not a data point.

"Excellent," Simms said.

"I'm calling because I've got a bit of a disturbing development," Salik continued. "While I was talking with Ms. Roy, another patient came in and was flagged by Dr. Li. The patient is a thirty-two year old male, admitted to using a drug that sounds a lot like opioid Z, last used about two weeks ago. Symptoms after withdrawal align with what we've been seeing."

"Okay," said Simms, drawing out the word. "What's the disturbing part?"

"Patient sought medical treatment for a severe rash on one side of his body and what Dr. Li is describing as 'degenerative neurological symptoms'. Memory loss, mood swings, periodic aphasia."

"So, we're looking at a progression of symptoms? Potentially worsening symptoms the longer they go without access to the opioid?" Simms said.

"Potentially, yes. But the news gets worse."

Marley felt a sudden tightness in her spine, a brittle moment as they waited.

"The patient's girlfriend is the one who brought him to the ER. She had their two-year-old son with them. The child is exhibiting signs of a rash on one side of his body."

Silence. Marley and Simms stared at each other, Salik's words hanging between them, the tinny sound of background traffic filling the space.

"The rash is contagious?" Marley managed to say, exhaustion, confusion, and horror warring for space. "A symptom from drug withdrawal is contagious?"

"It's too early to say anything definitively," Salik said. "Dr. Li and I are going to investigate. No facts yet, no proof. Nothing. But I thought you'd want to know the direction this is going."

"Thanks," Simms said, sounding tired. "Keep us posted."

The click and dial tone projected loudly in the silence of the empty office.

"Well, fuck me," Simms said, rubbing his forehead.

Marley leaned against the desk across from Simms. She looked into the mostly empty bag of popcorn, the fake butter smell making her suddenly nauseous.

"Now what?" she said.

Simms said nothing at first, just continued rubbing, as if he could wear this new information away.

"Simms?"

"We're a drug enforcement unit, Marlowe. Our job is to find who made this and who put it on the street. We get the drugs off the street, we get the bad guys off the street. End of story."

"But—"

"Look," Simms said, definitely sounding mad now. "This doesn't change anything. It's great Public Health is keeping us in the loop but our job is still our job, their mandate is still their mandate. We focus on the drug investigation, sewing up the loose ends of this drug bust we started three weeks ago. Then we move on."

He was scared. That's what Marley read from his outburst, from his insistence on not paying attention to this potentially critical development. But right now he was her supervising officer, and Marley knew she was already skating on thin ice.

"I'm going to write up and submit my report before I go."

Simms waved her away, suddenly very interested in the paperwork on his desk.

"Go home, Marlowe. The report can wait until morning."

Marley walked back through the office, leaving Simms to wrestle this new information into a box he understood. She sat at her desk and stared at nothing for a moment. Then she picked up her phone and scrolled through her contacts. She needed something to ground her flying thoughts. The phone rang in her ear three times before it picked up.

"Hey, Dad. What's cooking tonight?"

Devon walked through her house, the grogginess of a shitty sleep like a blurring blanket of fog in her mind. She registered the quiet, just the *clink* of ceramic and the *tink* of cutlery being moved around in the kitchen. Aimee must still be asleep. The kid hadn't yet mastered the art of quiet.

Devon entered the kitchen as the soft beep of the percolator said the coffee was ready. Carla looked up and held up the coffee pot in a question. Devon nodded and walked to the fridge to take out the cream.

The spoons sounded loud against the mugs as they stood side by side and doctored their first coffee of the day. Devon took a sip and leaned back against the counter. Carla did the same and Devon felt the softness of Carla's favourite worn blue velour sweatshirt against her arm. It was comforting somehow, the softness and the recognition of familiarity.

"Bad sleep?" Carla said.

"Bad sleep."

Devon acknowledged the ink in her veins, the hint of depression that seemed to steal in through the vulnerability of sleep and dreams. It pulsed weakly but consistently, a steady heartbeat of a reminder that she was not entirely okay.

A moment later, Aimee shuffled into the kitchen, purple pyjamas wrinkled and sagging, the bandage still taped to her forehead. She blinked a few times, looking at Devon and Carla standing side by side in the kitchen. She grabbed a plastic cup out of the draining board and filled it with water, then stood next to them, staring quietly and blankly at the kitchen.

Carla turned and caught Devon's eye, mouth pulled tight like she was trying not to laugh. Devon's heart lifted, the inkiness overpowered for a moment with gratitude for these two people in her life.

"We're a bit of a sad bunch this morning," Devon said into the silence.

"That we are," Carla said.

Aimee nodded gravely and took a sip of her water, sighing.

A car door slammed outside, which sent Aimee running to the big window. She peered out, face pressed to the glass, then started to dance before running to the front door.

"Must be Marley," Carla said, heading to the window. "Can't imagine anyone else that would make her that happy." Carla looked outside and glanced back at Devon. "Yep, it's her."

Devon glanced at the clock on the stove. Not quite six thirty. What was Marley doing here this early?

The sounds of Marley's laugh and Aimee's dancing preceded them into the kitchen. Aimee was carrying a large baker's box she placed up on the counter before climbing on the stool and raising the lid.

Devon looked up at Marley, who was leaning against the doorway into the kitchen. She was wearing wrinkled shorts and a faded Blue Jays T-shirt, her hair was messy from the wind outside, and her eyes looked tired. But she smiled when Devon looked at her, a happy and satisfied sort of smile, as if this early morning with a box of donuts and a kitchen full of people she barely knew but definitely cared for was not only normal, but wonderful. And it was. Unexpected but wonderful. Marley's smile turned from a smile to a grin, as if she'd read Devon's mind.

"Anyone up for a beach walk? The wind is nuts but radar says at least another hour or so until rain."

Ten minutes later, with some clothes thrown on, coffee divided into travel mugs, and Aimee guarding the box of donuts, they all piled into Marley's car. Marley wound them through town, the early morning traffic sparse, before turning onto a gravel road that led to an empty parking lot. Aimee solemnly offered the box of donuts to each person, the whole while gazing longingly at the one donut dripping with pink frosting. Donuts and coffee in hand, they walked down to the beach.

The sand was wet under Devon's shoes as they stepped out of the last of the protective tree line and the expanse of Lake Ontario was laid out before them, sand-less wind gusts stopping her in her tracks.

Marley looked back at Devon and grinned. "Oh, yeah. This should be fun."

Up ahead, they could see Aimee turning cartwheels on the beach, knocked down by the wind and coming up with a sticky-faced grin. The wind snatched up the sound of Carla's laughter and tossed it back to Devon and Marley.

They walked together, sounds of wind-whipped waves and laughter filling in for words. The sweetness of coffee and donuts and the wildness of the morning made Devon's heart light, careering around in her chest. And when a gust of wind knocked them back a step, they both laughed, and Marley took Devon's hand, fingers sticky. Devon's heart steadied and soared all at once. She felt a wild joy surface, manifesting itself as tears in her eyes and an unnameable ache, an anchoring she hadn't known before. It was Marley. All Marley.

The sun made a valiant effort to shine through the racing, dark clouds above, and the beach view lit up and faded as the sun fought for dominance. Aimee ran back to show them a fistful of rocks she stuffed in Devon's pocket before racing off again.

"Thanks for this morning," Devon said. "We were a bunch of sad sacks before you arrived."

"The last few days have felt so…heavy. For everyone."

"You included?" Devon said.

"Me included."

Marley didn't elaborate and Devon wanted to ask. About the tiredness in her eyes, her withdrawal, her recent silence around the case. But she held back and instead squeezed Marley's hand, a message of presence. A hope she could be an anchor for Marley, too.

Marley angled them down toward the waves and stopped. The lake was grey, each wave white-tipped and furious as it crashed and crested and crashed again. The skyline blurred out past the industrial shores of Burlington, Toronto lost in the waves and the haze of the summer air. The sky was dark far off over the water, ominous clouds signaling an approaching storm.

"Maybe I should be a meteorologist," Marley said, staring off over the lake, eyes fixed on the storm.

"You like storms?"

Marley glanced at Devon and gave her a fleeting smile.

"Yeah. Winter storms especially. But I was thinking more about the radar. I love watching the weather radar. I can look back at where the storm was, where it is now, where they predict it's going to go. The radar tells people to prepare or brace themselves or get indoors. Or hell, even just to take their laundry down. It's so…useful."

It wasn't hard for Devon to see the thread woven through this story.

"There's not much certain about first responder work," Devon said.

"No," Marley said. "I guess I'm tired…" Marley snorted. "That's a full statement right there. I'm tired." She shook her head and took a sip of coffee.

"What are you tired of?" Devon said, deciding to push. Marley seemed to want to bring this to the surface. Maybe she needed a little help.

"If you don't mind following this storm analogy with me," Marley said, turning to Devon with a hint of humour in her eyes, "I feel like I'm the guy who saunters in after the storm is over. I pick up debris and look at the damage and say 'yep, a storm sure did go through here'. Maybe I pass out a few raincoats even though everyone's already soaked, I talk to some people about lightning safety. And then I write a report."

"I'd like to take a guess, if you don't mind, about what you'd like to do with a radar." Devon paused and Marley nodded, looking curious. "I think you'd like one of those storm chaser vans with all the latest technology. And you'd drive that van through town, giving updates to anyone who would listen. And when you saw a storm coming on that radar, you'd turn on the siren, making sure every person heard it. Then you'd fill that van with people who didn't have anywhere safe to go, a whole fleet of vans if that's what it took to make sure no one was stuck out in the rain and no one got hurt. You'd use that radar every day to predict the path of the storm because you want to limit any damage to anyone."

Marley stared at Devon, wind whipping her hair into her face. Devon squeezed Marley's hand tightly and pushed a little more.

"You want a radar to predict Aimee's path. You want to have seen the approaching storm of Randolph West. You want to have intervened six months ago to keep her away from her father and deliver her safely into Carla's care." Devon paused. "All the Aimees. Everyone."

Marley blinked, and Devon saw tears surface. "Shit," Marley said. "Shit, shit, shit."

Waves hit the rocky shore and wind tugged at their hair and clothes. Devon held Marley's hand, trying so hard to be an anchor.

"All my instincts seem backward," Marley said. "It's like everyone around me understands the rules, but no matter how many times I look at my job description, I keep getting it wrong."

"Is it different than you thought it would be when you signed on to the force?"

Marley seemed to consider this. "Yes and no. I guess I thought there would be more room for different perspectives." She shook her head and stared back out over the water. "Assuming a police force could be flexible was a mistake."

Devon knew the weight of self-doubt, but this didn't seem like the moment to help Marley turn doubt into reflection, reflection into action. Marley wasn't a member of her team, a client, a colleague. Instead, she rubbed her thumb over the back of Marley's hand, tracing the lines of bone, dips of soft skin, and cords of tendons.

"You okay?" she said.

Marley didn't answer, but she leaned into Devon as they looked out over the lake, where the sun had lost its battle with the clouds and the darkness of the approaching storm had inched its way over the water.

"Storm's coming," Marley murmured after a while.

Devon looked for Carla and Aimee and saw they weren't too far off, Aimee running down the beach with her borrowed raincoat streaming out behind her like a kite. They caught up to Devon and Marley as the first rumblings of thunder reached the shore. They stood together and watched the clouds building, climbing higher and higher into the sky. Intermittent flashes lit up the cloud mass, now a boiling cauldron. The wind had died down a little, as if it had been sucked out over the lake and was now whipping this storm into a frenzy.

"Maybe we should get a little closer to the car," Carla said. "I won't be making any mad dashes if this storm hits sooner than we're expecting."

They all watched the storm as they walked back to the parking lot. A sheet of rain covered the lake, a painter's stroke of grey lines marking the approaching line of water meeting water. When a fork of lightning escaped the ever-darkening mass of clouds and struck somewhere across the water, Aimee made an odd sort of whooping sound and shook her fists into the sky, as if encouraging the storm. Daring it to do more. Devon met Marley's glance, both of them curious about Aimee making a sound when the thunder answered the lightning's call and the ground shook beneath their feet.

They weren't too far from the path that led back to the car. They huddled together, Marley looking less troubled than earlier, reflecting more of Aimee's excitement at the storm. The thunder was a continuous roll that seemed to reach out to them and recede. Lightning lit the sky in sudden, unpredictable bursts, and the line of rain moved steadily closer. Then a clap of thunder made them all duck and flinch. Aimee looked scared, then laughed.

Devon suggested they watch the rest of the storm from somewhere safer. And when the storm finally hit shore, fat raindrops making divots in the sand, they were eating donuts in the car. The storm bellowed and cracked overhead, and the rain came down impossibly heavy. And for those few moments, they were cut off from the world, cocooned together in the sweet, sticky heat of Marley's car.

## CHAPTER ELEVEN

*M*ikayla's skin itched, and her nails felt brittle. She dreamed of digging her fingers deep into the flesh of her face, neck, shoulders, armpits, breasts. Imagined she could dig under the itch and lift it out of her body, the grooved tracks on her flesh like her mother's small vegetable garden, ready for planting. But what if it wasn't all gone? What if more of this itch grew under her skin, seeding and spreading, an underground network of roots attaching to her flesh? She scratched harder and harder, ignoring the voices telling her to stop. Suddenly she couldn't scratch at all, her hands bound. She thrashed and fought, her vision blurred by whatever was growing out of her flesh, a jungle of poisoned ivy eating at her body. Then a calm voice and a blanket of nauseating warmth made her muscles go slack, the itch faded, and the jungle receded.

She woke to voices, the itch dormant but she could still feel it under her skin. The voices were confusing, but she heard Ava's name so she tried to focus. Something about vaccinations, shots, childhood diseases. Yes, yes, Mikayla wanted to say. Yes, vaccinate Ava against this. She's late for her booster, she'd had an ear infection the day of the appointment, but give her a shot against whatever was burrowing into her body. Please, give it to her. Mikayla wasn't sure if she'd spoken, if words passed the dryness of her lips, and the itching was coming back and she just wanted to cry and make sure her baby was safe. Safe from this, safe from her. Safe.

❖

"You haven't asked her about it? I thought we agreed this was a good lead."

Red was beginning to creep up out of the collar of Simms's shirt, a sign Marley was coming to recognize as agitation.

"Aimee was in the hospital two days ago," Marley said, dropping her bag at her desk, where Simms had been waiting to ambush her. "I thought she could use a break. Like I said, I plan on talking to her about Mace today."

Simms shook his head, like Marley was speaking nonsense. "Hospitalizations jumped forty percent in the last forty-eight hours. We can't coddle the kid just because—"

"Not coddling, Simms. Being cautious and following the recommendations of the intake worker who evaluated Aimee." Simms looked like he was going to argue, so Marley cut him off. "Are the newest hospitalizations from overdoses or side effects?"

"Mostly side effects, a handful of overdoses. Public Health is screaming for answers we don't have. Look, I don't want the kid to be upset, but I also don't want to be the reason some disease or whatever spread across this city because we couldn't get the job done."

Fear, a constant motivator.

"I hear you, Simms. I'll ask her today." Simms quieted, though he didn't look any less worried. "What other leads are we following?" she said.

She had become Simms's sounding board in the last week even though he'd worked longer with other guys on the drug squad. Maybe she listened better. Or maybe she wasn't stuck in tackling one problem one way.

Before Simms could start talking, an officer Marley didn't recognize interrupted. He was tall, hair cropped short, good posture. Marley pegged him as ex-military.

"Are you Simms?"

"I am. This is Constable Marlowe."

Titles and hard-grip handshakes were exchanged.

"Dennis Olsen. I'm Randolph West's parole officer." Marley's adrenaline kicked up a notch. "I was told you were the person to see."

"We're investigating West and his associates. That investigation is ongoing, as I think you know."

"I do. I'm here because West has followed all parole protocol. He's a model parolee." The way he said it, Marley didn't think he was giving a compliment. "And now he wants to see his daughter."

Marley opened her mouth to respond, the denial coming straight from her gut. But Simms beat her to it.

"I don't think it's a good idea."

"Neither do I, honestly. I've read the preliminary report, and I've talked to his child's intake worker. There's enough evidence to hold him off, maybe even indefinitely."

"So, why are we standing here?" Marley said.

Olsen looked at her, his expression more curious than concerned. "We're standing here because I'm trying to prevent a public blow-up. Randolph West has gone through all the appropriate channels. And now he's threatening lawyers and media if we don't act on his request."

"He can go through all the appropriate channels he wants," Marley said, not hiding the venom in her tone. "If it's not in the best interest of the child, the answer is no."

"The problem is," Olsen said, "that isn't documented anywhere."

Marley looked at him, stunned. "It must be."

"I'm happy to be wrong in this case," Olsen said. "But I have no documentation and no official reason to continue denying his request, even though I think a man who raises a child in a drug house should have no more parental rights."

Marley's head was pounding out a rhythm close to panic, disbelief locking down her ability to think. She turned to Simms, hoping he had an answer, but he was looking at Officer Olsen with a speculative expression. Marley had seen that expression before, a man on the hunt, seeing an opportunity.

"No," she said too quietly. Simms talked over her.

"Why does he want to see her?"

Olsen shrugged. "Said he wants to see his daughter, make sure she's being taken care of."

"We could use this," Simms said, almost to himself.

"No," Marley said, louder this time. Too loudly maybe, as both officers looked at her. "Aimee West is not a pawn. We go find the documentation to prove seeing her father would be detrimental to her emotional well-being."

"Of course," Simms said. But Marley could see he still had something in his sights. "Of course we find that documentation. But in the meantime, I'm wondering if it's an avenue that we use. A bargaining chip, even if we never actually set up a meeting between him and his daughter."

Marley thought Olsen's expression of disgust mirrored her own.

"I don't want him to see his daughter," Simms said quickly. "I don't. But tell him you're looking into finding someone who can give the go-ahead. Run him around the red tape, and let's see if we can figure out why he's so desperate to get in touch with his daughter. What does she know?"

The question hung in the air, and Marley felt the weight of not knowing the answer.

"Fair enough," Olsen said, still looking concerned. "I'll see how long I can hold him off, if you can work on getting that assessment going."

"I'll be on that," Marley said. She'd find ten different experts to give their assessment if she needed to. Whatever it took to keep Randolph West away from his daughter. Case be damned. The whole city be damned.

Simms was looking at Marley like he was reading her thoughts. Marley stared back.

"Stay in touch, Constable Olsen."

"Will do."

Olsen walked away, and Marley squared off in front of her supervising officer. She wondered, as they silently took measure of each other, how much longer she was going to hold this job.

"Call in the assessment, talk to the kid about Mace. I want an update by the end of the day."

❖

Devon watched as Aimee planted her feet in the grass and swung her arms up into a wide arc, reaching for the perfect summer blue sky. They'd been practicing breathing techniques in Devon's backyard, and Aimee had taken on the new information with the kind of zeal Devon had come to know as her core personality. Aimee had turned the exercises into a kind of dance, and Devon sat back in one of the patio chairs and watched the young girl dance her sadness, sketching her worries into the air.

"Do I need tickets to watch the show?"

Devon squinted past the glare of the sun. Marley was standing on the back deck, still in her uniform pants but with a plain white T-shirt and bare feet. Marley's smile turned to a laugh as Aimee leapt up the stairs and barreled into her with a hug.

"I'm happy to see you, too, Squirt."

Aimee ran back down the stairs and continued her dancing as Marley descended with a little more caution and sat next to Devon. She sighed as she placed a pad of paper and a pen on the arm of the chair.

"Tired?" Devon said.

"Perpetually. Eternally. Infinitely."

Devon waved a hand at Aimee. "I think there's a slot available in our backyard interpretive dance show if you want to act out your exhaustion."

Marley laughed. Devon loved the sound of it, the layers of contentment and ease mixed in with the tired. Marley leaned her head back against the back of the chair and closed her eyes.

"Napping *is* an interpretive dance of my exhaustion."

Devon watched sun and shadow play across Marley's face, wishing she could trace Marley's cheekbones, touch the laugh lines around her eyes, the worry lines around her mouth. Wished she could hold her just then, wrap her in sunshine and the warmth of a summer afternoon.

Anxiety surfaced, a leviathan from the deep. This could all disappear, thunder on a sunny day, the stab of a knife, a girl's choked voice, blood and rain in an alley. Devon felt the presence of her anxiety, a living thing that snatched at her calmness and happiness as if they were flimsy and insubstantial. As her heart raced in her chest and tears surfaced, Devon stole a glance at Marley. Her eyes were still closed. Good. She could master this. Devon pulled in a shaky breath, picturing the air penetrating deep into her lungs, filling her body.

Aimee danced closer, both her arms swinging together to draw the biggest figure eight pattern in the air. Devon anchored to that infinity sign, the never-ending loop. She picked up one hand and traced the pattern herself, breathing in as she drew one end of the loop, breathing out on the other. And again. And again. Until the leviathan of her anxiety receded, until she was back in this summer day, sitting quietly with people who made her heart feel happy and vulnerable. Both. Always both.

"I'll need to talk to Aimee this afternoon," Marley said, opening her eyes. Her expression changed when she turned to Devon. "You okay?"

"Yeah," Devon said. "Yes. I had a…moment. But it passed."

"Panic moment? The sky is falling?"

Devon looked up, the afternoon sun beginning to descend past the tips of the trees.

"It looked like it was falling for a minute there. Felt like it."

Marley looked up at the sky as well. "It's never fallen," Marley said, her voice contemplative. "But we all worry that it's going to." She was silent a moment, blinking into the sun. "Humans are weird."

Devon laughed, a belly laugh that discharged the last of her unexpected panic. "You just summarized my entire master's of psychology."

Marley grinned, and Devon returned it.

"We need a date," Marley said, seemingly out of nowhere. "Soon."

Devon felt her grin grow even wider. "Yes," she said. "Please."

The creak of the back door had them both looking over their shoulders as Carla came down the steps balancing a tray of iced tea. Marley jumped up to help, and Devon pulled over two other chairs into a semblance of a circle. Aimee gulped her iced tea, then hung upside down in her chair, making faces at the adults above her.

"This is awfully civilized," Carla said, just as Aimee overbalanced, and she and her plastic chair toppled to the ground. They all laughed and Aimee righted her chair, then started running laps around the backyard. "Okay, well, maybe *civilized* is the wrong word for my granddaughter."

"That kid is my kind of civilized," Marley murmured. Then sighed. "I'm sorry I'm going to have to break up this quiet afternoon with questions about Aimee's past."

Carla waved away Marley's apology. "It's all steps to closure. And what Aimee needs is closure."

"I guess so," Marley said.

Carla straightened up in her chair and cleared her throat. "Before we get the urchin back over here, I had something I wanted to talk to you two about." Devon read nerves and resolve in Carla's expression along with a hint of anger in the set of her mouth, a sign of vulnerability. "I've been on the phone with my boss up in Thunder Bay. She's been great, really understanding, but I'm out of sick leave and vacation time. So, we agreed I'd resign, and she's going to see if she can help me find another warehouse manager or distribution centre job down here."

"Hamilton's a good spot for it," Marley said. "You should find something pretty easily."

Carla snorted. "You try being fiftysomething and looking for a job. But my boss said the same thing. I'm trying to be hopeful."

"Does this mean you've decided to make the move to Hamilton permanently?" Devon said.

"Yes. It's a good city, I think Aimee and I could settle here, feel comfortable here." Carla looked from Devon to Marley and back again. "A lot of that is because of you two. And I know I'm asking a lot after everything you both have done for us. It feels wrong asking for more. But I'm going to need some help settling in. It will take some time to get a job, a place to live, an address so we can register Aimee for school. After-school care." Carla sighed and stared down into her empty cup. "It's a lot to ask," she said.

"I'm in," Marley said immediately. "I talked to my mom the other day, too. I think you two would get along. And it widens the support network a little."

"I'm in, too," Devon added. "Stay here until you find a space that works for you. Use this address to register Aimee for school."

Carla looked up. "It's a lot."

"I think you should take advantage of the fact that neither Devon nor I have any idea what we're getting into," Marley said, "but we're here and we're clueless but keen."

Carla laughed. "I appreciate it, both the offer and admitting you don't know what you've just agreed to."

"It's a perfect scenario," Marley said.

Carla cocked her head to the side. "It's an odd scenario. This whole thing has been odd since the get-go. But it feels right."

"I couldn't agree more," Devon said. "I'm happy you've decided to stay."

They were quiet then, all watching a more subdued Aimee, who was following a white moth around the backyard, gently trying to get it to land on the branch she was holding out.

"I hate to break up this quiet backyard scene, but I need to ask Aimee a few questions," Marley said.

"Might as well get it over with," Carla said, calling Aimee over.

The girl sat, and Devon watched as she seemed to read the energy of the adults. She sat quietly expectant in her chair. Devon recognized the empath in Aimee, the ability to read and absorb the emotions of others. A gift and a curse.

"Marley has a few questions for you, love," Carla said. "About your time living with your dad. Marley says it won't be a long conversation, and then I've got some good news for you. You can let me know when you're ready to hear it."

Aimee reached over to grab the pad of paper and pen from Marley's chair, then sat back and waited. Devon's eyes pricked with sudden tears at the incredible strength this kid demonstrated in this small gesture.

"Just a few questions," Marley repeated to Aimee. "You ready?"

Aimee nodded.

"Do you know someone named Mace?"

Aimee seemed to flinch at the name, her head dipping down in a scared, submissive gesture. But she didn't look away.

"Can you tell me where you've seen him?"

Aimee shook her head and wrote something down.

"Ah, okay. Mace is a woman," Marley said, looking surprised. Aimee wrote some more. "Other house," Marley read. "You met Mace at your other house. The one in Windsor where you went to school with Miss K?"

Aimee nodded.

"Did Mace live there with you?"

Aimee shrugged, like she didn't know how to answer the question. Devon wondered if it was hard to tell, with so many people in and out of the drug house, flopped on couches and in spare bedrooms.

"I think," Devon said, "Marley is trying to figure out Mace's relationship with your dad. If they worked together or if they were closer, like friends or boyfriend and girlfriend."

Aimee shrugged again.

"Did you ever see them hug or hold hands? Did they smile at each other a lot? Sometimes those are good ways to know how someone feels about another person."

Aimee shook her head definitively this time. Devon looked up at Marley, who seemed satisfied with the answer.

"Did Mace talk to you?"

A slow nod this time.

"Was she nice to you?"

Aimee shook her head, eyes solemn.

"Did Mace hurt you? Your body or your heart?"

Aimee didn't react at first, and the moment felt very fragile. No one moved. Devon thought maybe Aimee was holding her breath. She lifted one hand and started tracing a small figure eight in the air. Aimee followed the pattern with her eyes but still didn't respond.

Carla leaned forward and Aimee turned her attention to her grandmother. "Did Mace ask you to keep a secret, pet?"

Aimee closed her eyes. That felt like an answer to Devon. She was about to speak, about to pull out what she knew about how to talk to kids about secrets and shame when Marley started talking.

"Can I tell you what my mom and dad told me about secrets?"

Aimee gave a faint nod but didn't open her eyes. "They always told my sister and my brothers and me that secrets shouldn't hurt. Holding a secret should feel fun and exciting, like knowing what someone's getting for their birthday, a surprise visitor coming to school, or knowing who someone has a crush on. But secrets that hurt should always be shared with someone you trust. Sharing bad secrets is the only way to make them stop hurting."

A perfect explanation, Devon thought. She had a moment then, an odd break from reality where she could see, so clearly see her and Marley with their own kids, talking to them about secrets, laughing with them and loving them, trying to protect them from the hurts of the world. Devon blinked and the vision receded, as if it was tucking itself away for now.

"Three people you trust," Carla was saying to Aimee. "If you're feeling safe in your heart and your body, this might be a good time to share the bad secrets."

Aimee kept her eyes closed, hands still in her lap. She felt far away and Devon wondered if she was lost in tangled, painful memories. Out of reach and alone. A gentle wind came up, a summer breeze that moved across Devon's skin in a way that always made her thankful for days like this. She waited for Aimee to turn her face to the breeze, tilting her face up to accept the caress of wind. But Aimee didn't move. She was unswayed by breezes, disconnected from the world.

Devon watched Marley and Carla exchange a worried glance. But then Aimee opened her eyes, looked right at Marley, and shook her head. Then she stood, handed back the pen and paper, and walked away.

"Shit," Marley said after Aimee was out of earshot. "That didn't go well."

"We've always known she has secrets," Carla said, venom in her voice. Devon figured it was directed at her son. "I guess this means we're getting closer."

Devon said nothing, a stirring of helplessness that surfaced as anger surging through her system. Aimee needed professional help instead of interrogations that doubled as shitty therapy sessions. Yes, Aimee trusted them, but not one of them, including Devon, knew the best way to support a child through what was evidently some kind of trauma. Devon felt sick, felt complicit, felt powerless.

They watched as Aimee picked up the stick again, creeping through the long grass. A moment later, the white moth flitted into the air, and Aimee held the stick so carefully above it. But the moth flapped its delicate wings, evading Aimee's offer, and disappeared up into the sky. Aimee threw the stick at the fence, a strangled sound escaping her, then she collapsed onto the ground and started to cry.

Carla jumped from her chair and sat down next to Aimee, drawing her into her arms and rocking her. Devon's heart ached to see the brokenness of this wild child. Knowing this was part of her journey, knowing this had to happen, didn't make witnessing it any easier. Devon saw Marley crying quietly, her lips pressed together as tears tracked down her face.

"It's okay," Devon said, contrary to every piece of current evidence.

"I did that," Marley whispered. "I knew I shouldn't. I knew it wasn't right and I did it anyway."

They were all complicit; they could all do better. But Devon kept those thoughts locked down for now because they were too hurtful to share. Instead, she took Marley's hand and squeezed tightly as they sat, bearing witness and staying present, giving the only love they could to the crying child in that moment.

# CHAPTER TWELVE

You're not listening. It came back negative."

"That doesn't make sense, test it again."

"Three tests, all negative. We need to look at another avenue."

"And waste time and resources? No, it's a wild goose chase."

Marley sat back and listened to Simms and Salik as they became angrier and angrier with each other and listened less and less. They'd already wasted a half hour. Marley half listened to the argument, the rest of her mind spinning about Aimee, torturing herself with regret and shame, even though Devon had told her not to.

"Anything to add, Marlowe?"

"No," Marley said. Then, "Yes. What problem are we trying to solve?"

They looked at her blankly, like they were trying to work out what she was doing here. Marley was getting used to that look.

"Street drugs," Salik said. "Making people sick."

"Is that the problem? The main problem, the one that's keeping you up at night."

Salik looked surprised then thoughtful. "A new street drug making people sick enough to seek medical treatment during withdrawal is absolutely problematic. But it's this question of withdrawal symptoms being potentially contagious that's keeping me up at night."

"Two cases," Simms said. "Two cases of a rash. Call me crazy, but I think that's a coincidence, not a crisis."

Salik shook his head, unconvinced. Marley thought it odd Simms was talking stats to the guy whose whole job consisted of tracking Public Heath numbers but kept her mouth shut.

When nobody spoke, Simms tried again. He seemed desperate for someone to agree with him. "It makes way more sense from a logical perspective that the two people with rashes also ingested the drug somehow. That's why they're showing similar symptoms."

"The Ferrick boy is two years old. And we did a hair follicle test. No drugs in his system."

"Those tests aren't reliable, we all know that."

"A history of inconclusive or false positives, yes. Not false negatives."

Marley remembered reading about the fallout from decades before with hair follicle samples from kids that were used to remove them from their mothers. So many kids were dumped into the social services system from a faulty drug test. She was pretty sure the court cases were still ongoing.

"It sounds like a dead end to me," Marley said. Maybe taking Salik's side wasn't the best career move. "What other theories are on the table?"

Marley's question was met with silence. Simms looked satisfied, as if the silence justified his theory of coincidence. Salik stared at the table, and Marley thought this was a man whose mind never stopped. Neither did hers. She knew little about the world of rashes and contagions, just that her niece had broken out in a viral rash often when she was sick. Grace called it waving the red flag of sick as the poor kid's stomach and back were covered in red splotches.

"Is it possible we've got it backward?" Marley said.

"What do you mean?" Salik said.

"What if the drug overdose lowers the person's immunity or whatever. And they're around someone who is sick, with a virus or something. So they're more likely to catch it?" Her tentative theory seemed to impress Simms, maybe because it meant it wasn't something he had to worry about.

But Salik suddenly stood up. "I need to take this back to my office. I'll let you know if anything comes up."

Once he'd left, Marley and Simms stared at each other.

"I've got a meeting with the director of the safe consumption sites in an hour if you want to tag along."

Marley considered the offer. "I'm going to take a pass, I think. I need to get to the bottom of those evidence boxes."

"Okay," Simms said, slapping the file in front of him as if they'd come to some sort of conclusion or resolution. Neither of those things were true. "Keep me in the loop."

Marley checked her phone on her way back to the office. There were two texts, one from her mom and one from her sister, checking in to see how she was doing. Marley smiled to herself. They'd been talking. Marley tucked the phone back in her pocket and opened the door to the office. Everything was as she'd left it four days ago. No one else on the drug team wanted to take on this job. As Marley adjusted the mask on her face and pulled on gloves, she steeled herself for what other evidence of Aimee's neglect she might find.

Marley had logged more receipts when she came across a manila envelope with Aimee's name written across the top in black marker: Aimee Madeleine Parker West. Marley had never seen her full name, though she knew Alicia Parker was Aimee's mother. She'd always wondered why Aimee's mother had given her baby the father's last name since he wasn't in her life until Alicia became sick. And Randolph used that to his advantage.

Marley slid the contents of the envelope on the table. Aimee's birth certificate, printed on stiff paper. Born in Sudbury, Ontario on April 29, 2011. A small hospital card listing her height and weight with the words *It's a girl!* across the top. A tiny hospital bracelet. Her health card. A form letter saying she passed her infant screening test. A preschool assessment. Aimee's handprint in purple paint. Kindergarten report cards. Results from an allergist. Her first grade school photo, Aimee with a blistering smile that outshone the fake fireworks in the background.

Marley sat back in her chair. She'd come in ready to steel herself against evidence of Aimee's neglect. But here was documentation of love and care, concern for her well-being, a celebration of her daily existence. It hurt to see Aimee's loving childhood collected in an envelope and shoved into an evidence box. She couldn't feel it all right now, needed to contain the ache, so she pulled the evidence sheet toward her and meticulously catalogued the contents.

Before sliding everything back in, Marley checked the envelope. One piece of folded paper slid out when she tapped it, a one-page printed letter from Alicia Parker to Randolph West. It was short, formal, and sad, Alicia saying she was giving custody of Aimee to her father, who had proven he had turned his life around, had a job and a home in Windsor, and promised to raise their child right. Marley counted from the date of the letter to the date of the Fleming Street drug bust. Aimee had endured almost nine months of hell with her mother's hope and her dad's empty promises.

After a moment's hesitation, Marley put aside the envelope and finished cataloguing the last handful of paper evidence. Nothing stood out as interesting—offers from an internet provider, instructions from a coffee percolator, receipts from 7-Eleven for gas and energy drinks. Marley packaged it all up and put the evidence log on top with a scribbled note and signature in the margin saying she had taken possession of the envelope. She then sent out a text to Simms regarding the envelope, locked the door to the small office, and headed out the door, intent on bringing these small pieces of Aimee's life back where they belonged.

❖

Devon walked up her driveway, adjusting the bag across her shoulder and wishing it would sit more comfortably. She wished everything about her work clothes and this day felt more comfortable. She turned back at the sound of insistent knocking on glass and waved at Aimee, who was wedged in the dining room window as usual. Devon laughed as Aimee made a face, waved enthusiastically, then jumped down and disappeared.

Feeling a little lighter, Devon got into her car and backed out. She was heading to an all-day work training event. Her supervisor and HR thought this might be a good, slow introduction back into work. The session was being held off-site, so there was no pressure to walk back into her routines and responsibilities. She could show her face and start to reconnect to colleagues and her team. Devon kept reminding herself it was okay this didn't feel normal.

Devon pulled into the parking lot behind the hotel and convention centre on the outskirts of downtown and parked her car away from other vehicles. She was early, but she wanted a few moments before the barrage of greetings and questions and sensory noise of three hundred people. She pulled out her phone and reread the text thread with Marley from last night.

They'd talked about Aimee and Carla, about their jobs, their families, places they wanted to travel. Marley made her laugh. Being with Marley felt so much like she'd been starving and Marley was the nourishment she had been craving. Devon was grateful for Marley in her life. And more than a little terrified.

She checked the time on her phone. It was time to get in there. She thumbed out a quick email to her therapist to book an appointment. Thrilling-terrifying feelings were Ash's specialty. After a brief hesitation, she sent Marley a good morning text, then grabbed her bag and went into the conference centre. When her phone signaled a text, Devon anchored to Marley's message: *It's okay if today is weird, it's also okay if it's wonderful.*

It was both. Devon slipped into work mode as she registered at the makeshift desk, received a name tag, and headed straight for the coffee. She greeted people and exchanged a few hugs, letting her scared heart feel the genuineness of the moments, even amidst the chaos. She answered questions, raising her voice to be heard above the din and energy of several hundred regional health care workers set free from their hospitals and offices for the day.

Gloria, the nurse who had taken such good care of Aimee, took Devon by the elbow and guided her to a seat at her table.

"Pace yourself, Tiger," Gloria said in her ear. "There are sixty of us here from the hospital. I want you to get out of here alive."

Devon laughed and Gloria winked. The rescue felt good, she decided, as she sat at the table and prepared for her day. She could let her team look out for her, like she had tried so hard to look out for them. Ash, she thought, would be proud.

The day was good but overwhelming. Nothing about the day felt settled or familiar, but by the time the last speaker was wrapping up, Devon felt connected again. She was exhausted, but she welcomed the feeling of excitement in her belly, the reminder that she loved working in health care and the challenge of working within this complex, under-resourced, best-intentioned system. As she packed up and headed back to her car, Devon felt more excitement than dread for the first time in a very, very long while.

Devon checked her phone on the way back to the car, disappointed she hadn't had any texts from Marley all day. But then her phone signaled message after message, and Devon realized she was getting a day's worth of texts and notifications all at once. Confused and concerned, she scrolled through. Texts and a call from Marley. And, even more alarmingly, a missed call from her home phone.

Hands shaking, Devon unlocked her car and made herself breathe. She jammed her phone in the hands-free contraption on her console and called Marley. The ringing seemed to take forever, and the car was already stifling from having sat in the sun all day. Sweat gathered under Devon's collar and she had turned on her car and opened her windows by the time Marley answered.

"Devon, hey. Everyone is okay."

Relief flooded into Devon's system.

"I was at training, I guess I wasn't getting a signal but I didn't know it." Devon could hear herself babbling.

"It's okay. I'm at your place with Carla and Aimee. They got a letter from Randolph, and it freaked Carla out a bit."

"He delivered it? To the house?"

"No, I don't think so." The phone was muffled briefly, and Devon could hear Marley speaking to someone else. "Come home and we'll talk. It will make more sense when you see it."

"Yeah, okay," Devon said, heart rate dropping to normal. "I'll be about ten minutes."

"It's rush hour, sweetheart," Marley said. "Turn up your A/C and maybe listen to…classic rock? A true crime podcast? I don't know, what do you usually listen to in the car?"

Devon laughed as she pulled into traffic. "CBC Radio, but the drive home show drives me crazy."

"Totally. So Toronto-centric."

Marley talked and Devon listened as she navigated the clogged streets. The half-hour drive was easier with Marley's voice filling the car.

"I'm here," Devon said, pulling into the driveway.

"Oh yes. The Aimee alert has gone off."

Devon peered up through the windshield to see her waving furiously.

The house felt Aimee-level chaotic when Devon stepped inside. Homemade paper lanterns and streamers hung from the ceilings and walls. And it looked like when she'd run out of construction paper, she'd turned a blank section of wall into art using green painter's tape.

Thundering footsteps announced Aimee's arrival as she ran across the living room and launched herself off the chair into Devon's arms. Laughing, Devon caught the girl and swung her around.

"I missed you, too, Squirt."

Marley was leaning in the doorway between the kitchen and living room, smiling. She was still in her uniform, hands shoved into her pockets. The combination of Aimee's energy and Marley's smile eased some more of the tightness in her chest.

"Let the woman breathe, Aimee," Carla called from the kitchen. "She just walked in the door."

Aimee grinned but let go and ran into the kitchen. Devon put down her bag and toed off her shoes as Marley walked toward her. She stopped in front of Devon, a smile somehow sweet and mischievous on her face. Devon felt her breath go shallow as thoughts of her day, the panic, the worry entirely fled. Then Marley leaned in a little closer, tilted her face up to meet Devon's, and kissed her.

It was all sweetness, that kiss. It was gentleness and welcome, it was safety and softness until the very end, when Marley pressed herself closer, kissed her a little harder, then released her and stepped back. That was heat and promise, and Marley's smile was all mischief.

"Welcome home."

"Thanks," Devon breathed.

Marley laughed and took Devon by the hand, pulling her into the kitchen.

Carla was at the island, chopping cucumber like her life depended on it. Devon read stress in the lines around her mouth and the curve of her shoulders as she hunched over the cutting board.

"Hope you don't mind a little redecorating," Carla said sharply, waving her knife in the general direction of the living room, now full of Aimee's art.

"Not at all," Devon said, hoping Carla would look up. She didn't.

"And I hope you don't need to paint anytime soon because the little one went through all the tape."

Devon glanced at Aimee, who had stopped spinning on the barstool across the island. She held still and glanced between Carla and Devon.

"I can't stand painting, so that's not a problem."

Carla kept chopping vegetables, her anger clear in every slice and scrape.

Devon turned to Marley. "I think there's more painter's tape down in the basement if you and Aimee want to go check. It should be in one of the drawers by the work bench." She turned and smiled at Aimee. "I think there might even be different colours."

Aimee's eyes brightened but then she glanced at Carla.

"Go ahead, pet. You can go in the basement as long as an adult is with you."

Aimee leapt off the stool and ran to the basement door, followed by Marley.

"I'm sorry I didn't get your messages today," Devon said once the kitchen was quiet.

Carla scraped the chunks of cucumber into a bowl and twisted a bright red tomato off a cluster on the vine.

"I'm sorry I called you. I shouldn't have done that when you're just getting back to work."

Devon watched her work, trying to decipher what was driving her anger.

"I'm not upset," she said. Carla still didn't look up. "Not about you calling or about the redecorating or the tape. I'm not upset about you being here and everything that means."

Carla grunted and sliced through the tomatoes with grim efficiency.

"Marley said there was a letter," Devon said.

Carla didn't respond as she added the diced tomatoes to the bowl. She opened the fridge, pulled out a container of feta, and slammed it on the counter. Then she closed her eyes and took a long breath in and exhaled slowly.

"Randolph sent me a letter through his lawyer. Marley says she's unsure how it got here since it's not postmarked, and it didn't come through regular mail. He wants to see Aimee and says he's going to testify at some family court that I'm unfit to raise Aimee. He's going to use his own childhood as evidence I was neglectful."

Devon sorted through the information. None of it sounded right, the family court, Randolph's credibility as a witness, the accusation of Carla's neglect.

"What do you think is really behind it?"

Carla kept her focus on the plastic container of feta, ripping off the plastic seal and slamming the lid on the counter.

"My anger is telling me it's payback for keeping him from his father when he was a kid." Carla looked up, still clutching the feta container in her hand. "Did you know he started calling Family and Children's Services when he was eleven years old because I wouldn't let him contact his dad? He'd proven over and over he had no interest in kids, and I had a restraining order against him because he'd endangered the lives of my two children on more than one occasion. Took them to casinos and biker bars. He was a horrible person, a horrible parent. But Randolph didn't want to hear that. Randolph always thought his dad's life sounded glamorous."

Carla snorted and looked down, still clutching the feta container. She seemed to shake herself, a release of the past or guilt, Devon wasn't sure. Devon watched as Carla pulled out a hunk of feta and started slicing neat rectangles until she was finished. "I think he's trying to get Aimee away from us so she can't tell us what she knows."

Aimee and Marley stomped up the basement stairs. Devon smiled at Aimee, then glanced at Carla's face. Her expression had gone blank, as if she'd disappeared her anger and her worries and had nothing left.

Aimee stood at the top of the stairs, clutching three more rolls of painter's tape in her arms. She seemed worried, looking at Carla.

"We've all got some worries today," Devon said to everyone. "Some things we're finding hard."

Aimee nodded gravely then looked back at Carla. She put down her rolls of tape on the counter, then wrapped her arms around Carla's middle and squeezed. Devon watched Carla hesitate for only a moment, her eyes shuttering closed. Then she reached a hand back and stroked Aimee's hair.

"We're okay, sweet one. We're all okay."

Aimee tucked her head under her grandmother's arm.

"Let Grandma get supper on the table, and then you can choose what we do tonight, okay?"

Another nod from Aimee, then a tighter squeeze and Aimee let go.

Marley picked up the tape, a blue roll this time and held it up to Devon.

"How do you feel about tape poetry in your kitchen?"

Devon smiled. "I feel pretty great about it."

Marley held out a roll to Aimee. "Your pick, Squirt. Let's start with our names."

Devon and Carla worked side by side as Marley and Aimee turned pieces of tape into colourful words along the wall by the table. By the time dinner was ready, tension had eased, though not disappeared. Aimee dragged Devon and Carla over to see their words. They'd taped out all their names, then the words okay, worried, together, candy, spin, blue, yum, and stay.

Once they were seated, Carla said, "I would like to say grace tonight, if that's okay."

Devon probably didn't hide her surprise well but she and Marley both said "of course" at the same time.

Aimee looked curious as everyone held hands around the table. Instead of bowing her head, though, Carla read their names and the words on the wall, making it seem like a sweet plea to the world. Carla smiled at Aimee, and she beamed back. Then the four of them ate dinner together.

# Chapter Thirteen

Marley knocked on the door of the small, two-story house with white siding, then she took a step down and waited. She'd contacted Mikayla that morning, surprised and relieved she was back at her parents' house, reunited with her daughter and recovering from the overdose and side effects of withdrawal from opioid Z. Marley hadn't been able to forget Mikayla, and even though she couldn't explain to Simms how this meeting was going to help their investigation in any way, here she was.

Mikayla answered the door, her face puffy and pale and her smile shy.

"Hi, Mikayla. It's good to see you again."

"Hi," Mikayla said, her voice quiet. "Come in."

Marley stepped into the house, the smell of breakfast and burned coffee in the air. Mikayla's parents lived in a working-class area of Hamilton that swung between families and transients, depending on the decade. Marley knew it as a generally quiet neighbourhood.

"Ava is at school, and my parents are at work, so it's just me," Mikayla said, leading Marley into the kitchen.

"Thanks for letting me disrupt your day. I wanted to check in and see how you were doing."

Mikayla indicated the table, a covered butter dish, salt and pepper sitting atop a patterned cloth in the centre. Marley sat down, and Mikayla twisted her hands nervously.

"Would you like anything to drink? I could make you some coffee or tea?"

"Are you a coffee drinker?" Marley asked instead of an answer, trying to figure out how to put this young woman at ease.

Mikayla shook her head. "No. I've been trying different teas, though. Right now I like chai tea." She blushed and looked down at her hands.

"I'd love to try that, if you don't mind."

Mikayla walked to the sink to fill up the plug-in kettle, and Marley looked around. The house was neat, signs of a young child in the drawings on the fridge, a fleece hoodie draped over a chair, and a stuffed elephant with a tea towel draped over its head on the counter.

"I imagine Ava was happy to see you when you came home."

Mikayla smiled. "Not as happy as I was to see her. I think Ava thought I was just at work for a really long time."

"I guess kids don't have much concept of time."

"Thankfully, no," Mikayla said, her smile slipping. "And I'm lucky my parents took me back in." She tucked her hair behind her ears. "I lost my job and can't afford to pay rent. So, we're back here."

"How are you feeling these days? You were in pretty rough shape last time I saw you."

"Worn out. The combination of the rash and the hallucinations was…awful. Really awful. Nothing worked, so we just had to wait for it to get out of my system."

"Sounds like you pushed through a rough time," Marley said.

"Do you know what it is yet? The other guy who talked to me, the Board of Health guy or whatever, he said they were tracking it as a new drug."

"We don't know much," Marley said. "We know it's an opioid with side effects that begin on withdrawal and not before. We're still trying to figure out the rest."

The whistle of the kettle interrupted her, and Mikayla prepared the tea. Marley thought she looked troubled when she returned.

"The guy who sold it to me, he's sort of a friend." Mikayla looked nervous, as if expecting Marley's judgement or condemnation. "I know that's weird. He doesn't actually sell drugs anymore, he hasn't for a long time. He only got them off his cousin for me. When I asked for them."

"You said his name was Jaxon," Marley said.

"Yeah."

"Jaxon likes you."

Mikayla smiled shyly. "He came to see me after I was in the hospital. Was super upset, said he didn't know it would make me sick. And he said he didn't care if I never spoke to him again, he wasn't going to do anything that might hurt me."

"Sounds like he's trying to be a good friend."

Mikayla poured the tea into two white mugs with a design of ivy curling up the sides.

"Jaxon said something weird the other day. He asked if Ava was okay, if she'd had the rash or gotten sick or anything. He was really worried. He said if something had happened to my daughter because of him, he'd never forgive himself."

Marley felt her spine tighten at Mikayla's words. She took a small sip of her tea before she asked her next question.

"Why do you think he was worried about Ava?"

"Partly because he's a good guy. But I think his cousin told him something about the drug." She fiddled with the spoon in front of her. "Jaxon said when he found out I was in the hospital, he went to his cousin's. He was super mad his cousin had given him something that would hurt me. His cousin said it was experimental. That he was just a...preceptor or something?"

"A prospector?"

"Yeah, like these guys had given him these new drugs for cheap, and he was supposed to hand them out, get people interested, see what the reaction was." Mikayla looked into her mug, her expression blank. "I guess we saw what the reaction was."

Marley felt a little sick. The idea of prospecting wasn't new to her. The first time she'd heard it described was when someone likened it to the people alcoholic beverage makers hired to make the product look cool and fun. But opioid Z seemed to act on a whole other level.

"But Ava has been fine?"

"Yeah, she's good. I told Jaxon her vaccinations weren't up to date," she said, almost absently.

"Jaxon asked about her vaccinations?"

"Yeah. I don't know why."

Neither did Marley. But she really, really wanted to know.

"Mikayla, I think we're going to need to talk to Jaxon."

"The cops already did," Mikayla said.

"I know, they talked to him right after you were in hospital. I'm pretty sure they told him they were more interested in where the drugs came from and not in his drug-dealing past."

Mikayla took a sip of her tea and shifted in her chair as Marley let the silence stretch.

"He's a good guy," Mikayla said.

"He sounds like it," Marley said. "He sounds like he's trying to protect you. And his cousin."

Mikayla's expression was pained as she put down her mug of tea.

"Jaxon said he told the cops he got the drugs from someone he knew they'd already talked to, not his cousin. Figured he wasn't throwing anyone under the bus that way, you know?"

Like lying to the police was perfectly reasonable, Marley thought. She waited, hoping Mikayla would come to the right conclusion on her own. Marley took another sip of her tea, watching Mikayla war with herself.

"Cole Rogers," Mikayla finally said, sighing. "That's Jaxon's cousin's name."

"Thanks, Mikayla," Marley said.

"You're welcome."

They sat in silence, the sounds of cars and lawnmowers outside dulled to a steady summer buzz.

"Life is messy, isn't it?" Mikayla said. "Like, once you're not a kid anymore, it's just always messy."

Marley thought about how Aimee's life had been messy for most of a year now. The messiness of life didn't apply only to adults.

"It is," she agreed. "So messy. But sometimes you get to sit and talk and drink chai tea for the first time, and that's pretty good."

Mikayla smiled, looking happier but still unconvinced, and poured Marley some more tea.

❖

Devon added a lump of almost too-soft butter to the mixing bowl on the counter. Aimee looked up at Devon from her perch on the barstool, freshly washed hands poised. Music played in the background, a counterpart to the gentle rain outside.

"Go to it."

Aimee attacked the oats, flour, sugar, butter, and spices with her hands, squishing and squeezing the ingredients together for the fruit crumble. Devon's dad always said it tasted better hand mixed. Devon just thought it was fun.

"I thought I already did that," Carla mumbled from the table, peering at Devon's laptop screen. "Didn't I already do that?"

She was working on Aimee's school registration paperwork now that they had the envelope from Marley. Once Aimee was occupied with the huge bowl, Devon walked over to the table.

"Can I help?"

"It's these blasted tiny boxes. How am I supposed to see anything?"

Devon looked at the downloaded form on the screen. Then she pointed at the small magnifying glass in the top corner.

"Try that button."

Carla clicked the button and the form jumped in size.

"Okay, I need to remember that button. That button is my friend."

Devon laughed. "Mine, too."

Carla continued her slow typing, looking from her fingers to the screen and back again.

"Too old for this shit," Carla mumbled under her breath. "Maybe it's a test. If you're too old to see the font on the screen, you're too old to be raising a kid."

Devon glanced up to see Aimee still happily making crumble topping.

"If struggling with an online form is the biggest hassle you have as Aimee's guardian, I think you're probably doing pretty well," Devon said.

Carla flashed Devon a quick grin and went back to peering at the screen.

"Do you think they'll put her in a special class?" Carla said, her voice still too low for Aimee to hear.

Devon had wondered this herself. Aimee would need some specialized supports, especially if her mutism continued. But cognitively and adaptively, she was a sharp kid, and Devon saw no reason Aimee couldn't do well in a regular grade three class.

"I think your plan to meet with the school before September is a good one. See what they think and go from there." She paused and considered her next words. "If they want an assessment, I know some good people."

Carla looked up, and Devon kept her face calm.

"An assessment? You think there's a problem?"

Devon shook her head. "I think she's an incredibly bright little girl with a history of trauma resulting in possible selective mutism. An assessment can give better insight and could also give you and the school some ideas on how to best support her."

Carla's hands had stilled above the keyboard. "I'd like to get her into therapy. Soon."

Aimee was already on a waitlist for a trauma counselor through Family and Children's Services. Devon had itched at the six-month waitlist, her professional self understanding that waitlist was actually quite short but her personal self hating every second of the wait.

"I think it's a good idea now that you guys are a little more settled here."

"I can't afford it," Carla said quietly.

"I'd like to help," Devon said, equally as quietly.

Carla didn't respond, still staring at the computer screen. So much was on the line here, Devon thought, Aimee's continued journey through trauma, Carla's strength and pride. Charity was a complex, tangled offer and rarely the simple solution it seemed to be.

"Until I get a job with some benefits," Carla said with a hard expression. Devon knew her well enough to not take offense to that look. "It's not fair to make Aimee wait."

"We can look at some options tomorrow," Devon said. "You could meet a few of the people I have in mind and see who you think would be the best fit for Aimee."

But Carla shook her head. "No, I trust you. You know who will be a good fit for our girl."

A crack then in the woman's hard expression, showing vulnerability and a sharing. Possibly the hardest human emotions. And the most necessary.

"Okay. I'll look into it tomorrow."

They both looked up as Aimee thumped on the wood paneling of the island with her feet, holding her hands, thick with oats and butter and sugar, above the bowl.

"Nice work, kid," Devon said, going to help Aimee. "Your next goal is to cover the fruit with that delicious mess."

It was small steps, Devon decided, as she and Aimee covered the sliced apples, plums, and blackberries with the crumble. It was filling in one form at a time, making a phone call, showing up to one meeting. Deciding to trust. Opening your heart. Listening. Small, wonderful, difficult steps.

# CHAPTER FOURTEEN

Cole Rogers was a cocky kid, Marley's least favourite kind. Anger tingled up her spine as he swaggered and postured through their questioning. She wanted so much to knock him down fifteen pegs and make him show the fear she knew he must be feeling just below the surface.

"We've got some time to wait," Simms was saying. He seemed utterly calm in this interview. Either he wasn't anywhere near as agitated as Marley or he was way better at keeping it under wraps. "We know the name you gave us isn't the right one. We need to know who gave you those drugs. And everything you heard about them. In your previous interview, you tried to convince us you were just an innocent guy caught up in the drug trade. Well, we've come to realize that isn't factual. So, here we are, back again for the real story."

"I gave you the real story." Cole smirked.

Marley's anger surged again. "And yet we've got some people who say otherwise."

Marley saw a flash of uncertainty, he tried to hide with a fake smile. Marley wanted to tell him he wasn't very good at this and likely had no real future in crime. Not by a long shot.

"So? They're lying."

Marley sighed audibly, Simms shooting her a *cut it out* look. She supposed she wasn't being very professional. She was so sick of this game. We ask, they lie, catch them in the lie, repeat. Forever.

"We talked to your supposed source. They say they don't know you." Simms made a show of flipping through his notes. "And I quote, 'Never heard of him. Must be some pissant from up the mountain'."

An insult, apparently, in the drug world, as Cole's eyes flashed with anger and indignation. The hurt pride of a young kid.

"Fuck them, I'm not from up the mountain."

Simms said nothing.

"And I know people, right?"

Simms gave him a bland, indulgent smile, like he was trying to make the kid feel better about himself. Marley considered taking notes. Simms was good at this.

"You lose nothing by giving us the name," Marley said. "You're saying it's someone big in the drug world, that means we already know about him. We only care about finding out how the drugs filtered down to the streets. Your name's already on our radar, just tell us who to link it to."

Your standing in the street drug hierarchy was an odd thing to be proud of, but Marley was willing to bet Cole Rogers needed to hear some validation about his life.

"Terry Russo."

Simms's eyes lit up but Marley watched him cool his expression and give a low whistle. The kid tried and failed not to look pleased with himself.

"Russo must trust you," Marley said. "We hear he talked to you about this drug."

"Not him," Cole admitted, seeming like he was enjoying this. "But yeah, the guys trust me." He paused, like caution had recently occurred to him. Marley jumped in.

"They told you something about this drug, the new opioid."

"EZ? Yeah. Said it was mellow, like weed but a million times more intense. The guys said it was made to hook people in, you know? But none of the opioid overdose shit. They wanted customers for life."

Customers for life. The phrase made Marley cold. She thought about drinking tea with Mikayla yesterday. A customer with a drug wrapped around her brain, hooked into her body somehow. She felt sick.

Simms, however, had never lost his neutral, vaguely interested look. "Did they tell you anything more about the hook?"

"Yeah, but I didn't really listen. Something about chickenpox and vaccinations? Sounded stupid to me. And I didn't need to know, as long as I could sell the shit as safe with a kickass buzz."

"You must have sold a lot if you were with Russo's guys."

Cole shifted in his seat. "I do well."

"Can I offer you some advice, kid?"

Cole bristled at the word, eyebrows drawing down in anger.

"Sure, old man."

Simms laughed. "You seem smart. Smart enough to be running a business, not hanging on to someone else's coattails. Get out of the drug trade. Because I don't want to be the one arresting you. Waste of a life."

Marley watched the words bounce off Cole's cool, cocky exterior. She could only hope something was absorbed, or at least anchored somewhere in his memory.

"You can go," Simms said, for the first time sounding tired. "I don't want to see you again."

Cole took his time standing up, smirk firmly in place as he left the room, a junior officer waiting outside to have him sign paperwork and escort him out of the building.

"Jesus fuck, kids are dumb," Simms said after Cole was out of sight. "It's all a game to them."

Marley rubbed her eyes. She worked to put Cole, the drug trade, and the never-ending stream of poverty and bad life choices out of her mind.

"What are you thinking about the chickenpox thing?" she said. "The vaccinations."

"I'll send the info to the lab and follow up with Public Health. I'm not sure what we can do with it, though."

Marley sat back in her chair, somehow exhausted and energized all at once. Details from this case circled and buzzed, a cacophony of noise that refused to settle.

"Customers for life," Simms snorted, sounding disgusted. "It's a solid business plan. But Jesus."

It was, Marley had to admit.

"Any thoughts?"

"A few," Marley said, willing the buzz in her head to focus. She rubbed her forehead, which did nothing to clarify her thoughts. "I guess

I'm less interested in the drug guys with the business plan. We still don't know who masterminded this drug. We haven't talked to or heard of anyone capable of that. That worries me."

"We're missing something."

"That's the byline for our jobs," Marley said. "Who was researching Mace?" Marley said suddenly, the name dropping down through the chaos of details.

"Arnie's taking the lead on background searches."

"Mind if I talk with him?"

Simms waved his hand, clearly unconvinced it would go anywhere but too tired to do anything about it.

Marley wound her way through the noisy cubicles—laptops banging, doors closing, filing cabinets rumbling, and phones pinging. Police stations were an odd mix of old school and new school, a clashing more than a melding.

Marley found Constable Eric Arnold—Arnie—in the back corner, his cubicle dominated by two desks and three monitors, all the equipment set up like a wall between him and everyone else. Marley knocked on the edge of the fabric cubicle dividers.

"Hey, can I interrupt?"

Arnie glanced over from his monitors, his purple plastic-framed glasses catching the light. He was quiet, prematurely gray, and the only other out police officer on the force. Marley had tried to connect with him when she'd first started, but he'd seemed most content behind his monitors. Arnie was a friendly guy but distant.

"Mission accomplished."

"I'm sorry?"

"You asked if you could interrupt," Arnie said, without any real rancor in his tone. "I said mission accomplished."

"Ah," Marley said sheepishly. "Sorry about that."

"Not a problem. How can I help? You're still working on the opioid Z investigation?"

"Yes, and I'm stuck on this unknown woman, handle of Mace. Simms said the search for her real name came up blank, but I've got some other information. I'm wondering if we could cross-check it or whatever." Marley waved her hands at the monitors.

Arnie blinked. "Mace is a woman? My search didn't know that."

Marley remembered Aimee's reaction to the name, the blankness in her face. Then the tears.

"Randolph West's daughter identified Mace as a woman."

Arnie started typing, an intense sort of gleam in his eye that matched the glare from his monitors.

"Do you know where this identification was made? In Hamilton?"

"No, Windsor."

"Date?"

"Unknown. But likely between November and April this year."

Arnie kept typing. "Any data points are helpful. With three details, we narrowed the search by fifty percent of the population and pinpointed this person in time and space."

Marley let him work, feigning patience. She lasted three minutes. "Any luck?"

"Not yet," Arnie said. "But we'll get there."

"I like your confidence," Marley said, and Arnie flashed her a quiet smile.

"You said you had more information you wanted me to cross-reference?"

"Right. Yes. We just interviewed a low-level drug runner, and he mentioned hearing something about vaccines and chickenpox being associated with opioid Z."

Arnie blinked again, and Marley got the sudden impression of a computer server–like brain running at a constant, high level in this officer's head.

"Okay. So the search for Mace and drugs or chemical compounds came up negative. But you'd like me to see if Mace's handle comes up in connection with vaccines and communicable diseases. Is that right?"

"Dude, yes. You don't mind?"

Arnie shook his head. "This is my kind of fun. Give me this overnight, and I should have something by the morning. Email the best way to send you a summary?"

"Perfect," Marley said. "And copy Simms, if you could."

"Consider it done."

Marley walked back to her cubicle, feeling like maybe there was movement on this case. Maybe by tomorrow, they'd have more answers.

❖

Devon walked out of the hospital with Leo and Gloria, shift change coinciding with the end of her meeting. They all groaned when they exited the frigid hospital and the full weight of the three-day heat wave pressed on them.

"Brutal," Gloria muttered. "I mean, I love me some sun, but these temperatures are unbearable. What's a menopausal woman supposed to do?"

"It's seven o'clock at night, and it's still this hot," Leo said, pulling his bike helmet off his backpack. "I thought I'd get some kind of reprieve, but nope."

"Rest, stay hydrated, limit exertion during peak hours," Devon said, knowing they'd both said this multiple times to multiple people coming in with heat stroke today. Part of Devon's meeting about her transition back to work had been about emergency community outreach, heat waves included. "And make friends with someone with a pool," Devon added.

"Amen, sister," Gloria said, waving as she headed off to her car. Leo waved and angled toward the bike racks.

Devon watched them go, thinking about her earlier meeting with her boss. She had suggested they use this pause in service while Devon had been away as an opportunity to reevaluate the programs and services and what they wanted to continue. Devon suddenly saw this as the parallel to her mental pause, the chance to take a step back and breathe. Put a halt to what wasn't working and carry on with what was. She still felt the zing of energy and purpose, and she wanted to nurture that without losing herself in it. The task was enormous, but Devon felt up to it.

Devon closed her eyes for a moment. Sweat collected along her hairline. She could smell Tim Hortons and the ash of countless cigarettes. Traffic blared around the hospital, and a service vehicle beeped its intention to back up. The sounds and smells of being outside her home were invasive and sometimes unwelcome, but it was all a part of being out in the world again.

Without thinking, Devon picked up her phone. Marley had been busy today but not too busy to check in with Devon, making her laugh with a few texts. Devon thumbed out a text as she walked to her car.

*I feel like burger and a beer. If not tonight, then soon?*

Marley returned the text just as Devon was sliding into her way-too-hot car, parked for the last few hours in the sun.

*Date night! Now? Please say now.*

Devon laughed as she turned on her car, rolled down her windows, and blasted the AC.

*Now. Name the place.*

*Beer Haus. Twenty minutes. Race ya.*

Devon sent her a grinning emoji as her only reply and pulled out of the parking lot.

Eighteen minutes to get to the pub and six minutes to find parking made Devon late. Marley was leaning against the stairs leading up to the bar. She was wearing light, loose khakis and a blue sleeveless shirt. She looked golden and glorious, and Devon's pulse thudded with a deep reverberation of attraction and connection.

"You're tardy, Devon Wolfe," Marley said, her grin seductive and mischievous. She clucked her tongue. "And for our first date."

Devon considered apologizing but instead she leaned in and kissed Marley, tasting heat and smelling sunscreen on Marley's skin before she pulled away.

"I'm here."

Marley's eyes sparkled with surprise and satisfaction. "Yeah, you are."

Devon laughed, and Marley grabbed her hand and took her inside. The bar was dark and noisy and smelled like yeast and hops and good food. She followed Marley up two flights of stairs as they searched for a table for two, finally finding one on the middle patio. They slid on to the high barstools, voices and traffic creating a wall of noise around them. They shifted their barstools until their knees touched.

"Okay day at the hospital?" Marley said as they scanned the chalkboard list of local beers on tap.

"Better than okay," Devon said. "It felt good."

Marley reached over and squeezed Devon's hand. "That's great news."

"How about you?"

Marley shrugged. "Maybe some movement on the case? It's slow. And frustrating. And boring. And heartbreaking."

"That might be the worst combination ever for a job."

Marley tilted her head like she was considering it. "Sometimes it also smells bad. And people yell. But free coffee, so…?"

Devon laughed. She knew Marley had some deep-seated questions about her job and her choice of career, but tonight didn't feel like the night to pull it all apart.

Marley picked up the plastic menu.

"You're for sure going for the burger?"

"House burger and sweet potato fries."

Marley made a face. "I suppose you needed one flaw."

Devon shoved Marley with her shoulder. "Liking sweet potato fries is not a character flaw."

"What would you consider a character flaw, Dr. Wolfe?"

"Not hanging up wet towels after a shower."

Marley tilted her head back and laughed. "Some would call that criminal," she said, eyes shining.

The waitress came by, leaning in to take their orders. Marley stressed her desire for real French fried potatoes as her side for the chicken finger BLT and Devon rolled her eyes. Devon already loved this date. The way their legs tangled together under the table, the smell of Marley's skin, the warm breeze and the clink of their glasses and long, cold sips of beer when the waitress brought their drinks.

"This feels like it should have happened a month ago," Marley said.

"A lot has happened since the day I met you," Devon said. For a moment, the smell of the alley intruded, wet pavement against her knees, Marley's pale face, shirt streaked with blood.

Marley drew her fingers along the inside of Devon's wrist, bringing her back.

"Would you change anything?" Marley said, leaning in to be heard until their foreheads were almost touching.

"I didn't like you being hurt," Devon said. "But I wouldn't change anything else."

"Me neither."

They twined their fingers together, condensation from their glasses of beer making them slippery. Marley looked like she wanted to say something but was hesitating.

"What is it?" Devon said.

"I keep thinking there's one thing I would change. Time alone together." She looked up at Devon, like she was gauging her reaction. "But I don't regret having Carla and Aimee in my life."

Devon heard the layer of uncertainty, but she understood the tension Marley was feeling.

"I feel the same way, if that means anything," Devon said. "We hung out a fair bit together while you were unconscious," Devon said. "Does that count?"

Marley laughed, clearing the doubt from her expression. "It definitely counts toward our weird getting to know you phase."

"True. I learned you have tricky veins for IVs, and you look cute in a hospital gown."

Marley shook her head. "And I learned you hum almost constantly and have a mild addiction to Tim Hortons." She squeezed Devon's hands. "And you're always there when it counts the most."

"I'll always try," Devon said. The promise surfaced so easily, Devon forgot to feel nervous, She wasn't panicked by tying herself to someone else that could weigh her down. This didn't feel like a burden.

They pulled apart as the waitress brought their food to the table. Twilight descended as they ate and talked and drank, part of the noisy bar scene but also cocooned together. It was a night of sharing the pieces of their lives that had been overlooked in the intensity of their meeting and the ongoing drama playing out around them. Mundane, hilarious, and sweet stories shared over salty fries and sips of beer. Bouncing back in time, projecting into the future and landing solidly back in the present as the waitress dropped off the bill, leaving them to argue over it.

"I've got a list of things to pay you back for," Marley said, clutching the bill and pulling out her credit card. "This will help me sleep at night."

Devon felt the good-natured teasing in Marley's words and let it go. They had time to even the score. Moments later they were back on the street, the heat of the day still trapped by the pavement and the buildings even though the sun was down.

"Will you come over for a while?" Marley said. "I know we both have early mornings."

"Yes. Please."

The drive to Marley's felt long and quiet and oddly lonely. Devon tried to sort through the feeling and categorize it into something that made sense. After months of solitude, hiding away from the burden of others and what she thought was the proof of her failure, these last few weeks had been forging connections. Deep connections. And this first date night with Marley, she felt the connection like a live fuse in her chest. She wanted more, craved more of her laugh, the touch of her fingers, and even her uncertainty. Devon wanted more.

Marley was waiting for her at the top of the stairs down to her apartment. "You drive too slow," she said.

Devon laughed and followed Marley down the stairs. "I was texting Carla to say I'd be out late."

Marley looked over her shoulder as she unlocked her door. "Please tell me she swore at you."

"Close enough. I definitely got called 'young lady' when she made it clear I didn't need to check in."

"Sounds like Carla," Marley said, flipping on lights in her apartment. "It was good of you to check in with her, though."

"I didn't want her to worry."

Marley stopped in the hallway that led to the living room, a soft glow from a table lamp lighting her face.

"You're a good person, Devon Wolfe."

"I try, Bridget Marlowe."

Marley slid her hands around Devon's waist. Devon pulled her in, holding her close around the waist with one arm and cupping the back of her neck with the other. Without thinking, she began kneading the muscles in the back of Marley's neck, chasing the tension as Marley rumbled her approval. When Marley tilted her face up to Devon's, their lips met in a powerful, sweet kiss. The spark in Devon's chest flared and the words *finally, finally, finally* echoed through her head.

Kissing Marley was a kind of perfection. Devon let go of the need to know what was happening, let go of worry, let go of the need to breathe. Marley pressed their bodies together, heat flaring along Devon's skin where they touched. She kissed the sounds that came out of Marley's mouth as she spanned her hand across Marley's lower back and pressed her closer.

Then Marley was walking backward, tugging Devon to the couch where they fell into the cushions, laughing as their legs tangled, as they fought for breath and for control. Marley gave a sly grin as she pushed Devon back into the cushions, straddling her thighs. Devon loved that fire in Marley's eyes, loved the tussle for control and her willingness to give it.

She loved it even more when Marley leaned over her, caging her with her arms on either side of Devon's head and said, "Yes?"

"Yes," Devon breathed.

Yes to Marley's searing kiss, yes to the tilt of Devon's hips that made Marley groan and press her deeper into the cushions. Yes to the heat in her belly that felt dangerously and wonderfully out of control. Yes to tasting the skin of Marley's neck. Yes to Marley's thigh between her legs, to the rhythm of their breath and bodies together.

It felt like hours when the rhythm slowed, the kisses gentled. No connection lost, though, as Marley leaned back, cheeks flushed and eyes shining.

"I didn't ask how far you go on a first date."

Devon laughed, fingers tangled in Marley's hair, tracing lines across her scalp.

"I don't have any hard and fast rules."

Marley groaned and buried her face in Devon's neck. "Don't say hard and fast right now when I decided stopping was the best idea."

Devon laughed again, loving the feeling of Marley's breath against her skin. She gently massaged the back of Marley's neck, listening as their heartbeats slowed to a steady rhythm.

"I want you," Marley said, words muffled against Devon's neck. "But I don't want to rush this."

"Me, too," Devon said, kissing Marley's temple. "To both."

Devon closed her eyes, letting herself sink into the feeling of being wrapped up in Marley. She didn't know how much time had passed, but Marley's breathing was slow and rhythmic.

"You're falling asleep," Devon said quietly.

"Me? No," Marley mumbled. Then, after a moment, "Okay, yes."

Devon laughed, and Marley broke their connection and pushed back. She was adorably flushed and sleepy.

"I should head home," Devon said.

Marley sighed. "I guess." She looked hopefully at Devon. "It was a good first date, wasn't it? There will be a second."

Devon tugged her down for the gentlest kiss. "Definitely," she said when she let her go. She wanted Marley to hear the promise with her voice and her kiss. "Definitely a second date."

## CHAPTER FIFTEEN

Marley awkwardly pulled the door to the precinct open, wishing she'd said yes to the cardboard tray at the drive-thru window as she juggled two coffees and a bag of creamer and sugar. She was early to work after a heavy night's sleep and an early wake-up. Her body felt electrified today, her skin sensitive, her brain firing rapidly, her muscles feeling poised, ready to strike.

She knew some of it was her date with Devon the night before. Marley's breath caught in her throat as she could feel Devon beneath her, smell her skin. She tried hard not to grin and blush as she walked through the office, saying good morning and pretending she wasn't thinking of Devon.

She couldn't remember the last time she'd stopped with a woman when it had felt that good. Marley knew the dance, the progression of touch and movement, the search for skin, the need to be closer, feel more, and harder and…

And this wasn't helping.

Marley put the cups of coffee down on her desk, cursing herself for saying no to double-cupping the coffee, even though it was better for the environment.

"For me? You shouldn't have."

Superman swaggered up to her desk, grabbing a chair from another cubicle and having a seat.

"Come on in to my office," she mumbled at him. "And that's not for you, so don't touch."

Superman put a hand to his chest, feigning hurt. "Are you…are you cheating on me? Is there someone else?"

Marley rolled her eyes. "It's for Arnie. I gave him something to work on last night, and he said he'd have something this morning." Marley unlocked her laptop from the filing cabinet and started booting it up. The ancient brick of a machine took forever.

"You full-time with the drug enforcement guys, then? Like a promotion?"

Marley looked up at Superman, one of her only real friends at work. He had stood by her last summer when others had turned their backs. She heard the hint of real hurt in his tone. Maybe jealousy, too.

"Just this investigation," Marley said, refusing to give in to the surge of guilt. She wasn't doing anything wrong, and if Superman's ego was so fragile he couldn't handle her working for another division for a while, that wasn't her problem. Marley needed to see this case through, end of story.

"Then you're back to mighty street cop? Like the rest of us?"

"Yeah," Marley said, distracted as she logged in. "Then I'm back to the streets with you guys."

She opened her internal email account and scrolled through messages, most of them administrative or minute. But she zoomed in on Arnie's name, an email he'd sent at three in the morning. The message in the body of his email was short.

*We got her.*

Excitement surged in Marley's stomach as she double clicked the attachment. She was vaguely aware of Superman getting up to leave and mumbled a goodbye at him. Marley scanned the document, everything Arnie had found on Mace.

Holly Anne Mason, AKA Mace, born in Ottawa, Ontario, on December 1, 1995. Her mother was a stay-at-home mom and her father was a foreign diplomat with the RCMP. Arnie had made a note that "foreign diplomat with the RCMP" likely meant he worked for CSIS, the Canadian Secret Intelligence Service, but Arnie didn't have clearance to look into those files. He had noted, however, all the places she had lived up until she was eighteen: Alabama, Dubai, Germany, New York, Brazil.

Holly Mason had a combination of home schooling, private schooling, and international schools. She was a few credits short of graduating with a degree in computer science from MIT. In 2010,

Holly Mason seemed to drop out of the trackable record, and Mace made her first appearance as a handle in chat groups a year later. These groups all seemed political in nature, platforms that fed and shaped the disenfranchised and discontented.

Marley drank her coffee as she scrolled through the notes. Mace showed up on RCMP files for the first time early in 2012. Marley scanned this list, already familiar with Mace's illegal political antics. There were a few other notes and queries from regional police services, most in British Columbia, but nothing that jumped out at Marley as relevant.

The only other item of interest Arnie had helpfully highlighted for her was a Biology and Applied Human Sciences degree awarded to Ashlee H. Vincent from EdX, an international conglomerate of universities and colleges that offered everything from free online courses to master's programs. Marley was confused until she saw Arnie's note. Mace had used a fake name but her own Social Insurance Number to register for the courses. Apparently she'd tried to go in and change that number later, but Arnie had cracked the hack pretty easily.

Marley scanned the list of courses Mace had taken under the name of Ashlee H. Vincent: Proteins in the Body, Biological Secrets of Life, The Essentials of Cells and Tissues, Virology 101, Welcome to the Immune System, Using Math to Solve for Viruses. One course title that sent a chill along Marley's spine: The Power of the Virus: Looking At Disease from a New Perspective.

Marley stared at the screen. She was sure she was looking at the birthplace of Opioid Z. Yes, there was more to the story, including how Mace and Randolph West had joined forces and how and why it had shown up in her town and on her streets. But they only had the word of some Windsor drug dealers to connect Mace and Randolph. And Aimee.

Marley leaned back in her chair. She breathed, took a sip of coffee, and decided what to do next. First, forward the email to Simms and ask if he was available to meet. Second, take Arnie his coffee and offer her thanks. This was the break they had been needing.

Arnie was tapping away in his cubicle when Marley walked over. She wondered if he'd ever left. There was so much she didn't know about her colleague. But maybe he liked it that way.

"Hey, Arnie."

Arnie looked up and offered a small smile. "You got the info package on Mace?"

"I just finished reading it. Twice. It's exactly what we needed. Thank you." She handed him the cup of coffee and accompanying creamer and sugar. "I didn't know what you took in your coffee."

"Wow, thanks," Arnie said, his eyes lighting up at the coffee. "And not a problem. It was fun. She gave me a bit of a chase."

"Quick question. Was there a last known address on Mace?"

"Only her parents' address in Ottawa. I think she's gotten better at hiding her tracks in the last few years. I'm guessing she's using a stolen ID for things like credit cards and housing rental and cell phones. Did you want me to keep digging?"

"Maybe. Put a hold on it for now. I'm going to take this to Simms, and then we'll see."

"Yeah, okay," Arnie said, sounding a little disappointed.

Marley felt her phone vibrate in her pocket, and she fished it out. It was Simms, saying he and Crawford were meeting in the sergeant's office and they wanted Marley to join them for an update.

"I should get going," Marley said. "Thanks again, Arnie. I really appreciate it."

"Any time, Marley," Arnie said. "And…" He stopped and cleared his throat. "And I wanted to say that what you did at Pride last year was really brave. I volunteer on the Pride committee, just doing website maintenance, but it meant a lot to me that you spoke up." He adjusted his purple frames on his face. "Not all of us can."

"Thanks for saying that, Arnie. It's been pretty weird for me around here since then. So, that was pretty great to hear."

Arnie ducked his head and went back to his monitors, obviously a more comfortable place for him.

"Let me know if you need me to search for anything else around Mace. I think there's more if you want me to dig."

"Will do," Marley said.

Things were going right, Marley thought as she walked to Crawford's office. This case was moving, work seemed like a good fit for once, Carla and Aimee were safe, and she'd had an amazing first date with Devon. Marley hesitated outside Crawford's door, risking rebuke from her supervisor to send a quick text to Devon.

*Good morning. I can't stop thinking about date #1. And I really shouldn't think about date #2 while I'm at work.*

She was putting her phone back in her pocket when Devon's response came through.

*Thanks for the morning blush and smile as I walk into work. See you tonight?*

Marley confirmed she'd see Devon later, then tried to school her expression before she walked into the office.

Crawford greeted her with a wave to take a seat across from him at the desk next to Simms, who didn't look up from the laptop he had perched on the edge of Crawford's desk.

"Excellent work following this lead, Marlowe," Crawford said. "We're just going through it now."

"Thanks, boss," Marley said. She wondered why this was back on Crawford's desk but decided not to push.

"This is good. Excellent, even," Simms muttered, scrolling up and down through the document Arnie had prepared. "We've got Salik coming in so we can update, redacting the info he doesn't need, of course."

"This information does make it look like we've found our drug developer," Marley said. "And we've heard enough whisperings about viruses and vaccinations that maybe Salik can identify what's going on with this opioid."

"Thirty-two new cases of withdrawal symptoms in the last four days."

"It's increasing," Marley said.

"It is. Salik is hoping it will reach its peak soon. The production stopped six weeks ago, and the withdrawal symptoms were sporadic at first but then increased with less and less access to opioid Z. But with no real way of determining how much was already on the street before Fleming Street was shut down, Public Health is just guessing."

"It will get worse before it gets better," Marley said. "Still no deaths?"

"None, thankfully. But we've got some stirring hysteria this virus is infectious, something Public Health hasn't been able to prove or disprove."

"Shit," Marley said.

"Indeed."

"No known address for Mace? Nothing local?" Simms said, seemingly unaware of the conversation going on around him.

"No, I double-checked with Arnie this morning. We've only got the address of the parents in Ottawa. Arnie thinks she's using a fake ID. He's offered to dig but said it could take some time."

"Let's start with the parents," Simms said, then he looked up at Crawford. "Unless you think the RCMP need to hear it first."

*That's* why Crawford was involved. They'd discovered Mace's real identity, but since she showed up as a person of interest in several RCMP cases outside Ontario, there must be rules as to who had priority over the information.

"It seems to me if you were to call the parents at the same time I called the RCMP, that would satisfy protocol."

Simms shot Crawford a grin before he turned to Marley.

"Wanna make a phone call? I bet you're better with parents than I am."

Because she was a woman. Because she was softer, kinder, listened better. Because real cop work should be left to the guys.

Marley breathed, anchored to the tingle in her spine that had been there all morning. Something was happening, an energy, movement. This case but also more.

"We could also use verification," Simms went on, without waiting for a reply. "An updated sketch of Mace, since all we have is her scowling high school graduation picture."

Marley tensed but said nothing.

"We have verification through Miss West that she was in Windsor," Crawford said.

"That's not enough to go on. That could have been almost a year ago. We need details about that interaction. What colour her hair was, things she talked about, what kind of boots she was wearing, style of phone, tattoos. Details that might help us track her down."

Details Aimee might have. Still, she said nothing.

"Are you making a request to question a witness?" Crawford said.

Simms glanced at Marley, then back to Crawford.

"Yes."

"What do you think, Marlowe?" Crawford said.

"I don't make decisions for Aimee West. You will have to put a request in through her grandmother."

She was satisfied with the steadiness of her tone and how well she'd hidden her irritation. Simms didn't seem to feel the need to do the same.

"A witness literally living at your girlfriend's house, and you won't let her be questioned," Simms said, sounding disgusted.

So many ways to interpret that disgust. So many ways to take offense.

"It's not my decision to make, Simms. Put in the request and see what Ms. Slessinger says."

"Process," Simms spat out, going back to his laptop screen, like he could no longer stand looking at Marley. "We'll take time with process while this opioid thing continues to get out of hand."

"We'll follow process because that's what our job demands, Constable Simms," Crawford said.

Simms closed his laptop and stood up.

"Don't worry about calling the Mason parents," he said. "I'll do that myself. I'm sure Crawford could use you on cleanup duty tonight."

With that confusing parting shot and the slightest of nods to his boss, Simms left the room.

The ensuing silence was uncomfortable.

"Damned if you do and damned if you don't," Crawford said eventually.

"Sir?"

"Don't follow the rules, squad is mad. Follow the rules, squad is mad."

He was right. Marley felt like she was always chafing against a constantly shifting grain.

"I can't win, I guess."

"My advice, Constable Marlowe, is to discover what game you're wanting to play. That will give you the measure of whether or not you're winning."

He might not particularly like her as a cop, but her sergeant gave some good advice.

"What did he mean about cleanup duty?" Marley said, leaving the rest to think about later.

"I sent out an email this morning about the storm coming in tonight. A line of storms is coming up from the American Midwest starting late this afternoon. Heavy rain and high winds are predicted into tomorrow morning, so we're looking at potential street closures, flooding, and power outages. It's going to be all hands on deck tonight."

"Okay, I'm in. And sorry, I was pretty focused on getting Arnie's information this morning."

"Not a problem. Report in by six, we'll deploy as needed."

"Yes, sir."

Marley left Crawford's office and went to her desk. She took a moment, sipping her now cold coffee. Maybe it was the impending storm that was making her skin so sensitive, her body so restless. She got that sense again of something approaching, of movement outside her peripheral vision, a sizzling of layered thoughts and questions.

Marley sat up and opened her laptop, finding the Fleming Street file and starting from the beginning. Whenever this thing arrived, she wanted to be ready.

❖

The rain started out light as Devon drove home from work early in the afternoon, just droplets picked up by the wind and scattered across her windshield. The grey clouds and small gusts of rain-wind were almost playful, but Devon knew this was only the start. The storm was all anyone could talk about at work. Storm nights made for busy ER nights. Devon assumed it was the same for Marley, but she hadn't heard anything from her since that morning.

Moments from their date night had crept in while she'd worked: Marley's laugh, the press of her hands on Devon's hips, the way their hearts had thundered together, pressing closer and closer. These fragments of sensory memory felt like a dream, but Marley felt real. Their date was a beginning and a promise for more.

A gust of wind rocked Devon's car, a spray of leaves from the overhead tree getting caught on her hood. Devon peered up at the sky, to see if the storm was on them already, if it had crept over the city while she'd been daydreaming about her girlfriend. But the sky kept its playful light grey, the strength of the wind gust the only reminder that something was coming. She dug out the garage door remote. The potential for flying branches in a neighbourhood lined with old maples, oaks, and pine, seemed high, so tonight seemed like a night to use the garage.

Devon could tell Aimee had heard her come into the basement because the thumping of Aimee's feet grew in intensity as she pounded across the kitchen floor and flung open the door to the basement.

"Thought I'd trick you by coming in through the garage," Devon said while Aimee danced at the top of the stairs. "But nothing gets by Captain Aimee Pants."

Aimee rolled her eyes, then made a big motion with both hands over her head and clapped her hands together, almost like cymbals.

Devon climbed the last few stairs as Aimee repeated the gesture.

"Are you talking about the storm?"

Aimee nodded and took Devon's hand and dragged her into the kitchen. Carla was peering into the freezer with a frown on her face, though she looked up and smiled when Aimee and Devon walked in.

"Hey, Devon. Can I tell you how deeply disappointed I am you don't have tubs of ice cream we need to consume before the power goes out tonight?"

Devon laughed and put down her bag.

"I think we should go out and get ice cream so that we can do just that."

Carla's eyes glinted. "I'm thinking the same thing. It's a bit of a tradition in our family, big storms and ice cream."

"I'm guessing we need a few other things," Devon said, trying to remember what she had in the house for storm supplies. "Think there are any batteries left in the city? I think I'm low for flashlight batteries."

Aimee found paper and a pen and sat down to write a list while Devon and Carla called out items. Some were serious, like flashlights, bottled water, and food they could cook on Devon's gas stove even if the power went out. And some were less so, like the two flavours of ice cream because they couldn't agree on one and glow in the dark bracelets because Aimee had an idea for a lights-out craft.

Carla peered over her granddaughter's shoulder at the list.

"This is ridiculous," she said. But Devon could see the smile on her face, something of a rarity with Carla.

"Carla, how do you feel about doing a run around town to get our storm items, and Aimee and I will stay home and get started on the chocolate chip cookies?"

"You sure?" Carla said.

"As long as you don't mind going out," Devon said. "The rain isn't too bad yet, but take the car anyway, just in case it picks up while you're out."

"You okay with that, pet?" Carla asked Aimee.

Aimee made a twirling motion with one hand without looking up from where she was decorating the list with storm clouds and lightning bolts.

"Well, I wouldn't mind getting out for a bit, especially if we're going to be cooped up for a day or so."

"Done," Devon said.

Ten minutes later, Carla had backed the car out of the garage and headed to the grocery and hardware store, and Devon and Aimee got started on cookies. Aimee used a whisk to blend the dry ingredients, but she seemed to be more interested in making designs in the flour with the whisk tip. They had decided against music, preferring to listen to the wind outside. Devon was about to start mixing the butter and sugar together when she heard a knock at the door.

Aimee froze, her eyes zeroing in on Devon.

"Probably a neighbour," Devon said, trying to soothe Aimee's nerves. "You wait here, okay?"

Aimee went back to making flour designs as Devon wiped her hands on a towel and went to the front door. With a few open windows in the house and the wind outside, she had to pull hard, the door resisting against the suction of the house, as if it was fighting back.

Devon didn't recognize the young woman at her door. She was in her mid-twenties maybe, with straight, dark brown hair and big brown eyes made bigger with a hint of makeup. She was wearing tan capris and a light pink cardigan, and she smiled as soon as Devon opened the door.

"Hi, are you Devon?"

"I am," Devon said with friendly caution.

"I'm Eva Karagalis. Miss K. I'm Aimee's teacher."

Devon blinked. The woman's smile was brilliant.

"Miss K? Wow, hi. Yes, Aimee's mentioned you."

A gust of wind threw some rain sideways against the front porch.

"Do you mind if I come in?" Eva said. "Just for a moment, I know I'm dropping in at dinner time."

Devon's muscles felt tight, her jaw and neck and shoulders, her body putting up the smallest resistance, like something was a little bit out of alignment.

"Of course," Devon said automatically, politeness winning out over nameless doubt.

As Eva Karagalis stepped into the house, Devon took note of how tiny she seemed.

"Thanks so much," the woman said. "When I got back from vacation, I had a message from my principal about Aimee and some kind of trouble. I had to make sure she was okay." The slightest fidget, a nervous twitch. "Is she here by any chance?"

Doubt flared into suspicion.

"No."

"No?"

"I'm afraid you just missed her. She and her grandmother went out to pick up some supplies for the storm." She silently willed Aimee to stay quiet in the kitchen.

The woman blinked and looked out the window beside Devon's front door.

"It's supposed to be a big one," she said. She turned back to Devon, that huge smile firmly in place. "I drove from Windsor to see her, do you mind if I stay for a bit? I'd love to see her again and know she's okay."

Just as Devon was about to come up with a reason she couldn't stay, the oven beeped in the kitchen. It was actually the signal that the oven had come to temperature, but Devon decided to use the brief distraction.

"Can you give me a moment?" Devon said. "I've got something in the oven. I'll be right back."

The woman's smile faltered, but she stayed by the front door as Devon headed to the kitchen. The room was empty when she walked in. As Devon walked around the far side of the island, she saw Aimee crouched down, her face pale and eyes huge.

Devon crouched down in front of the young girl and put her arms around her. "It's okay," she whispered.

Aimee shook her head hard and leaned into Devon, pulling her closer. Devon could feel her shaking as Aimee put her mouth to Devon's ear.

"Mace," Aimee breathed.

Mace. Marley had questioned Aimee about Mace. Aimee had shut down, something about a secret. Shit, shit, shit.

"Come here," Devon said. She opened the cupboard under the sink and crouched down again. "Stay here, stay quiet."

Aimee scrambled under the sink and Devon closed the door. She walked over to the oven, opening the door and closing it again. Then she filled a glass of water.

Mace was looking at Devon's bookshelf, and she turned around when Devon returned.

"I brought you a glass of water. It's so humid outside."

"Thank you," Mace said.

Devon made no move to sit down, though the couch and chairs were only feet away.

"Do you know how long until Aimee is back? I don't want to impose, but it would be great to see her."

"An hour maybe?" Devon said. "They had quite a list."

Anger flashed in Mace's eyes, a bright spark quickly smothered by feigned disappointment.

"That's too bad. She's such a special kid, you know? I was really attached to her when she was in my class. And my principal said she had stopped talking? I couldn't believe it. She was such a chatterbox."

She must have read Aimee's file somehow.

"She is an amazing kid," Devon said, forcing a smile. "I couldn't agree with you more."

"And is she talking? I'd hate to think something scared her so much she stopped talking for good."

There it was, the lie that revealed the truth of this woman. "No," Devon said, using years of clinical practice to keep her voice calm. "Aimee hasn't started talking yet."

Mace took another sip of her water, relief in the set of her shoulders.

"I think it would be good if Aimee had a chance to meet with you," Devon said. "She's mentioned you more than once. But it doesn't look like tonight is going to work. And I think it would be good to give her a heads-up about something unexpected. It's best for Aimee, wouldn't you agree?"

Professional to fake professional.

"I suppose that's true," Mace said, eyes darting around the room, desperation heightened. "Could you text her grandmother? Maybe they are on their way home right now."

"That's a good idea," Devon said, pulling out her phone. She texted Carla first. *Stay away from house.* Then Marley: *Mace here.* Then, to distract Mace, she smiled and pulled up her photo gallery. "Oh, I should show you some recent pictures. She's such a ham."

Devon turned the phone and scrolled through a couple photos of Aimee making faces. She felt sick showing this woman pictures, but she needed to keep this trust charade going as long as she could.

"Oh! She's grown," Mace said, sounding more agitated than impressed. "What a cutie."

Devon pulled her phone back, still smiling, like she couldn't get over how cute the picture was. But she'd toggled between apps and saw that Marley had replied.

*Bad storm. On my way.*

Something must have changed in her expression, some hint that she wasn't buying what was going on. Because when Devon looked up, Mace had dropped all pretense of sweetness and concern.

"It looks like we've got a problem," Mace said. "How about some real answers now, Devon?"

Devon sighed and pocketed her phone, then sat in one of her living room chairs. She gestured for Mace to sit as well. It was the only strength she had, the only superpower she could draw on, her ability to talk and de-escalate and listen. It was all she had to protect Aimee.

"Yes, Mace, I think we have a problem. Why don't we sit and talk?"

## CHAPTER SIXTEEN

Marley was scrolling through case notes, jotting down random thoughts she was sure would make no sense tomorrow. Or maybe even now. She was just thinking her time might be better spent grabbing some food before starting what would likely be an all-night shift when her laptop froze, then logged her out and shut down.

"What the hell?" Marley said. She thought maybe it was just her own computer, but from the alarmed and annoyed sounds around the office, it was the whole network.

She was about to ask if anyone knew what was going on when Arnie ran by her desk, an open laptop balanced on his forearm.

"You need to hear this," was all he said as he beelined for Crawford's office.

Marley grabbed her phone and ran after him, a sense of dread building in her chest.

Arnie was already updating Crawford when Marley barged in.

"Full system breach, which probably isn't as bad as it sounds," Arnie said.

"It doesn't sound good, Constable Arnold."

"I think it's a cover, multiple hits at multiple access points, bits of data copied from numerous servers, all to cover what I think the hacker was actually after."

"Which is?"

Arnie glanced at Marley.

"The Fleming Street file."

Aimee. Carla. Devon.

"Can you tell what they looked at? What they stole?"

Arnie shook his head. "Not yet. I've locked down the network for now, but I need more time to dig into what's been tampered with. This is a high-level hacker that's been in the system for a least a couple hours now. They just tripped over my redundancy file closer, that's why it triggered a network shutdown."

"You mean those annoying emails we get if we open but haven't closed a file?"

"Uh huh," Arnie said absently. "It's an anti-hacking trick."

"A useful one," Crawford said. "Constable Arnold, the highest priority is ensuring the system is now safe, next highest is targeting what the hacker was after. Everything else we'll deal with later. Got it?"

Marley's phone vibrated in her pocket and she pulled it out, almost without thinking. A short text from Devon.

*Mace here.*

Here. In Devon's house. With Aimee. Here. In their database, in their network.

"Mace," Marley said, staring at her phone.

"That's my guess," Arnie said, glancing up. "We recently identify a high-level hacker wanted by the RCMP and now we get hacked? On the file she's attached to? I don't think—"

"*No,*" Marley shouted. "Mace is at Devon's house. *Now.* She's there."

Crawford immediately picked up the phone and put a call into dispatch for 9-1-1, stopping only to ask Marley the address.

Action—she needed to move, she needed to make the right decision, she needed to race home to Devon, to Aimee, to Carla. She needed to think, and Crawford was pounding her with questions as officers from the floor began crowding the office.

"Take a breath, Officer," Crawford said, his voice sharp. "And tell me what you know."

She squeezed her eyes shut. "I think they're all at home, at Devon's house. Carla, Aimee, and Devon. I just got a text from Devon. It said, *Mace here.*" She opened her eyes. "That's all I know."

"Are we assuming a hostage situation? Kidnapping? What's her motive?"

"Either," Marley said. "It could be either."

Locked in panic mode, Marley stared at the phone as Crawford dispatched squad cars to the neighbourhood.

"Constable Marlowe."

Marley stared, the chaos in the office too much.

"*Marlowe!*"

Marley looked up.

"You're with me," Crawford said, his voice low but not gentle.

They moved down the hallway, Marley following her commanding officer out of the building and towards the parking lot. It was darker than it should have been at six o'clock; wind howled and dark clouds lumbered across the sky, threatening torrential rain with every gust and stolen breath.

"Call Dr. Wolfe," Crawford said as they got into his car. "If this is a hostage situation, let's start by making contact."

Crawford started the car and turned on his lights but no siren as Marley hit the green call button on her phone.

It rang and rang and rang. Devon's voicemail picked up. "No answer," Marley said.

"Count to thirty, try again. We can signal urgency without scaring anyone into rash action."

He sounded so calm and reasonable. Marley counted in her head as Crawford navigated the street, turning on his siren when traffic became clogged. As they drove through an intersection against the light, Marley saw the traffic light swing wildly in the wind.

Marley hit thirty in her head and dialed again. No answer. Then her phone rang and Carla's number came up.

"Marley? Do you know what's happening? I just saw a message from Devon to stay away from the house. I'm out shopping. I don't know what's going on."

Carla sounded frantic. "We've got squad cars on the way now, Carla. I got a text from Devon, too." She took a breath. "Is Aimee with you?" She knew the answer but needed to ask anyway.

"No," Carla said, her voice catching. "She and Devon stayed home to bake cookies to go with ice cream I just picked up. For the storm."

"Where are you right now?"

"At the Centennial Plaza," Carla said.

"Only a few blocks away, then." Marley updated Crawford on

the critical information—only two people in the residence with Holly Mason.

"Tell her to meet Constables Atwal and Henderson at the corner of Royal and Lawton. We're setting up around the corner from the residence."

Marley relayed the message to Carla, who repeated it, her voice sounding stronger with some action and answers. Marley wished she felt the same.

"Is it Randolph?" Carla said.

"No, I don't think so. I'll be there in less than five, Carla," Marley said. "We'll figure this out."

"See you in five."

Crawford relayed instructions through his Bluetooth as he drove, calling for a hostage negotiator and backup. Four squad cars blocked the entrance to Devon's small side street of the neighbourhood. Wind spat wet leaves and flower petals at them as they exited the car, thunder in the background.

"This is what we've got, folks," Crawford said, his voice booming over the wind and thunder. "Suspected hostage situation, two people in the residence, thirty-seven-year-old Dr. Devon Wolfe and eight-year-old Aimee West. To our knowledge, the hostage taker is twenty-four-year-old Holly Mason, aka Mace. Mace is a computer hacker with a history of political interference but no known violent tendencies."

Marley shivered. What did Mace want?

"Marlowe, the layout of the house, please."

Marley snapped back to her sergeant.

"Yes, sir," she said. She relayed the layout to the other officers, using the similar houses around them to point out which windows led to which rooms.

When she was done, Crawford dispatched two officers to approach the house from the tree-covered backyard and two to station themselves with binoculars across the street. They needed intel, he said. Until they could make contact to find out the situation and the possible demands, they needed to know as much as they could about the occupants of the house.

"Marley, call again."

She did. Still no answer. Without being asked, she called again. Marley couldn't stand the stillness of the silence. She even welcomed the sounds of the storm, making it feel like something was alive and breathing around her.

"Marley!"

Marley turned to see Carla being escorted toward her by an officer.

"Carla," Marley said, hugging the woman tightly.

"What do we know? What's going on?"

"It's Mace, the woman who worked with Randolph to develop the new opioid. I got a text from Devon that makes us think she's inside with Devon and Aimee."

"Mace? That's the one we think asked Aimee to keep a secret? The one Aimee wouldn't talk about."

"Yes," Marley said. "We're trying to make contact and figure out who is inside and where."

"I left them in the kitchen, though I'm not sure that means anything. I've only been gone about half an hour. I took the car out of the garage, Devon said to."

"The garage?" Marley said. "I didn't know Devon used that garage for her car."

"She said she puts it in during big storms because she's seen a lot of branches come down in her neighbourhood in storms like this. Said to leave it open until I got back."

"So the garage door is open, and the downstairs entrance to the house is unlocked?"

"I think so," Carla said. "Marley, what are you going to do?"

She stared down at her uniform, her black boots, the utility belt around her hips. She was not this uniform, she'd known that for a long time now. But she could use this uniform, use her training, use the team around her to get Devon and Aimee to safety.

Marley dialed Devon's number again. She didn't expect a response. This call went directly to voice mail. She approached Sgt. Crawford. "Anything?" she asked.

"Movement in the living room but no positive IDs, the room is too dark. Reports of voices, both adults, but we can't hear what they're saying. We've got a clear line of vision into the kitchen but no movement."

"So, not much."

"Not much," Crawford confirmed.

"I'd like to go in."

"I don't think that's wise given how little we know. Have you called again?"

"Yes, sir. And I believe Devon's phone is now off, so we have no hope of making contact unless it's face-to-face."

Crawford stared down the street, even though they were camped out around the corner from Devon's house.

"Tell me what you're thinking, constable."

Marley felt a thrill of excitement and fear snake up through her belly.

"I'm going to go up and knock on the front door," Marley said.

"That's your whole plan?"

"Part one," Marley said, giving him a grim smile. "In twenty minutes from the time I walk in, send a team in through the open and unlocked garage. Stairs lead from the basement into the kitchen, right outside the living room. I'll try to signal what room we're in, but I can't guarantee it."

Crawford was silent.

"What's your plan for those twenty minutes, Officer?"

"I'm going to talk. Or listen. My guess is unless Devon is hurt, she's already got Mace talking. I'll seek out the demands, de-escalate as I can, and seek a peaceful resolution."

"And if none of that is possible?"

"I'll protect the vulnerable and wait for backup."

"Are you going in armed?"

"No."

"Good," Crawford said. "Leave use of force to your backup."

"Yes, sir," Marley said.

Marley let Crawford update the team as she walked back to Carla. She was standing with Superman, who was talking to Carla in a low, steady voice. Sometimes a constant, steadying presence was all you had to keep you grounded. She needed to be that for Devon and for Aimee.

"I'm going in," Marley said. "Constable Stills will stay with you and let you know what's happening." She looked up at Superman, and he affirmed her request with a nod.

Carla clutched Marley's arm. "Be safe," she whispered.

Marley nodded and went back to Crawford. She unclipped her gun from her belt and handed it over to him, holster and all.

"Any advice, sir?"

"You know the goals, Marlowe. Be smart, be ready, and trust your backup. I'll see you on the other side of this."

Without another pause, without taking a breath or looking at anyone else on the team, she started walking toward Devon's street. Rain was falling in fat drops that dotted the sidewalk. Thunder rumbled above and around. Marley caught a flash of movement out of the corner of her eye. A branch in the wind maybe, or the officer stationed across the street.

Marley walked up the stairs to Devon's front door. She checked her phone, the signal for Crawford to start the twenty-minute countdown.

Marley knocked on the door.

❖

Mace had just stared at Devon when she'd first invited her to sit and talk. Then she'd pulled out her phone and typed a long message or series of messages or something. Devon had just sat there, itching to pull out her own phone to check in with Marley and trying desperately not to listen for sounds from the kitchen.

After a few minutes, Mace shoved her phone into her pocket and looked at Devon.

"Where is Aimee West?"

"With her grandmother. Shopping."

Mace gave her a hard stare. Then she sat down across from Devon, leaning forward on her knees.

"You have a lot of reasons to lie to me, I understand that. But you shouldn't."

Mace began unbuttoning her cardigan, but Devon looked at Mace's face, not at her fingers on the pearl pink buttons. She didn't know what this was, but she knew she couldn't react. Neutrality, calmness, and connection without boundary-crossing would establish trust, and she'd need Mace to trust her if they were going to get out of this.

Mace was wearing a black tank top underneath her sweater, and her arms were covered in vibrant tattoos. One sleeve was a design entirely made up of blue and green fish scales, the other a series of concentric circles in black and gold and red. Beautiful and sinister.

Mace caught Devon looking at her tattoos and smirked.

"My sleeves aren't even the most interesting thing about me," Mace said.

"What is the most interesting thing about you?" Devon said, unsure if Mace would answer.

"My brain," Mace said immediately. "I think in ways no one else does."

"It's always been that way? Since you were a kid?"

"Since the day I was born. A day I remember, by the way. Hyperthymesia. Excessive remembering."

"I've read about that," Devon said, finding an inlet and following it. "It's a very small percentage of the population."

Mace's eyes lit up. "Now you've met one. But I'm not going to be added to your collection."

"What do you mean?"

"Doctors, psychologists, and psychiatrists used to try and collect me. Puzzle me out. Fix me. Scan my brain, make me jump through hoops, and write me up in their journals. But I'm not here to be collected, Dr. Wolfe."

Just as Devon was about to ask why Mace was here, her phone rang. Devon looked down at her phone, Marley's name illuminated on the screen, then back up at Mace.

"I'd like to answer it."

"I'm sure you would. Let it go."

They both stared at the phone until it went silent.

"Should I call you Mace?" Devon said.

Mace shrugged. "It's good enough."

Her phone rang again. She let it ring in her lap. Mace stared at it while it rang. Her slight shoulders relaxed when it was finally silent.

"Why are you here, Mace?"

Mace seemed to shake herself out of her stare trance. "Who did you contact? Who did you tell I was here?"

"Aimee's grandmother, Carla. And Constable Marlowe with the Hamilton police."

Mace did not seem particularly distressed by this news.

"Ballsy."

Devon said nothing.

"We got sidetracked. I wanted to tell you the reason you shouldn't lie to me. And I need to tell you before the police arrive." She pulled out her phone again. "We've got about twenty minutes is my guess." She tapped it, and Devon thought she heard the faint sound of static. "I put a small antenna on your front porch on my way in. Hope you don't mind. The cops make it so easy to track what they're doing, thankfully."

Devon kept her face neutral, though the adrenaline and anxiety she'd been keeping down spiked. She tried not to show how unnerved she was by Mace's calmness, at her planning, at her confidence.

"What did you want to tell me?" Devon said, trying to swing things back to the two of them. She needed this resolved before Marley came. And she knew, with every breath and scared beat of her heart, that Marley was coming.

"I'll show you."

Mace tapped her phone then turned it around so Devon could see. It was a photo of a small plastic yellow box, like a hard shell camera case. Inside was a series of wires and a motherboard and circuits. Devon's heart plummeted down through her stomach.

"What am I looking at?"

"You're looking at an incendiary device, Dr. Wolfe."

"Where is it?"

Mace took her phone back and smiled fondly down at the picture for a moment before looking back at Devon. "We'll get to that eventually." She threw her phone on the couch. "Where's Aimee?"

"She's with her grandmother, Carla. They went shopping."

"What has she told you about me?"

"She wouldn't talk about it. She refused to communicate when specifically asked about you."

"And what did you glean from that, Dr. Wolfe?"

"I assumed she has some kind of trauma associated with a memory of you. Aimee had communicated other difficult things to us, mostly about living with her father, but she shut down when it came to talking about you."

Mace's eyes gleamed, and Devon's stomach rolled with nausea. "What are you afraid of?" Devon said.

Before Mace could answer, Devon's phone rang. Marley. The chimes sounded loud and out of the place in this silence. The phone went quiet, the house went quiet. Then it rang again.

"Turn it off."

Devon powered down her phone and placed it on the coffee table between them.

Mace only glanced at it briefly, then her eyes took on a far-off look, like she was listening to something in her head. When Mace turned to the large window overlooking the street, Devon saw the small ear bud. She was listening to the police.

"Let's wait for Constable Marlowe," Mace said. "She's on her way in."

Devon tried to control her breath, which was suddenly shallow and far away. She tried to swallow, tilting her head back and staring at the ceiling, as Mace walked to the front window, standing to the side and peering out.

A knock sounded at the door. Breath fled.

"Let her in."

For the first time, Devon's fear flared to anger. She looked at Mace standing by the window. She was so small, no meat or muscle on her. Devon stood from her spot on the couch, adrenaline replacing the paralyzing anxiety in her system. She could do this. She could walk over and take Mace down. Pin her arms, bring her to the floor. A confusing array of images streaked across her vision as she advanced.

Mace held up her phone as Devon moved closer.

"No, Dr. Wolfe," Mace said calmly. A yellow box, circuits. Incendiary device. "Answer the door, then sit back down. My show, not yours."

Devon blinked, and the anger was gone, the vision was gone. She was a psychologist, not an officer.

Devon opened her front door.

Marley was pale, her hair windblown and her uniform dotted with rain.

"Hi, Devon. You okay?"

"Yes. Come in. Mace wants to talk to us."

Marley walked past Devon into the house. Devon looked outside at the wind-whipped dusk. No cars on the street, no neighbours. Just a lashing wind, rolls of far-off thunder, and rain. Devon strained to see Marley's backup, a desperate and scared visual sweep.

Nothing.

"Join us, Dr. Wolfe."

Devon closed the door. The storm and their rescue on one side, she and Marley and Aimee with Mace on the other.

Marley stood in the living room, hands by her side, an open expression on her face as she looked at Mace.

"Holly Mason, I'm Constable Bridget Marlowe."

"It's Mace. Are you armed?"

"Mace, okay." Marley put her hands up and spun in a circle. "No, I'm not armed. I have a radio and a phone. I'd like to connect with my commanding officer and let him know your demands."

"Where's Aimee West?"

Marley turned to look at Devon. "I don't know. Devon?"

"She and Carla went shopping about an hour ago."

Marley turned back to Mace. "What do you want with Aimee?"

"Just to talk."

"You're wanted by the RCMP for questioning in relation to several different charges. We know you broke into our police files today and are linked to this drug case. Why do you think we'd let you close to an eight-year-old girl?"

Devon could see Mace's agitation as she stared at Marley and looked back to the window.

"Because I'm the only way you're going to get real answers about what Randolph West cooked up. I read the files. Your labs are close but not that close. You want to know why the withdrawal symptoms are wreaking havoc on the addicts in your city? Tell me where the kid is. We'll talk. It's that simple."

"No," Marley said. "Not like this. I'm not bargaining with a kid, and my commanding officer won't either. Come down to the station and tell us what you know. It sounds like you've got information we need, and I think you know you can use that to reduce your sentence."

Mace gave a frustrated growl and ran a hand through her hair. This wasn't going the way she wanted. She flicked the curtain closed and walked over to where Devon and Marley were standing.

"How about an explosive device planted at one of the hospitals in the city?" Mace said. "It's going to be a rough night to evacuate to other facilities. High winds so heli-med is grounded. Potential flooding. Widespread power outages." Mace made a *tut-tut* sound and shook her head in mock sympathy. "That's a lot of injuries on your shoulders, Constable Marlowe, when all I want to do is talk to Aimee West for five minutes."

Devon's arms tingled then went numb, the sensation crawling up her chest. She looked at Marley, paler still in this light, with this news.

"I'd like to update my commanding officer," Marley said.

Mace waved an impatient hand. "Use your radio so I can monitor the conversation."

Marley spoke into the handheld radio attached to her shoulder. Static hissed back at her. She tried again. Mace frowned and looked at her phone.

"Must be the storm causing interference," Mace said.

Devon could see Marley's brain do something with that news. Something fell into place, but Devon couldn't think what it was.

"I'll just text," Marley said, pulling out her phone.

"No," Mace said, lunging across the space and slapping Marley's phone out of her hands. It hit the floor with a clatter as Marley took a defensive stance, legs bracing her body, presenting the smallest target. But Mace had already retreated back to the couch, looking shocked and agitated.

"Shit. Fuck. Just don't…don't do anything. Let me sort this out."

Mace was unraveling. Frayed nerves, action with no thought, no plan B.

Marley glanced at Devon, motioning for her to take a few steps back. She was reading Mace's agitation as well.

"I need to let my commanding officer know about the hospitals," Marley said. "It's your bargaining chip, let me use it."

Mace clutched her phone with one hand, the other covering her mouth like she wanted to scream.

"Three hospitals," Mace mumbled. Then she removed her hand. "Three hospitals. One of them is already at capacity tonight. Four hundred and eleven people, including patients and staff. One hospital and four hundred people."

Marley bent down slowly to pick up her phone, keeping her eyes on Mace. "Good," Marley said. "This is good. Let me tell them."

*Bad*, Devon thought, her chest so tight it hurt. All of this was so bad.

"Four hundred people for five minutes with Aimee West," Mace said, breathing through her fingers. "You tell your boss that."

Marley typed and Devon watched Mace. Her poise was gone. This interface was not what she had expected. Loss of control was a dangerous thing.

"How can we make this easier?" Devon said.

Mace looked around the room, stopping at Devon, then back to Marley. She was mumbling into her fingers, phone still clutched in her hands.

"How can we make this better?" Devon tried again.

Mace shook her head. "No one listens. No one hears what's underneath. My mind is huge, you know."

"Yes," Devon said.

"I know how humans operate. Everyone but me. I know they won't risk four hundred people for one. One kid. One stupid kid."

A gust of wind shook the house and lightning lit the room in a quick flash, thunder rising as the light disappeared.

"One. Stupid. Kid," Mace repeated.

Devon saw Aimee first. She had silently opened the door to the kitchen and stood very still. Maybe Mace wouldn't notice, Devon thought, but it was a wild, useless hope as Mace and Marley both turned their heads.

"Aimee West," Mace said.

"Not stupid," Aimee said, her voice raspy, head held high.

*Aimee, no.*

"We were friends for a while, weren't we?" Mace said. "I was the only one who listened to you, talked to you about school, told you how smart you were."

Aimee hadn't moved, her expression scared and determined.

"Aimee," Marley said quietly. "Come here."

Aimee glanced at Marley, then back to Mace. She shuffled sideways, keeping her eyes on Mace.

This brought Aimee closer to Mace, but now she stood between Devon and Marley. Devon put her hand around Aimee's shoulder, providing comfort and preparing to grab the girl and run. A quick glance at Marley told her that was also what she had in mind.

"Do you remember the time you stubbed your toe on the dresser?"

Mace said. "We thought it was broken. So we looked up all the bones in the feet. You loved the word 'phalanges'."

Aimee's small frame shook, but she stayed silent.

"And your arm," Mace said softly. Devon found the tone threatening, not soothing. "How many times did your arm hurt? And you were so brave." Mace stroked the inside of her own arm. "So brave," Mace repeated. "Especially when we linked your arm," Mace drew a line all the way up her arm, "to your throat." Mace's finger ended in a line across her neck.

Aimee stared as her body shook. The lights flickered, rolling thunder the only sound in the room.

Mace smiled. "See? You're a smart kid after all."

"You hurt me," Aimee said.

"No, that's not how we remember it."

Aimee leaned into Devon. Devon held her close to her side as Aimee found her voice. "You hurt me. Needles in my arm. Scratches over and over. It itched, and you told my dad it was allergies. He told the school. But I'm not allergic."

Mace looked furious and shocked. But Aimee wasn't done.

"You took my blood and my skin. You told me the names of the tests. But you said they were secret tests, I couldn't tell. Special medical tests. Chicken pox, *varicella zoster virus*, you taught me that." The medical words and Aimee's hurt rolled off her tongue. "I listened. *I'm* smart. My dad made drugs. You were supposed to make the body want the drugs. Always and forever." Aimee swallowed. "I know what you did. No more bad secrets."

Aimee clung to Devon's side, and Devon kept a tight hold on the girl's shoulders, even as her heart broke and hurt. Marley hadn't moved, nor had her expression changed. Devon wondered if she'd even heard what Aimee had said. But Marley was staring at Mace, her body on alert. She was waiting for the fallout.

"Let's end this, Mace," Marley said, the reasonable tone she'd been using edged with tension. "Put your phone down on the table, then turn around with your hands on your head."

Mace was pale, her eyes wide. She seemed incapable of movement, of processing anything, as the night got away from her entirely. She'd come to ensure Aimee's silence, but she'd been served Aimee's bravery.

Marley glanced at Devon and made the smallest movement with

her head. *Get away.* Devon began edging Aimee away, moving the scared kid away from her tormentor, away from the unpredictable scene unfolding in front of them.

"She's lying," Mace breathed out, voice shaky.

"We don't have your side of the story," Marley said. "I think it's time to tell it. Put your phone down. Let us hear what's in your head."

Devon heard the wrongness of the words even before Mace whipped her head around to look at Marley. Marley couldn't have known it was a trigger, some unhappy history with psychiatry.

"You don't get the *privilege* of being inside my head, Constable Marlowe. I'm going to walk out of here and disappear." She held her phone up between them. Her last bargaining chip. "Tell the four officers on the street to stand down. Tell the units at the top of the block to back off. Two minutes and I—"

The front door banged open at the same time as the basement door crashed. Police shouted instructions over the rain and wind as uniforms swarmed into Devon's living room. Devon scooped Aimee up and backed against a wall. She watched, horrified, as Marley and at least six armed police officers yelled at Mace to put down her phone.

Mace was frozen, eyes wide, incomprehension and horror etched in her face. She'd miscalculated, badly.

"Look," Marley said, holding her phone out to the side with one hand. Mace tracked the movement. Then Marley swung her other arm in a rapid, violent arc, connecting with Mace's forearm. She yelled sharply in pain as her phone flew across the room.

Everything surged as the officers reacted and Mace went down. An officer hustled her phone outside like it was the bomb itself. Devon clung to Aimee who was sobbing now, screaming, her fear unleashed. She could do nothing but hold the girl and watch the end of this horrible scene unfold in her living room.

Then Marley was there, sliding her hand up Devon's arm, shaking her lightly.

"Are you okay?"

"Yes," Devon said. "We're okay. Scared. We're both scared but okay."

Marley put her arms around them both in a tight embrace and squeezed. She'd ended this, Devon thought. They had ended this.

Devon realized she was saying the words out loud, whispering them to Aimee as Marley rocked them. She opened her eyes as the energy in the room changed. Mace, handcuffed and crying, was being led out of the house.

"Aimee," Devon said, ducking her chin down to try and get Aimee to listen, the girl's face still buried in Devon's neck. "They've arrested Mace, she's in handcuffs, the police are taking her away. You don't have to look, but this is happening. The scary stuff is over."

Devon could feel Aimee's tears collecting in her shirt. She held the girl and watched as Mace was taken out of her house.

"She's gone, Aimee," Marley said. "I know it doesn't feel like it right now. But you're safe."

Marley and Devon looked at each other, silently exchanging their worry as Aimee continued to cry brokenly, the same sound, over and over.

"What's that?"

Devon and Marley both clung tighter to the girl as her words became clear.

"I'm sorry, I'm sorry, I'm sorry."

Tears surfaced in Devon's eyes. "Mace made this happen, sweetheart. Not you."

"It's not your fault," Marley said. "None of this was your fault."

Devon closed her eyes as Marley squeezed them tighter. A moment later, Carla was there, finding space to wrap her arms around them all. They stayed like that for a long time, trembling and crying and hugging. Devon knew she didn't have enough words to make this better. She could only be here in the best way she knew how for Aimee and Carla and Marley. For now, that was enough.

## CHAPTER SEVENTEEN

Two in the morning, and Marley found it hard not to mark the passage of time. It had been seven hours since she'd walked into Devon's house to confront Mace. Six since they'd established Mace had lied about a planted incendiary device. Four since Devon and Aimee had given initial statements. Zero hours since Marley had stopped worrying she'd done something wrong. And only ten minutes since Aimee had finally fallen into an exhausted sleep and Devon had carried her to her bedroom, a weary Carla not far behind.

Marley sat with her head in her hands at Devon's kitchen table. The still brightness of the room was odd after the confrontation and chaos of the evening. The storm had reached its peak about an hour ago, shutting down power in neighbourhoods across the city. Devon's power had flickered on and off as thunder and wind shook the house. Occasionally the sky would light up, flashes of lightning or falling branches taking out a power line. The four of them had watched the storm together in subdued silence, eating bowls of ice cream after midnight. They had already survived their storm. What was happening outside was nothing more than a beautiful and distant display.

Marley looked up as Devon walked back into the kitchen. She was pale, eyes still red from crying earlier. Her shoulders sagged.

"Will you come to bed with me?" Devon's words were so quiet, a hushed request in the brittle morning hours.

"Yes."

They said nothing more as they got ready for bed, sharing space and intimacy in a way they hadn't yet had time for in their relationship. But even before Marley began taking off her uniform and putting on the pyjamas Devon offered, the night had already stripped them bare. The sheets were cool against Marley's skin as she got into bed beside Devon, the pillow soft on her cheek. She could just make out Devon's features in the dim glow from the bathroom nightlight. Devon's face was leached of colour, her expression tired and sad and pained as she lay on her side and looked at Marley.

"You're hurting," Marley said. She brought her hand between them and placed it on Devon's chest. She felt Devon's breath shudder, and Marley got the sense something very tightly bound inside Devon was coming loose.

"Can I tell you?" she said.

Marley heard the layers of questions. *Can I trust you with my burden? Will you hold my worries with me? Will you sit with me while it hurts?*

"Yes."

Marley listened as Devon spoke her pain and worry in broken, whispered words of fear and helplessness and the weight of every decision she'd made to protect Aimee. She didn't interrupt when Devon shifted unconsciously to talking about how she'd failed at work by allowing herself to get lost in the burdens of others. Marley heard Devon accept how close they'd come to disaster tonight, how they had danced at the edge of heartbreak and loss. And Marley kept her hand pressed close to Devon's heart as Devon walked herself through to an uneasy acceptance that she had done everything she could, and everything had been enough. To feeling like she could be enough.

Devon's voice faded away, and there was only breath and exhaustion left between them.

"I love everything about you," Marley said. "And I am so lucky to have you in my life."

Only then were there tears, and Devon cried like Marley guessed she'd needed to cry for some time now. Marley pulled her in closer and kissed Devon's forehead and stroked her back and tried to infuse every touch with love and understanding. Nothing in her life had ever felt more important than that moment, and as Devon caught her breath and whispered *I love you* into Marley's neck, she knew Devon felt it, too.

❖

Sunlight woke Devon only a few hours after she'd fallen asleep, still wrapped in Marley's arms. Her eyes were gritty from tears and tiredness, but her chest felt light and her thoughts calm. Everyone was safe, and Marley loved her. Devon studied Marley's face, inches from her own. Her breath was soft and even, her body still as she slept heavily. Devon wanted to wake her up with a kiss, but she held back and disengaged herself from Marley's arm. Marley didn't stir as Devon quietly left the room.

After a stop in the bathroom, Devon followed the sounds of murmuring into the kitchen. In so many ways, it felt like a regular morning, Carla making coffee and Aimee spinning on a barstool. She knew in so many ways it wasn't.

"Good morning, everyone."

"Morning," Carla said, scooping grounds into the coffeemaker. "Looks like none of us are good at sleeping in."

"Marley's doing a pretty good job of it," Devon said, stretching. She wandered over to Aimee and gave the stool an extra spin. Aimee's answering laugh, an actual laugh, was magic. Devon looked over Aimee's head to Carla and saw the light in her eyes. A good start to a long road ahead, for both of them.

"I just asked Aimee what her heart felt up for today."

"It's a good question after a rough night," Devon said. They had to acknowledge the night before. Silence bred secrecy and shame, and Aimee already carried enough of both.

Aimee stopped the stool from spinning, looking thoughtful.

"Donuts," she finally said. "Big pink donuts."

Aimee's voice was a delight, even with the smallest rasp of disuse. Devon kissed the top of Aimee's head, not hiding the tears in her eyes.

"That will be top of the list."

The three of them talked as Carla and Aimee made breakfast. Aimee wanted to see the beach after the storm, and Devon offered the car since she and Marley weren't going anywhere anytime soon. Aimee skipped down the hall to go and change for a beach walk, leaving Carla and Devon alone.

"She seem okay to you?" Carla said, rinsing out Aimee's cereal bowl.

"Today feels like a new start for Aimee. I think it's going to be a long road, but she's got you, she's going to have therapy, and she's going to be okay."

"Yeah," Carla breathed out, wiping down the counters that didn't need to be wiped. "We're going to be okay."

"We are." Devon smiled, feeling the words in her bones.

Carla gripped Devon's arm and went to get herself ready. Ten minutes later, with only one whispered argument between Carla and Aimee about whether or not they could turn Devon's raincoat into a kite, they were off. Devon listened to the garage door close, then the quiet Saturday morning calm descended on the house. She poured and doctored two cups of coffee, then went back to her room.

Marley was awake, light hair disheveled, blinking sleepily into the light.

"How did the sun come up?" she said.

Devon laughed. "It does that pretty consistently," Devon said, holding out a cup of coffee. Marley sat up against the headboard and moaned out a thank you as she took a sip.

"Did I hear Carla and the munchkin leaving?" she said as Devon climbed back into bed beside her.

"They decided on donuts and a beach walk."

"How did they seem? After last night."

"Good. Solid. And if today's a high and tomorrow's a low, that's okay."

Marley sipped her coffee. "For you, too?"

Devon took a moment with the question. So much goodness and connection and relief had come out of the awfulness of last night. It had been terrible. It had been necessary. And Marley had been there for every thought and every tear. She'd sat with her and made her feel safe.

Devon leaned over and kissed Marley on the corner of her mouth.

"Yes, for me, too."

Marley put her coffee down and turned on her side. "How do you feel about kissing me with coffee breath *and* morning breath?"

Devon laughed and also put down her coffee, then mirrored Marley's position. Instead of answering Marley's question, she leaned in and kissed her again, this time full on the lips but still very gently. Not tentative, just unhurried. The lightness of their touch was a beginning, the commitment to taking time to be together. Devon drew this promise on Marley's skin, tucking Marley's hair behind her ear, feeling the soft skin of her neck down to her collarbone and across her shoulder.

She ran her light touch over Marley's T-shirt as they kept kissing, finding Marley's bicep, over the crook of her elbow and the tendons of her inner arm, traveling over knuckles, between fingers. Devon skipped lightly over the fabric of Marley's boxer shorts and felt Marley suck in a breath as she touched the bare skin of Marley's leg. She hiked Marley's knee up over her hip, and Marley moaned into her mouth.

Devon pressed herself closer into the space she'd created as Marley's kiss became more urgent, and she pushed her hands under Devon's shirt and across her back. Devon's skin was inflamed, sensitive to every stroke of Marley's hand, the taste of her lips and her tongue. Pressure built in her thighs, in her chest, a need that rose up in an all-consuming clamour of her body. Before she succumbed, Devon pulled back to look into Marley's eyes. The want was there, the reflection of need and desire.

Then Marley rose just enough to capture Devon's mouth again, her kiss so intense Devon was lost. Then Marley bit her bottom lip. Devon grunted at the pain even as her hips thrust in response to Marley's fight for dominance. She felt Marley grin against her lips, and Devon rolled them both over until she had Marley caged beneath her.

"Take your shirt off," Marley said.

Devon considered ignoring her request, making her wait. But she sat up and yanked her T-shirt off, discarding it on the floor. Devon felt her body respond to the hunger in Marley's eyes. Marley lifted herself enough to remove her own shirt then they were kissing again, hands and fingers exploring and pressing and scratching against skin, trailing over ribs and breasts, with a light nail scratch across a nipple that had Devon straining for control.

Devon lowered her body over Marley, thrusting her hips against Marley and feeling her lift her hips in return. Every thrust brought Devon closer to the edge, with Marley's hold on her mouth and her fingers digging in to her back.

Marley pulled back suddenly, breaking their kiss, breaking their rhythm.

"Shorts off," she gasped.

"No," Devon muttered, tugging at Marley's earlobe with her teeth.

She didn't want to stop the kissing, feeling the heat at her centre as they pressed against each other.

Marley tilted Devon's head back, giving her complete access to Devon's neck. Marley licked from Devon's collarbone up to her jaw where she nipped, scraping her teeth against skin. Then, as Devon was distracted by the feel of Marley at her throat, Marley thrust her hips up in a powerful motion and flipped them over, reversing their position.

"Shorts off," she said again and yanked at Devon's boxers.

Then they were both naked, and there was no way to take in all the heat of their skin as they fought to be closer, Devon hooked her legs around Marley's powerful thrusts, needing the anchor to absorb every sensation.

"More," Devon groaned into Marley's ear.

Marley kissed Devon hard as she lifted herself just enough for Devon to move her hand over Marley's ribcage, across her stomach, down past the sharp jut of her hipbone and right to the centre of her. Marley's breath hitched as Devon opened her. She didn't have it in her to be gentle, but she restrained herself enough to start slowly, circling her fingers over the wet hardness as Marley made strangled sounds and thrust into Devon's hand. Devon loved the power of having utter control over Marley's body with every stroke of her fingers. Marley's eyes were closed, the muscles in her neck stood out, and she seemed so close to the edge.

Then suddenly Marley pulled herself away and put all her weight on one arm. The other hand drew a line down Devon's body, from her jaw down her chest to her hips and between her legs in one long, heated stroke.

"I need you," Marley said.

"Yes."

Then Marley was inside her, and Devon was lost. There was no thought, just the shifting of bodies until Marley's centre again pressed against her palm. She could not separate the sensations, heat and lust and that clamoring again in her body, muscles straining against the thrust and stroke of fingers until Devon felt like her head was going to explode. With one final yell and thrust from Marley, she did, her body unleashing an orgasm so powerful she closed her eyes as she shouted and rode out the tremors in their bodies.

It was sunlight again that woke her, this time accompanied by the slick feeling of sweat and the smell of sex. She was on her back now, Marley tucked against her side, head in the crook of her arm. Devon smiled at this culmination of who they were. Who they could be together.

"Our coffee is cold," Marley said against Devon's shoulders.

Devon laughed lightly. "We can heat it up in the microwave. Or make a new pot."

"Mmm."

Devon wondered if she'd gone back to sleep.

"And muffins," Marley said after a few minutes. "Will you make me muffins?"

"I take it you're hungry, love?"

Marley leaned back and smiled sleepily at Devon.

"I like that," she said softly. "And I'm absolutely starving."

Devon pulled Marley in for a long, sweet kiss.

"Then let's go make something to eat."

# EPILOGUE

The courthouse was beautiful and gloomy on the March day Aimee West gave her final testimony against her father and Holly Mason. Because she was a minor, it took place in a small, wood-paneled office with only the attorneys, a court recorder, and a child lawyer present. Devon had taken the day off to sit in the hall with Carla and Marley on uncomfortable benches, taking turns getting coffee and oatmeal raisin cookies from the vending machine one floor down. It had been a long day and a long time coming, but it was finally over. Aimee had emerged from the final meeting looking pale, her expression unsure. But her eyes had lit up when she saw who was waiting for her.

Aimee and Carla were in the washroom, Aimee having insisted on getting two dresses for today, one for the testimony and one for when it was all over.

"She seem good to you?" Marley said, a variation of the question they'd been asking each other all morning.

"She's strong. She's going to be fine." A variation of the answer they'd been giving each other all day.

"It's too bad she had to miss school today."

Devon shrugged. "Her teacher doesn't seem worried. She's the one who suggested mental health days whenever Aimee needs them."

Aimee had started fourth grade in the fall. The first few weeks had seen tears and tantrums almost every evening, though her teacher reported she was doing fine at school. She was quiet and watchful, but compliant, and she took part in the classroom activities and routines. Aimee's psychologist had suggested she was taking time to be a kid again. She was hyperaware she was not like the other kids, that she had experiences they didn't. Shame still surfaced with heartbreaking frequency, Aimee still working through her part in her father's drug business.

Devon pointed out that Aimee fell apart at home because it was her safe space. She held herself together all day and was working so hard to figure out who she was and how she belonged, so it wasn't surprising she lost the fight at holding it together every night. She knew she had people who loved her and would pick her up.

The tantrums had faded, and Aimee had begun to adjust. She made friends, she went to therapy, she started swimming lessons and an art class. She talked and yelled and sang and screamed and laughed. She found her voice and used it.

Devon heard Marley sigh and ran a hand over her back.

"I just want this to be over," Marley muttered.

"I know, love," Devon said, kneading the muscle in the back of her neck and shoulders. The case was weighing heavily on Marley, and it would still be a few weeks until it was resolved. But the outcome looked good, according to Crawford.

He had enough evidence against both Randolph West and Holly Mason to put them both away for a long time. The lawyers had lined up experts to show how the two had masterminded a drug that attached itself to the dormant chickenpox vaccine, waking up the virus just enough when the drug was withdrawn that it reacted with odd side effects. The scientists would give the explanation and Aimee's testimony would show how she'd been used as a guinea pig for testing. Marley wasn't sure they were ever getting out of jail.

Once the opioid Z fallout had run its course, the number of cases of post-withdrawal syndrome, as Public Health had called it, peaked in the summer, then rapidly dropped off by early fall. Simms was leading a province-wide case study, helping other regions and municipalities know what to look out for. He had offered Marley a chance to be a part of his traveling road show, but she'd declined the offer.

"I'm glad we're planning a trip," Marley said, sitting up a bit straighter. "I desperately need something to look forward to."

They were taking ten days in British Columbia, hiking in the mountains, eating a lot of food, and hiding out in a cabin in the woods together.

"Eight more weeks, then we're on a plane," Devon said.

"And we'll plan our lives after?"

"Every moment."

They had careers and homes and family to think about, including Carla and Aimee. They kept finding the joy, even in the scary details as Marley considered training for a new career and Carla talked about finding their own place in the summer. As their days blended and their relationship deepened, Devon acknowledged she'd never felt any love as deeply as the one she felt for Marley.

Marley looked like she was about to say something else when the door to the bathroom opened and Aimee walked out. Her dress for the testimony had been grey and navy. This one was dark pink with a light pink sash and Aimee had on a pair of white tights with pink and red hearts.

"Look!" Aimee yelled as she ran up to Devon and Marley and spun around. "It's a twirly dress!"

Devon and Marley laughed. "It really is," Devon said.

"Where to, Squirt?" Marley said, even though she knew the answer.

"Big lunch," Aimee said. "Then the art gallery. Then comfy snuggles, blanket fort, and a movie with popcorn and ice cream."

"I like the big lunch plan," Carla said. "I'm starving."

"Lead the way to the car, Miss Squirt," Marley said with a grand sweep of her arm.

Aimee took Carla's hand and they walked toward the main doors, peeking over her shoulder to make sure Devon and Marley followed. Devon took Marley's hand and swung it between them as they walked.

"She did it," Marley said. "She's going to make it through."

"We all are," Devon said.

Marley squeezed her hand in agreement as they pushed open the doors to the cold March air.

# About the Author

Jessica Webb spends her professional days working with educators to find the why behind the challenging behaviors of the students they support. Limitless curiosity about the motivations and intentions of human behavior is also a huge part of what drives her to write stories and understand the complexities of her characters and their actions. When she's not working or writing, Jessica is spending time with her wife and daughter, usually planning where they will travel next. Jessica can be found most often on her favorite spot on the couch with a book and a cup of tea.

# Books Available From Bold Strokes Books

**Entangled** by Melissa Brayden. Becca Crawford is the perfect person to head up the Jade Hotel, if only the captivating owner of the local vineyard would get on board with her plan and stop badmouthing the hotel to everyone in town. (978-1-63555-709-1)

**First Do No Harm** by Emily Smith. Pierce and Cassidy are about to discover that when it comes to love, sometimes you have to risk it all to have it all. (978-1-63555-699-5)

**Kiss Me Every Day** by Dena Blake. For Carly Jamison, wishing for a do-over with Wynn Evans was a long shot, actually getting one was a game changer. (978-1-63555-551-6)

**Olivia** by Genevieve McCluer. In this lesbian Shakespeare adaption with vampires, Olivia is a centuries-old vampire who must fight a strange figure from her past if she wants a chance at happiness. (978-1-63555-701-5)

**One Woman's Treasure** by Jean Copeland. Daphne's search for discarded antiques and treasures leads to an embarrassing misunderstanding and, ultimately, the opportunity for the romance of a lifetime with Nina. (978-1-63555-652-0)

**Silver Ravens** by Jane Fletcher. Lori has lost her girlfriend, her home, and her job. Things don't improve when she's kidnapped and taken to fairyland. (978-1-63555-631-5)

**Still Not Over You** by Jenny Frame, Carsen Taite, and Ali Vali. Old flames die hard in these tales of a second chance at love with the ex you're still not over. (978-1-63555-516-5)

**Storm Lines** by Jessica L. Webb. Devon is a psychologist who likes rules. Marley is a cop who doesn't. They don't always agree, but both fight to protect a girl immersed in a street drug ring. (978-1-63555-626-1)

**The Politics of Love** by Jen Jensen. Is it possible to love across the political divide in a hostile world? Conservative Shelley Whitmore and liberal Rand Thomas are about to find out. (978-1-63555-693-3)

**All the Paths to You** by Morgan Lee Miller. High school sweethearts Quinn Hughes and Kennedy Reed reconnect five years after they break up and realize that their chemistry is all but over. (978-1-63555-662-9)

**Arrested Pleasures** by Nanisi Barrett D'Arnuck. When charged with a crime she didn't commit, Katherine Lowe faces the question: Which is harder, going to prison or falling in love? (978-1-63555-684-1)

**Bonded Love** by Renee Roman. Carpenter Blaze Carter suffers an injury that shatters her dreams, and ER nurse Trinity Greene hopes to show her that sometimes love is worth fighting for. (978-1-63555-530-1)

**Convergence** by Jane C. Esther. With life as they know it on the line, can Aerin McLeary and Olivia Ando's love survive an otherworldly threat to humankind? (978-1-63555-488-5)

**Coyote Blues** by Karen F. Williams. Riley Dawson, psychotherapist and shape-shifter, has her world turned upside down when Fiona Bell, her one true love, returns. (978-1-63555-558-5)

**Drawn** by Carsen Taite. Will the clues lead Detective Claire Hanlon to the killer terrorizing Dallas, or will she merely lose her heart to person of interest urban artist Riley Flynn? (978-1-63555-644-5)

**Lucky** by Kris Bryant. Was Serena Evans's luck really about winning the lottery, or is she about to get even luckier in love? (978-1-63555-510-3)

**The Last Days of Autumn** by Donna K. Ford. Autumn and Caroline question the fairness of life, the cruelty of loss, and what it means to love as they navigate the complicated minefield of relationships, grief, and life-altering illness. (978-1-63555-672-8)

**Three Alarm Response** by Erin Dutton. In the midst of tragedy, can these first responders find love and healing? Three stories of courage, bravery, and passion. (978-1-63555-592-9)

**Veterinary Partner** by Nancy Wheelton. Callie and Lauren are determined to keep their hearts safe but find that taking a chance on love is the safest option of all. (978-1-63555-666-7)